QUIET WATERS

CYNTHIA CAIN

Clear Fork Publishing

Summary: Eighteen-year-old Brie Birlow is mourning the death of her mother while trying desperately to stay strong for her younger sister, Alex. But a near death experience, an apparition that seems to want her dead and the awakening of inexplicable feelings make her question her own sanity. With time running out, Brie must unravel her family's legacy in order to escape the inevitable darkness that awaits her.

Clear Fork Publishing

P.O. Box 870 - 102 S. Swenson - Stamford, Texas 79553 (325)773-5550 - www.clearforkpublishing.com

Printed and Bound in the United States of America.

ISBN - 978-1-950169-09-2

Clear Fork Publishing

Thank you to my mom, sister Cheryl and daughter Amy for reading my manuscripts and giving me great feedback. To my movie loving daughters Jenny and Rachel, who make me laugh, maybe this will wake the reader in you. To my editor Austin, who made the book even better with proper grammar and punctuation. (who knew it would make that much of a difference). To Mike for taking time out of his extremely busy schedule to create the artwork for the cover, it looks amazing.

And a very special thank you to Denise Meck, without her there would be no book. Her encouragement and enthusiasm gave me the courage and the confidence to pursue my dream.

ONE

Letting go

"It looks like we're in for a big storm," Dad says, leaning forward to get my attention. "You all right, Brie?"

I shrug and stare out the window. Dark clouds billow across the blue sky, swallowing everything in their path.

"I hope it doesn't last long," he says.

To me, the storm-blackened sky is the perfect backdrop for today. "I like the rain," I say.

He squeezes my shoulder and scoots back against the leather seat of the limousine. He never has much to say. Mom used to say his silence comes from living in a house with four women.

Grandma, on the other hand, is a nervous talker. "I just can't believe it's the end of September. With this heat, it feels more like July. And if that ain't bad enough, it looks like rain . . . the laundry!" She gasps. "Did it get taken off the line? Oh, great, here it comes." She waves her hands in the air. "Now what'll we do? We can't stand out in this. For goodness sakes, can this day get any worse?"

"I hope it rains forever," Alex mutters.

Grandma switches gears, now lecturing on the disastrous consequences it could cause. Alex keeps her head down while picking at the pink embroidered hanky Grandma had given her earlier in the day. Her short blonde hair doesn't conceal her expression as she mocks Grandma, bringing a short-lived smirk to my face.

Good thing Grandma is too busy ranting to notice. Dad does, though. He places his hand on Alex's. She looks up at him with the same pale blue eyes as Mom's. He shakes his head in disapproval. Alex glances at me and, for a moment, it's as if Mom is staring back.

Rain falls fast and furious as the cars come to a stop. The chauffeur peers over the front seat.

"Would you like to wait?" he asks. "It looks like it will clear up in a few minutes." He holds his phone up so we can see a red blob dart across the radar, narrowly brushing Kiel, Wisconsin.

Dad nods and Grandma mumbles, while my sister and I sit in silence to wait out the storm.

Within minutes, the downpour slows to a drizzle. The driver opens our door and we step out. The ground is squishy. At first, I stay on my tiptoes to keep my heels from sticking in the soil, but when the casket is pulled from the hearse, I shift my weight, letting my heels sink into the grass.

Dad takes my hand and follows behind the pallbearers, but my body won't move. My hand jerks away, bringing him to an abrupt stop. The sadness in his eyes adds to my sorrow. Tears roll down my cheeks. "I can't do this."

He takes hold of my hand once again and squeezes it tight. "We'll get through this, together," his voice breaks. "I won't let you go."

Even though he's not very convincing, I wiggle my shoes free from the earth's hold and walk alongside him.

Streaks of sunlight break through the clouds as people

gather together in the sea of vibrant flowers that cover the ground. The preacher begins with a prayer. Heads bow and eyes close, but not mine. Alex keeps her eyes open and stares up at me while leaning into Grandma's arm. Even though life has cheated me out of a mom at seventeen, it's even sadder to think Alex only had nine years with her.

Love you, bug, I mouth to her.

Love you too, she mouths back before closing her eyes.

Part of me wants to run, but then the scent of Mom's perfume drifts my way. After scanning the area, my eyes are drawn to a solitary man standing motionless in the distance. He's dressed in black with his hands clasped together in front of him. He keeps my interest, until Alex touches my arm, bringing me back to her.

The preacher's words fade as an unsettling sensation washes over me. Warily, I look up. The stranger is now only a few headstones away from us, standing in the same position as if he were made of stone. He appears to be close to my age; maybe someone from my high school? Or maybe he was one of Mom's students?

I turn to Alex to ask if she knows him, but something's not right. Everyone around me is moving at a snail's pace. Visually sweeping the area, I try to rationalize what's happening when, without warning, I become immersed in the stranger's dark, deep-set eyes. A warm rush of fear explodes inside of me. My breath catches in my throat.

The longer he dominates my attention, the slower the movements around me become. Until the world . . . just . . . . stops.

The beat of my heart echoes in my head as a whirlwind of colorless images flicker between us, making me dizzy. Trapped in the illusion, I'm his to control. My mouth drops open, but nothing comes out.

Impulsively, I reach out to him. A jolt from behind me

releases me from his hold. My body goes limp as the world scrambles back to normal. Dad grabs onto me just before I hit the ground.

I'm not sure how long I was out—or if I even lost consciousness. People whisper around me:

"What happened?"

"Has she been sick?"

"Should we call an ambulance?"

"No, she'll be fine," Dad says. I'm relieved to hear his voice.

I open my eyes to an array of stares.

"Hey, what's going on? Are you okay?" Dad asks.

Embarrassed by the attention I've just brought to myself. I ignore the onlookers and focus on Dad's face. "Yeah, Dad, I'm fine."

He helps me to my feet. "What happened, kiddo?"

"I don't know, just felt hot."

His arm falls around my shoulder. He whispers, "Your ole' dad will hang on to you." He motions to the preacher to continue. The attention turns away from me and back to the preacher as he concludes the service.

"Are you sure you're okay?" Alex murmurs, scooting closer to me.

"I'm okay," I whisper.

IN SUCCESSION, the mourners disperse. Aunt Edna helps Grandma back to our vehicle. That's when it hits me. It's over. The final goodbye is here and I'm not ready.

Grief surges through me, causing an onslaught of tears. I hold tight to Alex. Dad places his hand on the angel that adorns the caskets spray of flowers. Tears stream down his face. "I don't want you girls to ever forget how much she loved you."

"We won't, Dad."

I take three pink carnations from the flowers on top of the casket, handing one to Alex and one to Dad. *What am I going to do without her? There's still so much I want to talk to her about.*

Before turning to leave, Dad kisses his fingers and touches the casket once more. He whispers, "I love you, babe."

He pulls me and Alex into his arms and we walk away, leaving Mom there alone.

Before getting into the car, a chill quivers down my spine, but I don't look back.

TWO

Secrets

_____

The spacious main floor of our century-old farmhouse seems small when packed with all the people and plants from the funeral. I move from room to room, trying to find somewhere private. My hand brushes against the leaves of a peace lily. Two beady eyes peer out at me from within the plant. "Gibson, what's wrong?" I pull the calico cat from her hiding place. "You're such a good girl." She nuzzles my neck. "Too many people for you . . . huh, girl. Me too."

A boisterous laugh from a man behind me sends Gibson scurrying out of my arms and up the stairs to the second floor. I just want to be alone right now. I make my way toward the stairs.

"How are you doing, Brie?" a friend of Mom's asks.

I don't stop to answer. That's when Dad comes into view. Our eyes meet, and he acknowledges me with a slight nod. He keeps his eyes on me while I back up and plop down onto the bench next to the piano. Trying to ignore his stare, I pick cat hair off my shirt while listening to the stories being told about my mom. I don't know why it's important to Dad that I stay in here. I'm not comfortable around this many people; he knows that.

Alex comes into the room and sits next to Aunt Edna. "Look what I made," she says, throwing her arm into the air, almost hitting Aunt Edna in the face. "They're friendship bracelets. Amy, my friend, showed me how to make them."

Aunt Edna holds Alex's arm out away from her face, "These are simply stunning," she says.

"If you want, I can show you how to make them."

"I would love that."

Grandma walks by me, as if on a mission. She stops to re-arrange knick knacks, straighten pictures, and pick up bits of food off the floor. Although Grandma is six years older than her sister, Aunt Edna, they look like twins— same build, same hairstyle, and same blue eyes.

It's unbearably hot in the house; if I don't get out of here right now, I'll go crazy. I make small talk while sneaking my phone out of the basket on top of the buffet, then amble toward the back door in the hope that Dad doesn't notice.

A woman stops me just inside the kitchen. "You need something, hon?"

I shake my head, pushing through the screen door and stepping out onto the porch. Cars are parked on both sides of our long gravel driveway and adjacent to the house, in the five-acre pasture. It makes the outside feel just as claustrophobic. The old barn that sits a few hundred yards from the house would be the perfect place to hide out. I'm no more than a few steps from the house when the screen door slams behind me.

"*Hey!*" Alex yells. "Where're ya going?"

"To the barn."

"I'm coming." She hurries to my side.

"Where're your shoes?"

She shrugs, "don't know."

"Your feet are getting muddy."

"I'll wash them in the puddles on the way back."

I move her toward the grassy edge of the driveway "Did you eat?"

"Nah . . . not hungry."

"Me either."

My cell phone beeps. "I thought Dad said you couldn't have that today." Alex says.

"He doesn't have to know."

From Josh: How's my best friend doing?

Me: Ok I guess

Josh: I wish I were there

Me: Me too

Josh: Call me later if you can

Me: K

Alex runs her finger along the dust covered cars, leaving behind a trail of designs. "Who was that?" she asks.

"Josh."

She stops to pick a dandelion. "Mom's in heaven, right?"

"Absolutely."

"Amanda said heaven's not real."

"Amanda's stupid. You think they'd have so many churches if heaven wasn't real?"

"I guess not." I take the flower from her and weave it into her hair. "You're so smart, Brie."

"Yeah . . . OK."

She looks up. "How's it look?"

"Fabulous." I look out over our field.

A cluster of cottonwoods grows alongside the barn and down a hill, leading to several acres of soybeans, which have already started to turn yellow. A large cattle pasture, a small patch of woods and a creek encompasses the back acreage.

Several more efficient outbuildings have been erected on this land over the years. But my favorite place by far is the original, rustic red barn—with its peeling paint and spots so worn the wood beneath looks stained. The tired, rusty hinges screech as the door slides open. The smell of hay, leather, and aged wood fill the air. We sprint inside one of the stalls for the rope suspended from the rafter. Alex leaps for it, catching the bottom of her dress on a nail, but that doesn't stop her from grabbing the rope first.

"Hah . . . beat you."

I point to the rip in her dress. "Grandma's not going to be happy about that."

"I won't show her." She stands on the knot tied at the end of the rope. I give her a push. "Dad's not going to leave us, is he?"

"*What?* Why would you ask that?"

"I don't know."

"Dad's never going to leave."

"But what if he does?"

"He's not going to." I jump onto the rope, accidentally launching us both into a pile of hay. "And besides, you'll always have me."

"You're going away to college next year. I heard you talking to Grandma."

"That doesn't mean I'm moving away. They have colleges right here."

"You promise?"

"Yes, Bug, I promise."

She falls backwards into the hay. "I miss her so much."

"Me too." The memories are too painful to bear at this moment. Through the weight of sadness, I lighten the mood by finding Alex's ticklish spot. "Who's your favorite person?"

She dissolves into laughter. "Stop it."

"Not until you tell me!"

"You are!" She breaks free from my grip and jumps to her feet. "Not!" She chuckles, running out of the barn. She dodges around the parked cars. I catch up as she reaches the hedges at the corner of the house. I notice Dad and Grandma standing on the porch. I pull Alex down next to me, behind the bushes, not wanting to be seen by Dad. He had been adamant about us staying inside to help.

"Shhh . . ." I raise my finger to my lips. They must not have seen us, as they continue on with their conversation

"John, when are you going to tell her?" Grandma's voice is stern.

"I'm not—it's not time."

"You're running out of time, and Brie has a right to know."

Dad lowers his voice. "I can't do this to her now, she'd never forgive me. Maybe she never has to know."

"And who would that benefit?"

"I'm just saying, nothing has come of it yet. Maybe nothing ever will."

"Maybe nothing," she grumbles. "You knew from the beginning, and you promised Beth that you would tell her."

"I know what I promised my wife." He huffs. "And I will, but not today. Besides, this isn't the right time. We have guests to attend to."

I hear Aunt Edna's voice. "People are starting to leave."

"Ok," Dad answers, then closes the screen door.

Alex whispers, "What was that about?"

I shrug. Taking her hand in mine, we wind our way to

the porch steps. Grandma has her back to us, with one hand on her hip and the other rubbing the side of her face.

"Hey, Grandma," I say.

She turns on her heels and gasps. "How long have you two been here?"

"Just got here . . . Why?"

"You both better get inside with your dad."

"What's wrong?"

The lines in her face soften. "Nothing, now get inside."

I want to know what their conversation was about, but the worn-out look on her face keeps me from asking.

"Come on, Alex." I open the screen door and motion for her to go in first. Grandma turns away. I follow Alex inside.

AFTER THE LAST of the visitors leave, Grandma calls it a night and disappears to her room. I help Aunt Edna put away the rest of the food and wash the few remaining dishes in the sink.

"If you need anything, call me." She kisses my cheek. "Be strong for your family. They need you."

"I will." I follow her outside and watch her walk down the driveway. She waves before sliding into the driver's seat.

I shut and lock the back door, turn off the kitchen light, and make my way into the living room. Alex is asleep on the couch. Dad is in his recliner, snoring. I turn the TV off. I think briefly about calling Josh, but I really just want some time alone. I slip out onto the front porch.

It's eerily quiet. Even the familiar breeze that blows across our farmland is absent. I make my way to the steps and lean against the rail.

The horizon is ablaze with bands of oranges and yellows as the day slowly gives way to the night. Taking in the beauty of this moment, it's hard to believe that the day has been filled with so much instability.

While watching the colors disappear into the distance, tears once again stream down my face. I think about Mom and her last words to me: *Please forgive me for what I've done.*

THREE

Encounter

———————

"I don't know how true it is, but when you lose someone you're close to, is it supposed to feel like you're starting over? Not that I don't have all my memories. It just seems strange to have new ones without her in them." I keep my voice low.

"That's not strange," Josh whispers. "It's going to take time."

"So, it's normal to feel disconnected?"

"Yeah—I mean, it's only been a couple days since the funeral. I didn't think you'd be here today."

Josh sits next to me in math class. This class is my favorite—not only because it's the last period of the day, but because he can always cheer me up. Dad wanted us to get back to our regular routine, or as close to it, as soon as possible. *Like that was a good idea.*

"If it was up to me, I wouldn't be here. It sucked spending most of the day in the counselor's office, catching up on schoolwork." I sigh.

"I'm glad you're here."

"Josh, do you have something to share with the class?"

Mr. Grey, our math teacher, inquires while standing next to Josh's desk.

"No." Josh scrunches his face, making me laugh.

School goes on like nothing has happened. For that matter, so does everything. Not that I expect the world to stop at my loss, but I'm not prepared for the continuous normalcy of it all either.

Josh waits until Mr. Grey is back at his desk before leaning my way once again. "Hey, what're you doing tonight?"

I shrug.

"You want to go to the lake?" he asks.

"That would be fun."

"Eric and Jill are going and, to be honest, it's been a while since we all hung out. I miss you."

I smile, "You need a bestie fix?"

"Yeah, I do."

"I'll ask. I'm not sure if Dad has something planned for tonight or not."

Mr. Grey clears his throat. We turn our attention back to the worksheet.

The final school bell rings. Josh waits for me to hand in a few late assignments, then walks me out to my car.

"If you can go, want me to pick you up?"

"I'll text you."

"Okay," he hugs me tight.

HURRYING home in Grandma's hand-me-down, silver Toyota Camry, I blow through the stop sign at the corner of Waverly and Jones. "Oh, crap, all I need is a ticket." A few blocks later and still no sign of cops, I let out sigh and slow down. Alex is walking down our gravel lane, dragging her backpack behind her. I stop alongside of her. "Hey Bug, how was school?"

She climbs in. "I don't know."

"What'd you do today?"

"Nothing."

"You had to have done something," I say.

"My stomach hurt all day. I hate school."

"No, you don't. It'll get better. Trust me."

DAD SITS at the kitchen table, going over the farm's finances, when we push through the screen door. "Hey, Dad."

"Hey Brie, how was school?"

"Alright," I say, even though that's far from the truth.

"How about you, Alex?"

She grabs a cookie from the counter. "It was awful." She hurries out of the kitchen.

"What's wrong with Alex?"

I raise my brows. "She misses mom."

Dad looks down at the papers once again. "We all do."

The need to get away from here hits me hard. "Is it alright if I go to the lake tonight? It's been forever since I hung out with my friends."

"You have to get your chores done first."

"I will."

"And I don't want you out too late."

"I won't be."

On the way to my room, I text Josh: What time you going to the lake?

Josh: 7 - need a ride?

Me: no see you there

Josh: Awesome

I pause in the doorway of my parents' bedroom; it's

exactly how Mom had left it. My eyes water and my stomach knots into a ball.

Alex comes up behind me. "Whatcha doing?" she asks.

I sniff back tears before turning around. "Nothing."

"Sometimes I can still hear her." Alex looks on, teary-eyed.

"Hey, I got something for you." I guide her away from the door.

"What is it?" She wipes her eyes as she follows me into my room, then plops onto my bed.

"Remember this? My old jewelry box—I found it in my closet. You want it?"

"*Really?*"

"Yep, all yours. And everything in it."

She squeals with delight, dumping the contents out onto the bed. "You don't want any of this?"

"Nah . . . It's yours."

"But isn't this your favorite ring?" She slips it on her thumb.

"It's yours now. Wanna help me make dinner?"

"No thanks." She gathers everything up. "I got my own things to do."

I change into a pair of shorts and t-shirt, and then pull my hair back into a ponytail. Alex is in her room, trying on jewelry and singing as I walk by.

"You might want to open your window, let some air in here."

"K." She clasps another bracelet around her wrist. "This one's so cool."

"Hey, bug." She rolls her eyes up. "You need to get your chores done."

"K."

Monday, Wednesday, and Friday, one of the chores that

had been added to my list when I turned twelve was to make dinner. It was fun at first, but now I would rather clean the barn than cook. Mom had said it was essential to learn, but admitted to me later on that she didn't like to cook either.

"Where's Grandma?" I ask, pulling out a pot and skillet from the cabinet.

"She's not feeling well," Dad says.

"What d'you mean not well? Where is she?"

Dad must have heard the unease in my voice. He puts his pen down and looks up at me. "She's upstairs lying down. She just has a headache."

"Should I get her something?"

"I'm sure she'll be down in a little bit. This week has gotten to all of us."

"I know."

Alex runs through the kitchen and out the backdoor. "Slow down." Dad yells, gathering up the papers in front of him. "I'll be outside if you need me." He stacks the papers on the counter and heads out the door.

Our kitchen is big and old. Dark cupboards with chrome handles line two walls, top and bottom. The marred and stained countertop doesn't do the room justice. Dad once promised Mom that he would update the space, but it never got done.

I plunk the ground beef into the skillet and squish it with the spatula. Tonight, we're having spaghetti. It's one of my favorites because it's easy to make. Alex comes through the door with a basket full of laundry from the close-line. She plops it onto the floor and sits at the kitchen table to fold the clothes.

"What're you doing tonight?" she asks.

"Going to the lake with Josh."

"Can I go?" she pleads.

"Did you forget about Aunt Edna? Didn't you promise her a movie or something?"

"I know," she lets out a puff of air. "But I love the lake."

"You can't break a promise."

"But it's so hot," she whines.

"We can go to the lake tomorrow, or Sunday."

"You pinky swear?" she holds out her little finger.

We lock pinkies. "I swear."

"What are you swearing to?" Grandma asks, coming into the kitchen.

"Brie is taking me to the lake tomorrow."

Grandma takes a quick peek at the noodles boiling, profound sadness is engraved on her face. I wonder if she'll ever be back to her old self. "How're you feeling?" I ask, even though I already know.

"Better," she says with a slight, unconvincing smile.

"Alex and I have everything under control."

"I bought some garlic bread at the store. It's in the cupboard."

"I think we can manage. Now, go sit down," I order.

Grandma looks at Alex and nods in my direction. "Bossy, isn't she?"

"I could've told you that," Alex says.

"I think I will go sit down for a bit." She leaves without another word.

"That's weird." Alex's face tightens. "She didn't even ask about school."

"She's just tired. She'll be talking your ear off before you know it." I try to ensure her.

Alex drops the folded clothes back into the basket and pushes it into the living room. She comes back to set the table. I mix together the meat, spaghetti sauce, and noodles, then set the bowl on the table. "Wanna tell Dad dinner's ready?"

"Dad!" she screams through the screen door.

"Holy crap, Alex, I could've done that."

When Dad opens the door, Gibson bolts inside and in-between his legs. "Damn cat," he grumbles.

Alex scoops her up into her arms. "Where've you been?" She scratches behind Gibson's ear.

"Get that cat out of the kitchen," Dad orders, making his way to the sink.

Alex kisses Gibson's head as she takes her into the other room. When Alex comes back, Gibson bolts into the kitchen and under the table. Dad must not have noticed.

"Smells good," Grandma says, making her way to the table. "If this heat keeps up, we're going to have to take dinner outside, under the shade tree."

Alex jumps to her feet, plate in hand. "Can we do it now?"

Dad looks at her out of the corner of his eye. "Sit down." He turns to me. "Brie, go get the fan from the other room."

"Isn't there supposed to be a cold front moving in tonight?" Grandma asks, wiping the back of her neck with a napkin.

"Yes, it's supposed to get downright cold later on tonight. And it can't come soon enough," Dad says. "This heat is taking its toll on the cattle."

Once the fan is on, we settle down to eat. Without Mom, our normal dinner routine feels abnormal. She was the one that kept the conversation going, but now it's oddly quiet.

Gibson rubs against my leg and purrs. I dig a piece of meat out of the spaghetti and discreetly drop it to the floor.

She gobbles it up. Alex looks over at me and smiles as she, too, drops a small bit of food to the floor.

BY THE TIME the kitchen is cleaned up and the laundry is put away, it's six o'clock. When Aunt Edna picks up Alex, she convinces Dad and Grandma to go with her too. I hurry to change into my swimsuit and stuff extra clothes into a bag.

Even though Fireman's Park in Elkhart usually closes after Labor Day, they're keeping it open longer this year because the weather is unseasonably hot. Throughout the ten-minute drive, I have to snake through patches of dense woods and then speed down to the lake. The beach is crowded. Luckily, there's a parking spot next to Josh's car. It's a tight fit. I reach for my bag, inhale deeply, and squeeze out the door.

As soon as Josh sees me, he jumps up and runs my way. "Need help with anything?"

"No, I've just got my bag."

He turns around in front of me and walks backward.

"What are you doing?"

"Got a surprise. . ." he stumbles, I grab onto his shirt, but that doesn't stop him from tumbling to the ground.

"Oh my God, are you okay?" I can't help but laugh.

He laughs. Jumping to his feet, he grabs onto me. "I meant for that to happen."

"Yeah, sure you did." I brush the sand off the side of his face. "Just like when you fell out of the hayloft? I think you were backing up then, too."

"Ouch! That was Gibson's fault." His dimples deepen.

"Oh, that's sad," I chuckle. "Blaming a cat."

I believe, Josh could have his pick of any girl, with his good looks and funny sense of humor. I love him very much . . . in a brotherly sort of way. Or at least that's what I keep telling myself. Especially after the falling out we had a few years ago.

He asked me out one other time since then, but I'm not sure I want to jeopardize our friendship again. I think he must feel the same way, as the subject of dating hasn't been brought up in a long time. "Come on," he says, taking my hand in his. He leads me over to where Jill and Eric are. The four of us have been friends since elementary school.

As we approach, Jill shouts, "Happy Birthday!" On the blanket is a huge, decorated chocolate chip cookie.

"My birthday's September 29th – that's tomorrow," I say, thinking how my birthday won't be the same without Mom.

"We know, but we thought we would surprise you tonight," Josh says. "This way you get to celebrate twice."

Josh and Eric were out of town the day of Mom's funeral. Josh was upset he couldn't be with me. He called me every chance he could. Both of them were invited to visit a college out east, and their families had already made their travel plans several months in advance. Both Josh and Eric have a good chance at a basketball scholarship. Jill had been there for me, but honestly, most of the week was a blur.

Jill hands me her gift. I tear off the purple paper and open the box. Inside is a beautiful bracelet with two charms attached. Jill points to a heart surrounded by three crystals. "The heart is supposed to be you, and each of the crystals represents us, your friends. This one, of course, Wisconsin's state flower, the violet, is to remind you where your home is."

Jill is the most sentimental person ever. She puts so much thought into everything she does. "I love it!"

Eric hands me a gift. "This is from us," he nods toward Josh.

I'm a little leery about this one when I see the grins plastered on their faces. Carefully opening it, I expect something to come flying out. But instead, I'm taken aback by the iPod inside.

"Gotcha!" Josh laughs.

"You guys shouldn't have."

"Since Eric destroyed your last one . . ."

Eric interjects, "I think it was your fault, too."

"Thanks, I love it."

"Now can we eat the cookie?" Eric asks. "I'm starving."

It's amazing how much he can eat. You would think he'd be huge—not the skinny, six-foot-tall, athletic guy that he is. Jill cuts the cookie into four large pieces. My appetite hasn't been very good over the last few weeks, so I scoot my share over to Eric. He takes it without hesitation.

With a mouth full of cookie, Eric says, "Hey, did you hear Jill is going to New York for Christmas?"

"You are?" I ask.

"Yeah. My mom's taking me to visit my aunt in Manhattan."

"Awesome," Josh says.

Their conversation fades, as the realization hits me that my mom won't be here for the holidays. As my emotions become jagged again, I drop my head into my hands.

Josh whispers in my ear, "You okay?"

Before I have a chance to answer, Jill tactfully shouts, "Hey, come on! Let's go for a swim."

I look up and mouth to her, "Thanks."

Inaudibly, her lips move, *No problem.* She runs for the water with Eric.

I lay my head on Josh's shoulder. His arm falls around

me. "You really are my best friend. You do know that, right?" he says.

"Yeah, I do." My mind races with thoughts of Mom. "I just wish I could stop thinking for a while."

"Remember when I broke my foot and was benched the entire basketball season? You kept me busy to keep my mind off it. Not to mention all those *fun* chores you let me do." He looks down at the scar on his hand. "Found out the hard way that barn cats don't like to be bathed."

I snicker, "I'm sorry, I didn't really think you'd try it. But I'd give anything to have that on video."

"I know that doesn't compare to what you're going through, but I'm here for you. No matter what you need."

"Thanks, Josh."

"Keeping busy—your words." He pulls me to my feet. "Let's go for a swim."

I nod. "Okay." For a little while, I do manage to stop thinking and have fun.

As night falls, the wind picks up and clouds fill the sky. The temperature drops fast. It doesn't take long for the beach to clear out, giving us the place to ourselves. Eric and Josh go looking for firewood while Jill and I walk back to my car to change into dry clothes.

"You're kinda quiet tonight. You okay?" Jill asks.

"Yeah, it's just been hard."

"I can't even imagine. You know, it's good that Josh is here,"

"Yeah, he's a great friend," I say, climbing into the backseat.

Jill changes her clothes behind the open car door. "You know, you and Josh belong together."

"I can't believe how cold it is." I say, trying to change the subject.

She leans down to look in at me. "Why're you so scared?"

"I have no idea what you're talking about."

"Josh isn't going anywhere; you're not going to lose him," Jill says.

"You don't know that…Besides we've tried dating and it didn't work out."

"Oh my God, that was in seventh grade. That doesn't count." Jill chuckles.

"Yeah, and we didn't talk all summer after that." My emotions are all over the place, and right now I'm better off staying friends with him. "Anyway, I think Josh is good with just being friends, too."

"I don't believe that. I see the way he looks at you and how happy both of you are when you're around each other."

"We're friends."

"Okay, whatever you say."

WE TAKE in the warmth of the fire as we sit together on the blanket. Our conversation becomes an amalgamation of gossip, sports, and college dreams. I drift in and out of the conversation while thinking about my future.

Jill gasps when she looks down at her phone. "It's officially your birthday."

"It's midnight already?"

When she starts singing a terrible rendition of happy birthday, Josh and Eric join in.

I laugh. "That was totally awful!"

"We should karaoke some time," Eric says.

"Yeah . . . like *that's* a good idea." Josh's brows rise.

Jill pulls her phone out of her pocket. "No service. I'll look it up when I get home."

"I was kidding," Josh adds.

"I wasn't." Eric looks at me, "You're in . . . right?"

"I'll watch," I say. "But seriously, I have to get home."

Eric and Josh put out the fire. Jill and I gather up our things and make our way to the car.

Jill shrieks when Eric grabs her from behind. "Will you stop doing that?"

Eric laughs. "Never."

"You guys are so cute together." I chuckle.

She whispers in my ear, "So are you and Josh."

My cheeks warm; I look away. I brush the sand from my feet and slip my flip-flops back on. Eric and Jill wave as they drive away.

Josh hugs me. "I'll follow you out of here."

In this moment, I miss Mom more than ever. I know I won't wake up to her singing the Beatles' birthday song or enjoy her birthday pancakes or spend the entire day being pampered. She made every birthday special. "I'd like to be alone, just for a little while," I say.

"Are you sure that's a good idea right now?" There's a touch of hesitation in his voice.

I had shared so many of these memories with him that he must know how I'm feeling. "It'll be like ten minutes," I try to ensure him. "Just need to chill a little." He pauses, and our eyes meet. "Josh, Please."

"I'll stop over tomorrow."

"Thanks."

"Text me when you get home."

"I will."

He hugs me again. "Happy Birthday, Brie,"

Tears fill my eyes; I turn away, not wanting him to see. "I'll talk to you later."

Before getting into his car, he yells over at me. "Will you at least get in your car and start it up before I leave."

I nod. Keeping my eyes from him, I get in my car and turn over the engine.

AS HIS TAILLIGHTS slowly disappear in the distance, I take a deep breath and rest my hands on the steering wheel. Mom—and all her party ideas we had talked about for this year—consume my thoughts. My eighteenth birthday was supposed to be awesome. "I miss you, Mom."

I reach across the seat for the bracelet Jill had given me and attempt to fasten it around my wrist, but it falls in between the seats. Before I can retrieve it, a funny feeling comes over me. Lifting my eyes to the windshield, I come face to face with the stranger from the funeral.

Closing my eyes, I mumble, "It's all in your head. No one's there. Just breathe." After a few more encouraging words to myself, I force my eyes open just a smidge.

His steadfast glare pierces through me. Quickly closing my eyes, I throw the car into reverse and hit the accelerator.

My heart pulsates in my throat. I slam on the brakes and jam the shifter into drive. Short bursts of random music blast from the speakers, causing my ears to ring. I smash down on the accelerator. The car thrusts forward only a few yards before coming to a sudden stop. My head hits the steering wheel the same time the window next to me shatters, sending pieces of broken glass into the side of my face. Blood trickles down my cheek.

Forcing myself to look out the windshield, I feel the world close in. And there—standing rigid against the front of my car—is the stranger.

"*What do you want!?*" I'm barely getting the words out when the car's engine dies.

The stranger beckons to me, urging me to leave my car.

"*No, go away!*" The more I resist, the more compelling his command becomes. "This can't be happening. Please stop!"

Like a puppet, my hand involuntarily opens the door and I step out. His stance never changes as his body moves toward the lake. Powerless against his control, I trudge through the sand toward him.

Chills crawl up my spine when my feet plunge into the water. "Don't do this. Please let me go."

Impassive to my pleas, he urges me further into the lake until my feet can no longer touch. Rendered immobile from the neck down, I inhale one last breath and am completely submerged. The more I fight to free my limbs, the faster air is expelled from my lungs. I gasp under the intense pressure, ingesting the water. Panic rips through me. My body convulses, trying to hang onto life.

My thoughts briefly turn to my sister and the promise that I would never leave. With that thought, my frozen limbs are freed. Desperately, I extend my arm in the direction of the surface, but it's too late.

Shrouded in stillness, my body halts the fight and gradually descends to the bottom of the lake. I want to live—I don't want to die like this.

FOUR

Awakening

I cough, releasing the liquid from my lungs and replacing it with the cool night air. The burning in my chest tells me I'm alive. Frantically, I try to clear away what's obscuring my vision when a hand touches my shoulder. I blindly strike at the air.

"Brie, calm down—It's me, Josh." Tears come without warning, and his voice escalates with panic. "*Brie!* Seriously it's me."

The haze slowly clears. Josh hovers over me. "Just lay there and breathe," he says, soaking wet and gasping for air.

A sharp pain knots up in my stomach; my mouth waters. Rolling over, I throw up—over and over until I'm spent. I collapse onto my back. Scattered thoughts whiz through my head.

"*Dammit*, Brie, what were you doing!?" His voice echoes a gravel rasp. "Is this why you wanted to be alone? Trying to kill yourself—is that it?"

Ever increasing confusion consumes me. I try to push

up onto my knees, but the world around me spins, making me lay back down.

"No . . . I was . . . I don't know . . ." I manage to choke out.

"What was going through your mind?" He runs his trembling hands through his wet hair. "Why would you do this?"

Nervous anxiety trundles through me as I lay still, waiting for the pounding in my head and the ache in my stomach to ease. "I'm—I'm sorry, it's not—I mean, it is—but you saw him. Why does he want to hurt me?"

"What're you talking about?"

"That man that . . ." I can't even say the words.

"See who?" He scans the area. "There's nobody here but us."

"No . . ." I try to get up again, to protect myself. "He's here . . ."

Josh touches my shoulder. "Brie, look at me . . . we're alone." When I see the pain in his eyes, tears cloud my vision. "No one's going to hurt you."

"Then how do you explain . . ." I throw my hand up in the direction of my car, and I'm horrified to see my car crumpled against a tree. "That's not right." A large branch lies on top of the car's dented roof.

"You took off so fast you didn't even try to stop when you hit the tree."

"That's not how it happened." I rub my eyes, trying to wipe away any deception. When my hand brushes against a lump on the side of my face, I flinch.

"We need to get you to the hospital."

"No, I need to get home."

"You hit your head hard. You need to go to the hospital. Besides that, you're bleeding." He carefully helps me to my feet. Once I move, pain shoots through me, making my mouth water again.

"I'm going to be sick."

Barely making it to the car, I push him away and throw up. I rest against the bumper and lean into my hands to wait for the nausea to subside.

Josh digs through his duffel bag, pulling out a sweat-shirt and a pair of sweats. "These will warm you up."

Without hesitation, I change into the dry clothes. They're huge but it's better than being wet. Josh pulls out another shirt and a pair of shorts and changes.

He helps me into the car and rushes to the driver's side. The inexplicable events of the night muddle my thoughts. My lips quiver. "You're not going to tell anyone about this, are you?"

"What if I didn't come back?" Sadness crosses his face as he stares at me. "What if this happens again? I'd never forgive myself if anything happens to you."

"I want you to say you believe me. I'd never try to kill myself."

"You scared the hell out of me."

"You think I would do that to my family? Come on, Josh, please. I'd never do that, and you know it." The thought of my family, especially Alex, thinking I would hurt myself is unbearable. Placing my hand on his arm, I sigh. "Josh, please."

He eyes the bump on my head—the bump that I can feel growing bigger by the second. "How're you going to explain all this?" His voice breaks.

"We can tell everyone that my car got stuck, and that I had the accelerator pressed to the floor while you tried to push me out. The tires gripped the pavement faster than I anticipated and the car lunged forward, smashing into the tree."

"Then how do you explain almost drowning?"

"We won't tell them that."

"I don't know." He sighs.

The nausea and headache return with a vengeance. "I'm not feeling good."

"Hold on, you'll be fine." He shifts the car into drive and speeds toward town.

When we pull up in front of the hospital, I hold my position. "I'm not getting out until you promise me that you'll stick to our story."

"You mean your story?"

I can see his reluctance. To put myself in his position, I'm not sure what I'd believe either. The seconds I wait for his response feel like hours.

Finally, he nods. "I guess."

I trust him. I have to.

AFTER I'M CHECKED over thoroughly, Josh is allowed to come back to my room. He sits in the chair next to the bed.

"So, what did the doctor say?" he asks.

"Waiting on tests."

"How you feeling?"

"Okay, I guess."

Suddenly, Dad bolts through the door. His voice radiates with panic. "What on earth happened?" He rushes over to the side of my bed.

"Sorry, Dad, I didn't mean to worry you. The car, it's not good."

"Don't worry about that." He brushes my hair away from the lump on my head. "Oh, Brie, are you sure you're okay?"

"Just tired is all."

He relaxes a bit when the doctor comes in and tells us I have a mild concussion, but everything else checked out fine

"You're going to have a pretty good headache in the morning," the doctor warns.

He isn't telling me anything new; it hurts to even blink.

"I want to keep her here a few hours for observation."

"I want to go home," I argue, wanting to forget this night ever happened.

"Now, Brie, we have to listen to the doctor. He knows what's best."

With a heavy sigh, I roll over to stare at the wall.

"I'll check back in a little bit," the doctor says before leaving the room.

"So, could you explain to me exactly what happened tonight?" Dad questions Josh.

"It was just an accident, not Brie's fault."

"I'm sure it was, but I would like to hear it from you."

I hold my breath, glancing over my shoulder at Josh. I'm relieved when he tells him the story we agreed on.

Dad is silent. His eyes move from Josh to me, as if questioning the story. Before anything else can be asked, Josh jumps to his feet. "I better be going . . . Uh . . . I'm sure Mom is wondering where I'm at." He leans in and whispers, "I trust you."

Thanks, I quietly mouth.

"See you, Mr. Birlow."

Dad nods as Josh leaves the room. He then turns his attention to me. "You have anything to add to the story?" without commenting, I close my eyes to avoid answering. "We'll talk about this later," he says.

A few hours later, I'm released from the hospital.

The ride home is quiet. It's late, and I'm tired. Dad must be tired too. He keeps a steady hand on the wheel and his eyes glued to the road. We arrive home around four in the morning. I walk through the kitchen door and into Grandma's arms.

"Thank God you're okay," she says, squeezing me tight, you scared ten years off my life.

"I'm sorry, Grandma."

"Are you hungry?"

"No, I just need some sleep."

She lightly touches the side of my face. "You let me know if you need anything."

"I will."

Tired and sore, I make my way up the stairs, grab pajamas out of my room, then head to the bathroom for a much needed shower. Before stepping into the tub, I look in the mirror. The cuts on the side of my face look horrible. Worried that they might scar, I rummage through the medicine cabinet for something that might soothe the redness—peroxide, iodine, bandages . . . none of that will work. I close the cabinet and eye the bruise, which I'm sure will take days to go away.

I think about Josh and the differences in our stories. Maybe he's right. Hitting my head so hard could have caused confusion. With that thought, an unsettling feeling rushes through me. My mind flashes back to the stranger.

FIVE

Reasoning

My head is pounding even before I open my eyes, reassuring me that last night wasn't a dream. Slowly propping up on one elbow, it takes a moment for the haze to clear. Brushing my hand over the bruise makes me cringe. The bump feels gargantuan.

Thinking back on the night, I remember clearly what I saw, but in the light of day, Josh's story does make more sense. I hang my legs over the side of the bed and slide my feet into slippers. Upon standing, the room spins, making me sit back down. It takes a few moments for the light-headedness to pass before I can try to get up again.

Passing by the mirror on my dresser, I'm shocked to see how dark the bruise has become. It's going to take some creative hairstyles to cover this up, but for now a ponytail will do.

I make my way downstairs and into the kitchen. Grandma comes through the back door with an arm full of groceries. "How are you doing this morning, darling?" she asks.

"I'm fine."

"You look a little pale."

"I'm fine. But where's Alex?" I ask.

"She's helping your dad with chores."

"Is she ok? Does she know?"

"She's fine. Your dad told her you had a little accident but nothing serious."

"I'm so sorry."

"Its fine, you're fine." She sets the groceries on the counter. "But you've got to take it easy today. Your dad wants you to rest."

"I need some aspirins."

"Go lie down, I'll get them." She follows me out of the kitchen and into the living room toward the couch. "And I'll get you something to eat." She hands me the remote. "Now, you rest."

The night plays over in my head as I lie on the couch, flipping through the channels on TV. There's got to be more to the story.

Grandma brings me a tray of scrambled eggs, toast, juice, and two aspirins. Setting the tray on the end table, she hands me the aspirins, then the juice. "These will make you feel better." She places her hand on the side of my face. "You gave us all a scare last night." She takes the blanket from the chair and lays it across my legs. The fatigue that she carries on her face seems even worse today.

"Are you alright, Grandma?"

"I'm fine, honey. Just a little tired is all."

"I can take care of myself. Why don't you go lie down?"

She smiles, "I like taking care of you. Keeps me busy."

"Keeping busy keeps you moving forward . . . Right?" I say, repeating the same words she's spoken to me several times over the years.

A weary smile crosses her face. "Promise me that you'll be more careful."

"I will."

She kisses the top of my head. "I love you, Brie."

"I love you, too."

"You need anything else?"

"No."

"You get some rest. I'll be in the kitchen if you need me."

I kick off the blanket and reach for the tray. My stomach growls. Gibson bounds onto the couch, nudging my arm. "Smells good, doesn't it, girl?" I give her a bite of egg; she gobbles it up, then comes back for more. "That's it for you."

Once I've got a full stomach, my eyes grow heavy. I move the tray to the floor and nestle into the couch. Gibson jumps down to sniff around on the tray. "Sorry girl, I ate it all."

Each time I'm about to doze off, Grandma comes into the room to check on me. Eventually though, I fall asleep.

MY EYES open to Alex crouched down, leaning in close to me. "How're you feeling?" She sighs.

"Good."

She squints while eyeing the bump on my head, "Does it hurt?"

"Not really." I pull her onto the couch next to me. "I want you to know I wasn't in any real danger."

She traces the pattern on her shirt. "Are you sure?" She sucks in a wobbly breath.

"Yes, it was just a freak accident."

"I did your chores today."

"You did? So, what do I owe you?"

"Just always be here." She wraps her arms around my neck and buries her head in my shoulder.

I hug her tight. "I'm never going to leave. You don't have to worry about that."

She keeps her head pressed against my shoulder. "Promise me again," her voice breaks.

"I promise I'll never leave you."

She sits up to stare at me. Her lashes brim heavy with tears.

I smile. "Now don't worry."

Her bottom lip quivers as she forces a grin. Gibson bounds onto the couch and nuzzles against her. Alex sweeps Gibson into her arms and cuddles her close.

"See, she doesn't want you to be sad either." I wipe away her tears. "Why don't you go see if Grandma needs any help?"

"You want me to bring you something?"

"Nope, I'm good."

She sets Gibson on the floor before disappearing into the kitchen. I hope that I've relieved some of her fears. I know I told myself that I'd like to skip my birthday this year but I'm a little disappointed that no one, not even Alex, has mentioned it.

There's a light tapping on the front door, then Josh peers in. "Anyone here?"

"You don't have to knock."

He drags in two large boxes. "I just have one question . . ." He stops in mid-sentence; his mouth drops open.

"What?"

"Wow! I've never seen anything so big." He stares at the bump on my head.

"It's not that bad."

"Have you seen it?"

"Okay, stop."

"I'm just kidding." He sets one of the boxes on the table. "Have you ever cleaned out your car?"

"A few times."

"I stopped by the garage where your car was towed and cleaned it out for you." His brows rise. "All the stuff barely fit into two boxes."

"I only carry things I might need."

"Oh, right, what about this?" He pulls out a shoe. "Why do you have only *one* shoe in your car?"

"That's where it is."

He shakes his head. "What about these?" He pulls out an arm full of clothing.

"You never know when you'll be stranded."

He laughs. "You had enough stuff in your car to be stranded for days and never wear the same thing twice. With the exception of the one shoe, you're set."

"It wasn't that bad."

"Reality check—it was." His brows shoot up.

"Josh, about last night . . ." I stop when Grandma comes into the room.

"Well, hello Josh. I didn't even hear you come in." She says.

"Hey, Mrs. B."

Beatrice is my grandma's name but everyone just calls her "B." She feels my head again. "Do you need more aspirins, dear?" She'll only let me get up to go to the bathroom. She told me that with a mild concussion I need to stay down.

"My head doesn't hurt too bad right now."

"What about you, Josh? Would you like something to drink?"

"Thanks, Mrs. B, but I'm good."

"I'll leave you two alone, then." Grandma says.

"I got you something." Josh hands me a small wrapped box.

"For what?"

"Your birthday, silly."

"You got me something already, remember?"

"This is from just me."

"Josh, you shouldn't have."

"But I did. Now open it." His excitement shows as I open the box, revealing a white-gold charm. "It's your zodiac sign, the Libra. I was with Jill when she bought the bracelet. Seeing how you're into all that, I thought you would like it."

"It's so beautiful." When our eyes lock, a strange sensation stirs within; I look away, feeling the color deepen in my face. "The bracelet, did you find it? I dropped it in-between the seats."

He digs through a box and holds it up. "I told you I pulled everything out of your car, even a few things I didn't want to." He fastens it around my wrist and then attaches the charm. Josh isn't into astrology; he says it isn't logical. But he lets me read his horoscope to him occasionally.

"It's perfect. Thanks, Josh."

"You're welcome."

His marbled brown eyes seem to see right through me. I drop my gaze. "My phone—was it in the car?

He pulls it out of his pocket "Yep."

"Thank goodness." It's dead but at least it isn't at the bottom of the lake. "You going to stay awhile?"

"Sure, as long as you rest."

"You're kinda acting like my dad," I tease.

A slight grin appears on his face. He falls against the back of the couch. "Aw . . . I've just been roasted." His tongue rolls out the side of his mouth.

I chuckle. "You're so weird." I nuzzle against him. "Be my pillow, now."

He wraps his arm around me. "Seriously, though, how you feeling today?"

I look up at him and can tell right away that he's asking more about my mental state than my physical state. I choose to act imperceptive. "Sore."

"You started to say something about last night?"

"Just wanted to thank you again."

"I'm glad I was there." He gently touches the side of my face. My heart flutters as my cheeks heat up. "If there's anything you want to talk about, I'm here."

"I know."

Grandma startles us when she comes into the room. "Thought maybe you two would like some lemonade."

Hastily, I turn away and argue with myself in silence. *What just happened? —Remember what happened last time we tried this—*

She hands Josh a glass. "Thanks, Mrs. B." He moves to the chair next to the couch. Grandma runs her hand over my cheeks and then my forehead, "You look a little flushed." She fluffs up the throw pillow then digs two aspirins out from her apron pocket. "You don't want to wait until the pain gets too bad." She once again covers my legs with a blanket. I wait until she leaves the room to kick it off.

"I bought Davis's old truck," Josh says.

"You mean that ugly truck that's been for sale forever?"

"Yeah, it just needs a little work. My boss said I could work on it at the garage in my spare time."

"That's funny. I never pictured you in a purple truck." I laugh.

His lips twist into a goofy smile. "It's plum."

I chuckle again. "And . . .that's better?"

"I'll make it look good."

"Let me guess, pink racing stripes," I tease. We both chuckle.

"Besides," he says, "I could have it running by tonight, and I thought maybe if you wanted, you could drive my Toyota. You know, if you want."

"You didn't buy the truck 'cause of me, did you?"

"No," he says way too fast. He sits rigid in the chair. "I've been thinking about it for a while."

Not wanting to add to his obvious discomfort, I accept. "That would be awesome, but I have to clear it with Dad first," I say.

He relaxes a bit, "Are you tired?"

"Not really."

"Want to watch something on TV?"

"You can watch whatever you want; I'm just going to lay here."

"The basketball game is on. The Badgers are doing great this year. Wanna watch that?"

"Sure." I move over. "It's more comfortable on the couch," I say.

I lay my head on his shoulder and attempt to watch the game, but the stranger permeates my every thought. I feel like I'm on the verge of a mental breakdown and need something plausible to hang on to. "Josh, if I tell you something, can you promise to keep it a secret?"

His attention shifts to me. "Of course."

"You can't laugh."

"I won't."

"Weird things have been happening to me since Mom died—things that I can't explain." My voice pitches with fear. "I think I'm going insane."

"You're the sanest person I know."

"Then why is it that what you told me happened last night is not how I remember it?"

"Is this about that man again?" he asks.

"I'm telling you he was there."

"I saw the whole thing, Brie."

"I *need* you to believe me."

"I believe you," he sighs uncomfortably, "it's just, what happened last night really scared me."

"You don't think it scared me? I'm living it. You know it's not the first time I saw him."

"*What?*" His voice booms.

"Shhh . . . I don't want Grandma to hear." I glance toward the kitchen door. "You've got to keep this to yourself." His face is stuck in an incredulous expression, making me think twice about confiding in him. "You still don't believe me . . . do you?"

"It's not that . . . it's just . . . ."

"Ridiculous?"

He hesitates. Now, I regret telling him.

"Thanks a lot, Josh. I thought I could at least trust you to listen."

"I don't want to fight with you."

"Yeah . . . Ok, just forget I said anything." I turn away.

"I'm sorry, you're right. You should be able to tell me anything." His arm falls around me once again. "I've just never been that scared before."

"Me either." The thought of it still scares me.

"When else did you see him?"

A wave of apprehension flutters through me, but I can't go through this alone. "I saw him at my mom's funeral."

"Did he say anything to you?"

"No, he was just standing there, staring at me."

"Did anyone else see him?" he asks.

I shake my head. "It's hard to explain . . . but I'm not making this up. And yes, when he's around, weird shit happens."

"How many times has this happened?"

"Two...I'm going crazy . . . right?" I pick at my fingernails while biting back tears.

"No, you're not. You've just been under a lot of stress."

"So, what you're saying—it's all in my head?" That's the last thing I need to hear. Now I wish I never said anything.

He slides his hand over mine. "I believe that you saw something, but can't stress cause this? I mean, look at what you've been through. I've heard about people having weird things happen when they lose someone that they're close to."

"It was too real to be an illusion."

His expression softens. "I bet if you google it right now, you'll find all kinds of people who've had these experiences. Stress sucks."

A bit of relief trickles through me. "You think that's all it is?"

"I know you're trying to be strong for your family, but you and your mom were really close."

"This has been the hardest year of my life." I sigh.

"I got an idea; let's go to Appleton next week, just to get away from here for a while. I think the art walk is that weekend too." I meet his hopeful gaze. "I know how much you liked it last year."

"You mean . . . like a date?" I gulp.

"No, I mean like a friend taking his friend for some fun."

"Oh sorry." My cheeks heat up once again. We've always done things together. Why am I questioning it now?

"I think you hit your head harder than you thought." He nudges me.

I push him off the couch. "I have to agree."

"Good thing you're cute, even if you're insane."

"Ha! You're funny."

"I've got to go to work." He kisses my cheek. "I'll call you later."

"Okay."

He's calmed my anxiety and made sense of the last few days. As the sound of his car disappears into the distance, I suddenly wish that he could've stayed.

SIX

Almost Perfect

———————————

My dream ends abruptly, and I'm shaken back to reality. Alex is a hazy blur. "Wake up, Brie."

"What time is it?" I yawn.

"Seven." She's leans in close.

"Why didn't you wake me earlier, and why are you so close?"

"Dad said you needed to sleep. Does this hurt?" She touches the bump on my head.

"Ouch, yes."

"Sorry."

"Where're Grandma and Dad?"

"In the kitchen. Grandma wanted me to tell you dinner's ready."

"You haven't eaten yet?"

"Nah, we wanted to wait for you." She jumps up and hurries into the other room, giggling.

As soon as I enter the kitchen, everyone shouts, "Happy birthday!" Dad, Alex, and Grandma begin singing to me, all off-key, but it's enough to make me cry. A birthday cake is on the table, along with several wrapped gifts.

Dad comes over and puts his arm around me. "What's wrong, darling?"

"I thought you all forgot. I thought I didn't care, but I do."

He chuckles. "Oh, sweetie, we would never forget."

"Yeah, Brie, we love you. And look, I helped make the cake." Alex points to the table.

A two-tier, round, slightly lopsided, white cake sits in the middle of the table, decorated with multicolored sprinkles and the word "Brie" piped onto it in pink icing. "It's beautiful." I sniff back tears.

Grandma sets the rest of the food on the table. "Come on, let's all eat so we can enjoy our dessert."

Dad pats the chair next to him. "Come sit by me, Brie." He overfills my plate with meatloaf, mashed potatoes, and corn. He obviously thinks I'm starving.

"I can't eat all that."

"You have to be hungry."

"Have you ever seen me eat that much?"

"Good God, John, you're not feeding cattle," Grandma says.

"I guess I'm overdoing it a little." He sets the plate in front of me. "You don't have to eat it all."

After dinner, Grandma clears the table while Dad lights the candles. Alex runs to turn off the kitchen light. Mom had always insisted that it be dark when the candles were lit. She used to say it made it easier for your wish to find its way to the stars.

"One more time." Dad, Alex and Grandma, sing, "Happy birthday to you . . ."

I close my eyes and make a wish—not just for me, but for all of us. One big breath and all the candles go out.

Alex hurries to turn on the lights, then hands me her gift. She brings her hands up to her face in excitement. "It's not clothes."

I chuckle. "Uh-huh."

Inside the box is a pale pink sweater, a pair of hoop earrings, and a matching necklace. The sweater is made of angora. I hold it up to my face to feel the softness.

Her eyes widen. "You like it?"

"No—I love it." I wrap my arms around her, squeezing her tight. "When did you find time to go shopping?" We'd been pretty much inseparable over the past few weeks.

Alex confesses, "We didn't go to the movies last night."

I point to Dad. "You actually got him to go to shopping? I'm impressed"

Dad nods. "Yeah. Once a year, I guess I can tolerate it."

Next, Grandma hands me her present. "This is from Aunt Edna and me, she wasn't feeling well tonight." Four gift cards are inside. A fifty-dollar gas card, a fifty-dollar card to the drug store, a twenty-five-dollar gift certificate to her favorite buffet, and a one-hundred-dollar gift card to the mall in Appleton.

"Grandma, this is way too much."

"Now, it's not every day you turn eighteen. You deserve it."

I hug her. "I love you."

She pats my arm. "I love you, too—very much."

"Okay, mine next," Dad interrupts. "I didn't realize how much this would be needed." He hands me a long, slim box.

I untie the ribbon and open the lid. "You can't be serious?" I hold up a set of keys.

"I figured it was time for you to have your own car."

"Oh my God, this is awesome." I throw my arms around his neck.

He squeezes me tight. "It's out in the barn. Come on, let's go take a look."

"But I'm not dressed."

"It's okay, just put on some shoes." Grandma says and hands me a jacket. "Don't want you getting chilled."

Dad grins. "Let's go see the car."

I shriek with excitement when the gray Pontiac Grand Prix comes into view. I run for the driver's side, open the door, and slide onto the leather seat. I clutch the steering wheel while looking up at Dad. "This is amazing."

"Come on, let's all take a ride," Dad says. "You better let me drive—you still look a little pale."

I start to get in the backseat when Grandma stops me. "Oh no honey, this is your day. You get in front." I hurry around to the passenger side. Grandma and Alex slide into the backseat. Watching Dad and his excitement makes me feel good. It's the first time in months I've seen him enjoy anything.

As he drives, he demonstrates the built-in GPS, along with all the other features on the car. He tells us a story about when he bought his first truck and a few misadventures he had with it. Grandma chimes in with a few first-time car stories of her own. We return home an hour later. I never did get to drive, but that's okay. Dad parks the car by his truck.

"It's time for cake?" Alex squeals, hustling to get out of the car.

"Now, you wait for me," Grandma says, shutting the car door behind her.

"When you feel up to it, I'll show you how to change the tires and check the oil." Dad says.

I joke, "You mean it's different than the truck or

Grandma's car?" At fourteen, I'd been taught how to replace tires, change oil, check fluids—not only in the cars, but also farm machinery.

"I just want to make sure you're safe."

Before heading inside, I turn to look at the car once more. Dad comes up beside me. "I hope you know how much I love you." He takes my hand in his. "I remember when you were little, you always insisted on holding my hand wherever we went. You remember that?"

"Yeah—I love you, too."

"You're a great daughter. I've been blessed to have you in my life." He smiles. "I just thought you oughta know that."

"You're pretty awesome too, Dad."

There's one last gift on the table. Dad goes over, picks it up, and hands it to me. "This is from your mother. She had wanted me to give this to you on your birthday. I promised her that I would."

My chest tightens. "Oh, Dad, I don't think I can open it."

"It's okay. Take your time, open it when you're ready."

Mom loved to wrap gifts and must have wrapped this one herself. The seams of the paper are placed precisely together, giving it a flawless look. Even the ribbon that winds around the box comes together on top to form a perfect bow.

Tears sting my eyes. "I'm going to take my stuff upstairs." I hurry for my room as tears stream down my face. Unable to open her gift right now, I carefully set it on my dresser.

"Everything okay?" Dad yells from the bottom of the staircase.

"Yeah, Dad, I'll be down in a minute." It takes me a little bit to stop the tears.

. . .

BY THE TIME I make my way downstairs, Alex and Grandma have the kitchen cleaned, and Dad is sitting on the couch, watching TV. I go over to join him.

"Did you have a good birthday?" he asks, putting his arm around me.

"It was almost perfect." I sigh. Not wanting him to feel bad I quickly recant my words. "I mean—it was perfect."

"I know what you meant. But I believe that she's here, taking in this moment with us."

Alex comes into the living room, carrying two bowls of ice cream and cake. She hands one to me, then plops down next to me.

"You want a piece of cake, John?" Grandma yells from the kitchen.

"No, I think I'm going to pass right now." He pats his belly. "Ate way too much dinner." He winks.

Grandma comes over and gives Alex and me a kiss. "It's been a long day. I'm going to bed."

Dad stands and heads for the door. "I need some fresh air. I'm going into town for a little while. Don't stay up too late, girls." He shuts the door behind him.

"Where you think Dad goes?" Alex asks.

"I don't know," I say. But I do know. He'll come back sometime in the middle of the night and stumble up the stairs. It's been like this since the funeral.

"Can I sleep with you?" Alex asks as we take our empty bowls to the kitchen.

"Yeah."

"I'll beat you." She runs for the stairs. My body aches but that doesn't stop me from trying to get to the top first. We hurry to the bathroom, quickly brush our teeth, wipe our faces, and then run to my room.

Alex screams, "I got here first." She jumps onto the bed.

"Shhh . . . you'll wake Grandma."

I throw her one of my shirts. She changes, then flops down onto the pillow next to Gibson and stares at Mom's gift. "What do you think is in it?"

I shrug.

"Why don't you open it and find out?"

"I will, but I don't want to ruin the wrapping paper just yet."

"It sure is pretty, isn't it?"

"Yes, it is."

She snuggles close to me and within minutes she's fast asleep.

As I lay there, staring at the gift on my dresser, a cricket begins chirping from somewhere in my room. It quickly becomes impossible to ignore. Quiet, so as not to wake Alex, I tiptoe in the direction of the noise. Before following the sound into the hallway, I grab a shoe.

The noise stops when a strange light appears from beneath the attic door. The shoe slips from my hand, whacking my big toe. "*Dammit!*" I grab for my foot, when the air around me warms. Panic replaces the pain.

I know I shouldn't open the attic door in case it's a fire, but I need to confirm my suspicion before waking everyone in the house. I swallow hard while reaching for the doorknob. Abruptly, the door flings open, knocking me to the floor. It slams into the wall with a loud thud. I stare into the darkness of the attic and wait for Grandma to show up, but it soon becomes apparent that no one is coming.

Suddenly, a strange glow eradicates the darkness. It draws me in with visions of Mom. I slowly stand to move toward the light. Crossing the threshold of the attic, I feel the brightness wrap around me, filling me with a sense of peace.

"Mom? Mom is that you?"

The feeling doesn't last long—without warning, the attic door slams shut, extinguishing the light. Anxiety rips through me. I try desperately to open the door, but it won't budge. *"Help me!"* I beat on the door. *Someone has to hear me. Why is no one answering?*

An uneasy breeze blows down from the staircase. An awareness creeps over me that I'm no longer alone. The hairs on the back of my neck stand. "It's not real . . . It's not real . . . It's not real."

An icy draft moves up my bare legs, stopping at the small of my back. Inescapable fear hits hard when I turn and come face to face with the stranger.

My body stiffens with terror. Unable to move, or scream, or even breathe, he lifts his hand to me. Tears edge from my closed eyes and course down my cheek. I flinch away as his cold fingers brush against the bruise on my face.

Slowly opening my eyes, I become immersed in his sorrow. A strange, comforting sensation sweeps over me. Confusion replaces my fear, and it becomes clear that he doesn't want to hurt me—or at least, not right now. He turns, ascending the stairs like a flicker in the dark, never actually moving any part of his body. He coerces me to follow.

Halfway up the stairs, a haze of jumbled images obscures my vision. The cries coming from the unknown explode in my head. Pain pierces my heart. I drop to my knees.

Without delay, the stranger's hand is upon my shoulder. With his touch, the pain subsides, the voices quiet, and the images fade. He encourages me on.

Guiding me to the corner of the attic, he turns and stares into my eyes and for a split second. I think I know him.

His radiance dims as he withdraws. "*Wait!* Why am I here? What am I supposed to do?" My plea doesn't stop him from disappearing among the boxes and old junk piled around me.

SEVEN

Memories

The luster given off by the moon shines through the port-hole window in the adjacent corner of the attic. Just enough light enables me to move a few things around so I can figure out why I've been brought here. I search for a flashlight when I stumble onto an old, battery-operated camping lantern. I flip the switch. To my relief, it works. It takes a moment to summon enough courage to keep strong before I scan the area. *Okay, just focus.* To keep from thinking about the stranger coming back and the fact that I'm up here alone, I concentrate on the stuff around me.

The first thing that catches my eye is an old steamer trunk. I set the lantern down and open the lid. The smell of mothballs makes me sneeze. Old hats, dresses, and other strange looking clothing are inside. It's funny to see the fashions that were considered in-style a century ago. A pair of buttoned, high-top boots is buried beneath a shawl. They would be cute with jeans, so I lay them aside.

Several pieces of jewelry lay in the bottom. A silver bracelet, embellished with a green stone, is too pretty to leave behind. I shove everything back inside the trunk with the exception of the boots and the bracelet and then close it tight to continue on.

Opening a box that is filled with paperback books, I skim through them. They're mostly westerns, a few mysteries, and a set of outdated encyclopedias. It takes all my strength to push the box up against the eave to get it out of my way.

I'm amazed at all the junk we keep. Tennis racquets, baseball gloves, a bat, and a pair of skis are among the sports paraphernalia. Then there's glassware, dishes, and other outdated kitchen gadgets. I pile together all the stuff that doesn't seem to have any significance as to why I'm up here, giving myself some sense of accomplishment.

Several large manila envelopes are stacked on top of one another to hold up a three-legged chair. I move the chair aside to pick up an envelope. *Brie Birlow, fourth grade,* is scribbled in Mom's handwriting across it in black marker. Tucked inside are school papers I'd written and pictures I'd drawn that year. A class picture makes me smile, as I see the faces of a few friends that have since moved away from the area.

Looking through the envelopes and pulling out the yearbooks transports back, it's funny to read some of the comments people wrote to me—especially Josh. He always started off his comments by writing, 'To my girl.' Even in elementary school he was a little strange.

At the bottom of the pile is an old photo album. I'm sure the people in the photos are my relatives on Grandma's side. They look remarkably like her.

I set the photo album, the boots and the bracelet from the trunk, next to the stairs. I want to take them to my room when I'm done.

For most of the night, I rummage through boxes, sacks,

containers, and even a few pieces of luggage, finding nothing that can explain all the creepiness.

I throw my hands into the air. "*Okay, I give up.*" I turn toward the stairs, when the light from the lantern flashes on the hinges of a large trunk. I remember this decoupage flowered trunk. It used to sit at the foot of my mom's bed. It was her 'hope chest,' as she called it. She told me she kept her most cherished possessions inside. It was brought up here years ago to make room for Alex's bassinet.

With a heavy heart, I open the lid and carefully lift out my mom's wedding dress. Tissue paper floats to the floor. The gown is strapless and made from the most beautiful chiffon material. The only embellishment on the dress is a row of pearls used for buttons sewn down the back. Simple but elegant, just like Mom.

A glint of my reflection catches my eye in the full-length mirror next to the trunk. I hold the dress up with one hand and twist my hair up on top of my head with the other, trying to imitate her wedding picture—the one that still hangs in the hallway.

When the memories become too much to bear, I push a large bag filled with stuffed animals off a chair, wipe the dust away with the sleeve of my shirt, and lay the dress down.

It's bittersweet to look at the unorganized mess in the trunk. Mom had to have packed this herself. Some days she would spend hours putting pictures into an album or sorting out recipes. Other days, she would pile papers, pictures, and recipes into a box and stuff it into the closet. She'd say that she would get to it another day. It used to irritate me when she made me help her search for something that she'd misplaced. Now, I'd give anything to have that time back with her.

The first photo I take out is of my parents and me. In

the picture, Dad is holding me with one arm while holding Mom with the other. He's looking at her instead of the camera. They look so happy. For several hours, I look at pictures and read the poetry that Mom had written.

The springs of a spiral bound notebook entangle in the trunk lining. I yank on it, causing the lining to rip. A small hardcover book falls out. The first several pages have been ripped out, leaving behind only ragged edges. I flip through the remaining blank pages and discover a cut-out within the pages. Tucked inside is a necklace.

The pendant is unusual—two silver ropes twisted around each other three times. In between the knots are two black stones. A strange inscription is etched in the silver around the stones.

I say the words out loud, "Totus Malum." My leg suddenly cramps. Dropping the necklace, I grab at my calf to massage the pain away. *Crap!* It hurts beyond belief. It takes a few long minutes for the pain to ease. As soon as it does, a wave of exhaustion takes a hold of me. Looking up at the porthole window, I notice the sky beginning to lighten.

Inhaling deeply, I stretch while eyeing the piles of stuff that I'd gone through—its small compared to all the things that haven't even been touched yet. Right now, though, the need for sleep weighs heavily on me.

Gathering up the tissue paper to place it neatly within the folds of the dress, I lay it carefully into the trunk just like I'd found it.

Picking up the picture, the book, the necklace, and the lantern, I descend the stairs. To my surprise, the door opens with ease. *That's weird.* I set the lantern down, peek into the hallway, and then bolt to my room.

I hide the picture, necklace, and book in my top dresser

drawer before slipping into bed. I'm just about to doze off when Alex whispers, "Hey, Brie, you awake?"

I don't answer.

"Brie," she says again, this time shaking me.

"Yes, Alex."

"I had a bad dream about Dad."

Panic strikes, when I realize that I hadn't heard him come home last night. Even though I'd been preoccupied, I'm sure I would've heard his truck come down the driveway. We jump from the bed and run to his room. He isn't there.

"Where do you think he is?" she asks.

"I'm sure he's fine—he's probably just outside already." We hurry down the stairs when Dad's voice comes from the kitchen. "See, I told you he was okay," I say with a sigh of relief.

"I can't go back to sleep now," Alex says, following me up the stairs.

"Why don't you read or something."

"Wanna play a game?" she asks.

"It's way too early for that."

"But I'm not tired."

"Tell you what, let me sleep until it's time to go to church, then we'll go to the movies or something."

"I thought we were going to the lake?"

"Yeah . . . I don't think that's a good idea today."

She stares at my bruise. "I guess you're right."

"A movie then?"

"Okay." She goes to her room.

I go into my room and collapse onto the bed.

IT SEEMS like I've just closed my eyes when Alex comes into my room and jumps onto my bed. "Brie, it's seven."

"It can't be."

"It is."

She's barely visible through the slits in my eyes. "Can you just give me a few more minutes, Bug?"

Grandma yells from downstairs. "Alex, you're not bothering your sister, are you?"

"*No!*" she yells.

"Then come down here, I could use some help."

Alex begs, "I wanna stay here with you."

"Go help Grandma while I get dressed, then I'll come save you."

She blows out a big breath. "Fine."

"*Alex!?*" Grandma's voice roars.

"I'm coming." She moves like a snail toward the door. "Hurry, Brie."

"I will."

Thoughts of the stranger cross my mind. I try to shut them out by thinking about other things, but my mind keeps going back to the attic. I wrestle with the idea that this might be all in my head. Anxiety trickles through me. To calm the panic, I hurry to get up, but my sore muscles slow me down. I take a moment to look over the things I stashed in my drawer when Alex yells my name.

"I'm coming," I yell. Immediately upon stepping into the hallway, it feels like a million little needles are vibrating against my skin. The closer to the attic door, the more intense the tingling becomes. Almost hurting now, I race past it and down the stairs.

EIGHT

Losing Control

"You sure you're up for church today?" Grandma asks.

"Yeah," I shrug.

"Well if you get too tired, I want you home."

I nod.

Sunday: the day for family. At least, it used to be that way. Mom and Dad would take us to church every week, but when Mom got sick, Dad stopped going. Grandma doesn't believe in organized religion. She says it isn't her thing. She has always encouraged us to go, telling me that when I got older I could decide how to feed my faith—just as long as I believed. Grandma prays often and reads the Bible nightly. She says that God knows what is in her heart.

After breakfast, we hurry to get ready for church. Alex rummages through my horde of shoes while I dab makeup on my bruise. "Can I wear these?" she asks, holding up a pair of red pumps.

"I don't think those go with your outfit."

"Can I wear these?" She holds up a pair of high tops.

"Those are too big."

She comes over to me, wearing a pair of rhinestone-embellished sandals. "How about these?"

"They're too big."

"Nah-huh, not if I squeeze my toes."

I laugh. "Fine."

Dad comes into my room. "Where're you going?" he questions.

"Church." Alex grins.

"I don't know what good you think that'll do," he says.

I lower my voice and move closer to him. "Dad, don't you think with Mom gone, it would help Alex?"

He reeks of alcohol. "I don't know, do whatever you want." He throws his hands into the air. "At least you'll be safe there."

"What's that supposed to mean?"

"Look at you. I mean, after Friday, it's going to be hard to let you out of my sight."

"What's wrong?"

Dad's words slur from his lips. "You really have to ask that? Aren't you even paying attention to what's going on around you?" He stumbles over a pair of shoes on the floor. *"Dammit!"* he yells. Picking them up, he heaves them into the hall.

Alex stares at me open-mouthed. I don't know how to respond. "Come on, Alex, we're going to be late." I snatch the keys from my dresser and push past him and down the stairs.

"What's wrong with Dad?" Alex asks, following me to the car.

"Just crabby, I guess."

"I don't like him like this."

"Neither do I."

My irritation disappears when I get into my new car, loving the way it looks and the way it smells.

Alex puts on her seatbelt and then opens the center

console.

"What're you looking for?" I ask.

"Nothing." She continues rifling through the car.

"Do you have to go through everything?"

"Yes!"

I gaze at my reflection in the rearview mirror. The make-up I'd plastered on doesn't look the greatest in the sunlight. "Does this look bad?"

Alex responds, without looking up. "It looks good."

"You didn't even look."

"I already did this morning," she says.

WE ENTER church and are immediately met with condolences, hugs, and questions. I'm thankful when service is about to start. Everyone settles down, and the pastor begins. Suddenly, a sharp pain spirals in the pit of my stomach, making me hot. I lean into my arms trying to contain the pain. Then, ever so softly, my name echoes around me.

"What?" I whisper to Alex.

She looks confused. "I didn't say anything."

My heart races when my name comes to me again. The world around me slows. "I have to go to the bathroom. I'll be back." The ache in my stomach intensifies as the voices in my head grow louder.

The pain leaves as fast as it hit, and the voices quiet to a soft buzz. Wetting several paper towels, I place them on the back of my neck. With a deep breath and feeling somewhat back in control, I head out the front door and into the cool morning air to sit on the steps. I'm convinced it's a lack of sleep making me feel this way. I'm going back to bed the instant I get home.

. . .

THE WEATHER in Kiel is always a challenge, especially this time of year. It changes so fast that you never know how to dress. In a few weeks, the weather will turn cold and stay that way. This past week has been the hottest on record, so it's a relief that's it's finally cooling down. Closing my eyes, I lean against the rail to try catching a catnap, but every little noise keeps me from dozing off.

As the hour-long service comes to an end, I make my way back inside to find Alex. There's a meet-and-greet following the church service, and I don't want to stay for that.

Alex runs over to me. "Where'd you go? I looked for you."

"I needed some air."

"You could've told me. I was worried."

"Come on, we better get going." Alex heads in the opposite direction of the door. "Alex, where're you going?"

"I want a doughnut."

"Hurry up."

Though I'm struggling to stay polite and avoid everyone, panic stirs inside of me once again. It becomes unbearable quick. I push my way through the crowd to find Alex.

She's holed up next to the doughnuts. "Come on, we need to get home."

"I don't want to leave yet."

"We have to get our chores done if you want to do something this afternoon." I reach out for her, and she pulls away. "Alex, I'm not joking."

Mrs. McCleary heads our way. If you get sucked into one of her conversations, it takes hours to be released. This time, I grab Alex hard, pulling her in the direction of the door.

"Gosh, Brie, you don't have to be so mean."

"Well, if you would listen to me."

Tears fill her eyes. She yanks her arm away from me and runs. Silent stares come from the people around. I hurry out of the building.

Alex won't talk to me on the way home. Not that I can blame her. I'm so irritated, I can't say anything either. We pull up in front of the house. She barely waits for the car to come to a complete stop before jumping out and running up the porch steps. I'm quick to follow.

"How was church?" Grandma asks.

"Fine!" I rush past her and bolt up the stairs.

"Is something wrong?" she yells.

"No."

Alex slams her bedroom door, I can't remember the last time we argued, but for some reason, I'm so angry. As soon as my head hits the pillow, I drift off to sleep.

MY SLEEP ENDS ABRUPTLY by a noise outside my bedroom window. The clock on my dresser proclaims the time: One p.m. Still exhausted, I try to close my eyes again, but then the look on Alex's face when we argued comes to mind. Guilt tugs at my heart and forces me to get up and apologize.

From the upstairs hallway window, I can see Alex getting into Aunt Edna's car. I tap on the window glass, but she doesn't look up. Heaving a heavy sigh, I lean against the wall and slump down until I come to rest on the floor. A spider scurries across the floor, disappearing under the attic door, which brings the stranger and the search I'd started earlier to the forefront of my mind. A lingering haze of sleep makes it impossible to think about that right now.

NINE

Taken Identity

I'm brought to a standstill when my name seems to be the focus of a discussion coming from the kitchen. I keep quiet to hear the conversation clearly.

"You need to tell her soon," Grandma says.

"Why are you in such a hurry?" Dad demands.

"I'm just thinking about Brie. If she finds out on her own, it's going to be worse."

"You have no idea what you're talking about."

"You know as well as I do that this is not going away on its own. You have to be honest with yourself, too."

Dad groans, then the screen door slams shut. I wait a few seconds before entering the kitchen.

"Hello, Brie," Grandma says, not looking up.

"Hey, Grandma, what were you and Dad talking about?"

She keeps busy mixing together the leftovers from the week. "What did you hear?"

"I heard you talking about me. You said I had a right to know. This isn't the first time I've heard you two talking about this."

"Can you get me some butter out of the fridge?"

"Grandma, please . . . tell me."

She fills a casserole dish with the mess she has just created. "You'll have to ask your dad, but first you need to take your laundry upstairs."

I grab my clothes, run them up to my room, throw them onto my bed, and then go to find Dad. Whatever he is keeping from me might explain some of the creepiness. Or at least give me some kind of direction.

The noise from the conveyor gives me his location. Dad throws hay bales onto the conveyor belt. Dan, one of the hired hands, stands in the loft to take them off and stack them up.

"Hey, Dad!" I holler over the ear-piercing roar of the conveyor.

"How was church?" he yells.

"It was good. I have to ask you something." Even though I'm screaming, the sound coming from the antique machinery drowns out my efforts.

"What is it?"

"Dad, I really need to talk to you," I shout even louder.

He motions to Dan. "I'm shuttin' it down for a few minutes. Take a break." He turns off the conveyor, takes off his gloves, and comes over to me. My ears ring even though all goes quiet as the equipment comes to a halt.

"Okay, you have my full attention. He stares at me with weary, bloodshot eyes and still reeks of alcohol. I'm worried about his drinking, but that's not what I want to discuss right now. "I need you to tell me the truth about something."

"Have I ever told you anything other than the truth?"

"I know you're keeping something from me. I overheard you and Grandma talking."

His jaw stiffens, and he shifts his weight from foot to foot. He takes a deep breath and sighs. "Let's go for a walk." He keeps his eyes on the ground. "I want you to understand, Brie, sometimes things aren't as we would like for them to be. And facts can be covered up, though not on purpose."

"Okay . . ."

"Your mother wanted to be the one to tell you. I'm just sorry we didn't do it sooner. I know she felt guilty about it."

"God, Dad, you're scaring me."

"I'm scared, too, but I want you to remember that I love you very much. That'll never change." He stops to face me. Seeing the look in his eyes makes me want to cry even before I know what he's going to say. "I don't know how to put this, so I'm just going to say it." He nervously twists the gloves in his hands. "You were six months old when I met your mother. And I loved both of you from the first time I laid eyes on you."

His words make no sense. "That's impossible."

"You are very special to me and even though I'm not your biological father, you will always be my daughter." The creases in his forehead deepen. "I wanted to tell you before you found out on your own. Your mother thought it would be better when you were old enough to understand."

"Understand . . . understand what, that you lied to me?"

"I know this is difficult, but you have a right to know."

"Difficult? You're kidding, right? This isn't difficult. This is a lie." I turn away.

"I can only imagine how hard this is. It's hard for me, too. I'm so sorry we didn't tell you sooner."

With my back to him, I mockingly answer, "You're

sorry. Well then, I guess it makes everything okay . . . right?" I glance back and can see the sorrow in his eyes. Anger once again explodes inside me. I turn away.

"Brie, look at me." His hand touches my shoulder.

"Why now? Why would you tell me this now?"

"Because you need to know. I promised your mother that if an opportunity ever presented itself, I wouldn't hold back."

I jerk away from him. "I don't believe this."

"Brie, nothing has changed between us. I love you more than ever."

Through a blur of tears, I whirl around to stare at him. "What about my real dad? Does he know about me?"

"All I know is that he left before I came into your life. As far as I know, he has never tried to contact anyone."

"So, he just left."

"Your mom wrote you a letter. I promised her I'd give it to you. It's at the house in her top drawer, under the Bible she kept in there."

I run away from him and his lies, through the kitchen door, and up the stairs into my parents' room. I'm not going to find anything, I'm sure of it. Slowly opening the drawer, my body trembles. Under the Bible, there it is—a white envelope with my name written in Mom's hand-writing.

The envelope isn't sealed, even though it looks like it had been at one time. My heart races as I pull out the letter to read what seems impossible.

DEAR BRIE,

If you are reading this, then you know the truth. I wanted to tell you myself--I'm sorry that I didn't. I guess I didn't know where to begin, and as time went by it didn't seem important. I know this must come as a shock to you. But don't you ever forget how much you are loved. I've enclosed information on your father, Sean, and his family. I know that he didn't want to hear from me, and he made that very clear when he left, but I think you have a right to find him if you want to. I know this can't take your pain away right now--but keep in mind that even though John might not be your biological father, he has been a great dad to you and loves you. I hope one day you will be able to understand and forgive me for not telling you sooner.

I love you very much, Brie. Keep true to yourself and remember I will always be with you.

Love forever,
Mom

THERE'S nothing else in the envelope. I search the entire dresser and come up empty handed. I then search through the nightstand, throwing papers onto the bed. Grandma comes into the room and gasps, "What on earth are you doing?"

"Nothing."

"It doesn't look that way to me. Put that stuff back," she orders.

"No—this is my mom's. I have a right to it."

"Brie, stop it. This is your dad's now. How would you like someone going through your things, making a mess?" She picks up the papers from the bed, stacking them neatly in a pile. I focus on the closet next.

"*Brie!*" Grandma yells. "What're you looking for?"

Dad comes into the room, yelling. "*What's going on!?*"

Without answering, I grab the letter from the dresser and rush past him to my room, slamming the door behind me. The emotional stress of this new secret is too much to handle. I lie across my bed and cry.

Within minutes, there's a light tapping on my bedroom

door. Dad enters. "Brie, listen, I know this is hard—but I want you to know. I love you. That'll never change. We probably should have told you years ago, but I didn't want to lose my little girl. I guess that was selfish. I hope—well— I *do* hope you can forgive me." The floor creaks. He comes over and sits next to me on the bed.

"I just don't understand why you needed to tell me now. Why didn't you just leave it alone?"

"It was your grandfather. He made your mom, grandma, and me promise that we would tell you before your eighteenth birthday. He was adamant about you knowing."

"Why?"

"I'm not sure . . . and to be honest with you, if it wasn't for your grandma, I probably wouldn't have said anything."

"I wish you wouldn't have."

"Your mom was going to tell you when you were seven, but then your grandfather passed away. You were devastated, so she waited."

Grandpa had always been a big part of my life up 'til then. My love for puzzles, trivia, and walking through the woods came from him. He had told me the best way to get out of tough situation is to use your brain and know your surroundings.

Dad continues, "Then again, when you were eight she was going to tell you, but then found out she was pregnant. You were so excited, and she didn't want to ruin that in any way."

He goes over to my dresser and brings Mom's gift back to me. "She started to tell you several times over the years, but something always stopped her. And then when she got sick. I guess she thought you had enough on your plate."

He places the gift in my hand. "This was part of that past."

I stare at the gift and my heart breaks a little more. "I still don't understand."

"I don't have the answers for you, but I do know that it's better that it came from me." He kisses my forehead. "I'll leave you alone. Now get some rest. I've got your chores covered today."

"Thanks, Dad."

I slide the bow off Mom's gift and then peel back the tape, careful not to rip the paper. A tiny white box holds a red velvet sachet with a gold drawstring. Inside is a beautiful, princess-cut diamond ring with three smaller diamonds on each side of the larger one. I slip it on my finger. It's a perfect fit. If this was part of Mom's past, could this have something to do with my real dad? Wondering if she was wearing the ring in the picture from the attic, I go over to my dresser to take a closer look.

Her hand isn't visible in the photo. It's then that the necklace catches my eye; I hold it up for a closer look. It's unusual and beautiful. I clasp it around my neck and vow never to take it or the ring off, since both belonged to Mom. I flip through the journal once again. Upon a closer inspection of one of the blank pages, I notice indentations. I hurry over to my desk and use the flat surface of my pencil to lightly shade over the area.

Words appear. 'Those who are cursed must find their own way. To bring it to their attention too soon would cause them great pain and even death.' The indentation at the bottom of the page isn't as prominent, but I can make out a few words. 'Knowledge, files, ancestors, stones.' The next word makes me shiver. 'Brie'

I hold on tight to the necklace while looking down at the stones within it, but a peaceful lull carries away my concerns. My agitation dissipates, giving way to exhaustion.

I lie across my bed, reading the letter again and thinking about everything that's happened. One thing's for sure though. If Grandpa was adamant that I know about my real dad, then Grandma must know why.

TEN

Under Attack

———————————

I'd slept most of the day away and do feel better. Even the body aches have improved. I make my way downstairs. Dad and Grandma are in the living room, watching TV. Alex is lying on the floor, talking to Gibson.

"Come to join us?" Grandma asks, reaching out for my hand. "Well, isn't that pretty." She stares at the ring on my finger. Out of the corner of my eye, I see Alex trying to get a glimpse. I look over at her. She quickly turns away.

"I'm glad you opened it," Dad says.

"Me too."

"Are you hungry?" Grandma asks.

"A little."

"There's a casserole in the refrigerator."

Dad follows me into the kitchen. "How're you doing?"

"Good."

"I have dreaded this day forever." He hugs me tight. "I do love you."

"I love you, too."

"This sure has been a heck of a start to your eighteenth year."

"Yeah, it has."

"Now, get something to eat."

"I will." I'm relieved that he's decided to stay home tonight.

Before pulling the casserole from the refrigerator, I poke at it. It looks disgusting. Instead, I opt for a bologna and cheese sandwich.

While sitting at the table, the day plays over in my head. It's hard to believe that there's another family out there that I'm related to. Even though this is my family, I'd like to at least know who they are.

Rinsing my plate while I look out the window, I notice something dash across the yard, disappearing into the barn. "*Dad!*"

He bolts through the kitchen door, startling me. "What's wrong? Are you okay?"

"Geez, Dad, I'm fine. I just saw something run into the barn."

"Don't scare me like that—I thought—never mind. It's probably just those pesky raccoons." He disappears into the other room, then comes back with a shotgun. "Stay in here, I'll be right back."

We've been having problems with raccoons getting into the garbage and making a huge mess. I'd always thought they were kind of cute—that is, until I had to clean up after them.

Now, to make amends with Alex. I sit alongside of her on the floor. "Today wasn't good for me," I say.

She twirls a string in the air for Gibson to bat at, ignoring me.

"I'm sorry I yelled at you earlier. I wasn't myself."

"You promised me we'd go to the movies."

"I know and I'm sorry about that too." I move her hair

behind her ear. "Besides didn't you spend the day with Aunt Edna?"

"Yeah . . . So!?"

"What'd you do?" I inch closer to her. When our noses touch, she snorts out a laugh.

"Can I see your ring?" I hold my hand out to her. "It's beautiful . . . Can I try it on?"

The sound of gunshots compels us to our feet. We bolt into the kitchen and out onto the porch.

Dad runs toward us, yelling for us to get back inside. Through shallow gulps of air, he manages a few words. "The thing you saw . . . was a . . . was a dog."

Alex gasps. "You shot a dog!?"

He pauses to catch his breath. "Believe me, darling, this wasn't a pet." He glances at Grandma. "Call the police, there's at least two more out there and they might be rabid."

She reaches for the phone. Dad leaves the kitchen only to come back with another gun. "You girls need to stay here." He pushes through the screen door.

The chicken's squawk lets us know that the dogs have found their way into the coop. Grandma assures us that help is on the way. Alex and I hurry to the kitchen window. We can't see the dogs, but Dad stands with his gun raised and takes a few shots.

Alex leans in close to the window. "Wow, where do you think they came from?" Her breath fogs the glass.

"I don't know, maybe someone dumped them off."

A dog jumps at the window, baring his teeth. Alex screams, making me jump. She hangs onto me with all her might.

"We're fine. They can't get us." A police car approaches, stopping next to the house.

The dog that had appeared in the window is running

toward the woods. The cop pulls out his gun and brings the dog down. The dogs split up, heading off in different directions.

"Okay girls. Come in the living room now." Grandma says.

Alex whines, "I wanna watch."

Grandma stands firm. "I'm not asking."

"Come on, Bug."

It doesn't take long for Dad to come through the door followed by Josh.

"Did you get them all?" Alex asks.

"I think so." Dad answers while heading into the other room.

"What're you doing here, Josh?" I ask.

"Just got off work. Thought I'd stop by and see how you're doing."

"I'm okay." I say.

"I texted and called, but you didn't answer."

"Something's wrong with my phone."

Dad comes back with a box of shells to reload his gun. "I'll be outside if you need me." He heads for the door.

Josh quickly asks, "You need some help?"

"I won't turn it down."

"I can help too." I say.

"You need to rest," Dad argues.

Josh snickers while whispering in my ear. "Yeah, little darlin', you rest, us men have it handled."

"Just like you handled spring calving?" I smirk. "I believe you threw up."

"That was a totally different, I didn't feel good that day."

"Sure." I roll my eyes to Dad. "I slept all day, I'm fine."

Dad reluctantly agrees, "Okay, if you think you can handle it."

"I can." I wonder what I just got myself into.

"I'm coming too." Alex says.

Grandma interjects, "You can stay in here with me."

"But Grandma . . ."

"No but's—now come on." Alex follows Grandma into the living room. I slip on a pair of boots to follow Dad outside.

"We have to burn the dogs, since we don't know whether or not they have rabies."

"Uh . . . okay . . . *Ew*."

"This would be a good time to burn all that debris I've piled up in the pasture," Dad says as we walk into the barn. He starts the tractor while Josh hooks the bucket up. Dad motions to me. "You and Josh take the ATV down to the pasture and get the fire started. I'll meet you down there."

Josh jumps on the back of the ATV. "Sure you don't want me to drive?"

"No way . . . you scare me." I hit the throttle, and as we fly out of the barn, Josh grabs me tight.

"I scare *you*!?" he screeches.

We arrive at the burn sight in no time at all. "See, that wasn't so bad." I say.

"Maybe for you."

WITH THE DRY BRUSH, it doesn't take long to get a roaring fire going. I look over to watch Josh heave a few tree limbs into the fire. When he catches me staring at him, he smiles.

"Hey Josh, I got to ask you something."

"Sure."

"You know what I said yesterday, about the stranger?"

"Yeah."

"What if I tell you he's not in my head?"

His brows furrow as his voice rises. "You didn't try to hurt yourself, did you?"

"*No!* I wouldn't do that. I've *never* done that."

He reaches out to me. "I know, it just . . ."

I pull away. "It's just what?" I don't give him a chance to answer. I hurry over to where Dad is edging the tractor closer to the fire. He lifts the bucket up to dump out the remains.

"I think that's all of them," he says, handing Josh and me gloves.

We exchange a silent glance before helping Dad with the remains. It surprises me to see a beautiful black and white husky dog—not a mangy, deformed, skinny one. This animal must have belonged to someone not long ago.

"Do you think this is someone's pet?" I ask.

Dad responds. "It might have been at one time—but by the way it acted, I'm pretty sure it's been on its own for a while."

"This is so sad."

I watch as Josh helps Dad throw more debris into the fire. I mull over what Josh had said. It upsets me that he would even *think* I would do something so horrible.

The stench coming from the fire makes me sick. "I'm going to take a shower," I say while pinching my nose.

"I've got this, Josh. You can head back with Brie."

"Okay." He eyes me, as if hoping for my approval.

I motion toward the ATV. "Whatever."

We're quiet on the ride back. I park next to the porch and run up the stairs. Josh grabs onto me before I can make my way inside. "I don't think you'd really do that, you know. To you or your family."

I swing around. "You're the only one I've told about this, and you made me feel stupid."

"I didn't mean to do that."

"Well you did."

"I'm sorry." He steps back. "I shouldn't question it, but put yourself in my place."

"I'd believe you," I quickly add, even though I'm not hundred percent sure I would. "I never lied about any of this."

"Okay," he nods. "I just don't want anything to happen while I'm gone."

"Where're you going?" An ache ignites in the pit of my stomach.

"Another college tour. Dad thinks we need to visit as many as possible."

"When will you be back?"

"Friday, since he's making a family vacation out of it. That's what I stopped by to tell you." He leans against the house. "Please, tell me what else has been going on."

If he didn't believe me about the lake and he was there, then there's no way he'll deem the ghost in the attic as real. "I was just thinking about the lake."

"I still think it's stress." He takes my hand in his. "Tell you what—give it a week and try to relax. If things aren't right by the time I get back, we'll deal with it together."

A new train of thoughts and feelings arise inside of me. I give him an impromptu squeeze. He hugs back. "I'll miss you," I say, feeling weighed down by the thought of him leaving.

"I'll miss you too." He kisses me on the forehead. "And promise me that if anything happens, you'll call me right away."

I nod.

"And Brie, you're *not* stupid or crazy."

As I let go of him, our eyes meet. I can see the concern on his face. I don't want him to worry, so I muster my calm and reassure him. "I'll call you if I need too, but I'm sure I'll be fine."

"Make sure to text me when your phone gets fixed," he says before leaving.

I nod again.

ALEX IS TUCKED in my bed, reading to Gibson. "Looks like you two are comfortable." I grab clean clothes out of my dresser.

She looks over the book. "What'd ya have to do with the dogs?"

"Nothing you want to hear about."

"You coming to bed?"

"Going to take a shower first."

The hot water soothes my aches and pains even more, but does nothing to quiet my thoughts. The week plays over in my head. I can tell that Josh doubts me, but his 'stress logic' gives me a false sense of security.

Coming out of the bathroom, I trip over Gibson, who's lying by the door. She yowls. "I'm so sorry girl." I reach down to pet her; she bounds to her feet and hisses. Her eyes widen, and her ears lay flat against her head. "What's wrong, girl? Did I scare you?"

She strikes at me with her paw. "Gibson, stop it." I reach out to her again, but she's quick to back away and scurry down the stairs.

"Weird cat."

ELEVEN

Déjà Vu

The week flies by until it's already Friday. I've been so busy with school, chores, and spending time with Alex, I didn't even have time to go back in the attic or to talk to Grandma about what she might know. Not to mention, Jill had stopped over almost every night. I'm pretty sure Josh had something to do with that, even though he adamantly denied it. He blew up my phone while he was away. But now, I'm convinced that Josh was right— the stress I'd been under caused me to go temporarily insane, as nothing weird has happened since he left.

Even though things seem to be getting back to a different sort of normal, I miss the way it used to be. There's not a day that goes by that I don't think about Mom or find myself talking out loud to her when I'm alone, as if she's there listening to me.

Dad is lost without her. He spends the majority of his free time away from the farm. As soon as chores are done, he disappears, coming back after we've all gone to bed. I had hoped that this would pass, but it seems to be getting worse.

I'm still curious about my real dad, I'd at least like to know his name or if he has any family around here.

Grandma is in the kitchen cooking breakfast. I grab a piece of bacon and lean against the counter. "Grandma, can I ask you something?"

"You know you can ask me anything."

"Is Dad going to be okay? He's been acting strange."

"He'll be fine." She cracks eggs into the pancake mix. "I think it's just going to take time."

"But ever since he told me about my real dad Sean, he barely talks to me."

"He loves you very much, but he has a lot to deal with. Just give him time." She flips the bacon in the pan.

"Do you think it'll ever be the way it used to be?"

"Your mom and dad were very close. Just like all of us, he needs to find a way to get through this."

"Was it like that for you when you lost Grandpa?"

She sighs. "I guess with most people it is."

I look down at Mom's ring. "Did you know Sean?"

She answers without hesitation. "I only met him a few times."

"What was he like?"

"To be honest with you, your mom left right after graduation. Didn't tell anyone where she was going."

"Not even you? You and Mom were so close."

"Nope, she left without talking to anyone."

"I can't imagine Mom doing that. Why would she just leave?"

"Your mom was a strong person. But when she met Sean, she seemed to change. We fought a lot during the few months they dated. She pulled away from her friends, family, everyone who cared."

"What do you remember about him?"

"I know you must have all kinds of questions, but I

don't know a whole lot." She takes out the last of the bacon, pours a little bacon grease onto the hot griddle, then spoons pancake batter onto it.

"Will you tell me what you do know?"

"Your mom didn't elaborate on him. Whenever I asked, she would change the subject."

"Is he still around here?" I ask.

"No, he left shortly after your mom came home."

"What did he look like?" I grab another piece of bacon.

"I have to admit he was handsome, from what I can remember. I'm not sure if there are any pictures of him around here or not." She smiles. "You do look like him though."

"I wish I could meet him." I didn't realize I'd said that out loud until Grandma stops to stare at me.

"Okay, that's enough. You look out there," she points the spatula toward the window. "That's your father out there."

"Oh, I know." I sigh. "But you can't blame me for wanting to meet him."

She flips the pancakes. "Sometimes, Brie, it's better to leave things alone."

"Do you at least know what his last name was?"

"I know what you're thinking. Believe me, if he had wanted to get in contact with you, he would have. And he hasn't."

"Then why did I need to know about him?"

"Your grandfather thought you should know."

There's something in her voice making me think she knows more than what she is telling me. "Yeah, I know that . . . but why?"

"I don't have time for this." She moves me toward the door. "Go out and see if there is anything you can help *your dad* with before school."

"He doesn't want my help."

"Brie, stop it, just go out there."

"Ugh . . ." I push through the back door and make my way over to where Dad is stacking wood. "Hey, Dad, is there anything I can help with?"

"No, I think I have it all under control." He is fast to respond.

"Do you hate me now?"

"No, Brie, I don't hate you. I love you very much."

"Then why are you so mad all the time?"

"I'm sorry, I'm not mad. I've got a lot on my mind," he snaps.

"Oh, yeah, not mad, right. You know, you're not the only one hurting. With the way you're acting, it's just making it worse."

He wipes his brow with the back of his hand while he glares at me. "What do you want me to do?"

"I don't know." I throw my hands in the air. "Something." I'm completely frustrated.

"Well there's a fine idea." He continues to throw wood onto the pile.

"Whatever!" I yell. He doesn't even try to stop me from leaving. Up the porch and through the back door. "See, Grandma, he wants to be alone."

"Just keep trying."

"That's easy for you to say."

I head upstairs to see if Alex is ready for school. She's still curled up under the covers in my bed.

"You better get up. You're going to be late."

"I don't feel good," she whines.

"What's wrong?" I place my hand on her cheeks. "Oh, my God, you're burning up."

I yell for Grandma. Alex sobs.

"You're going to be fine, but you need to calm down."

"I can't," she cries. "It hurts all over."

"Grandma will make you feel better."

"What's wrong?" Grandma asks, coming into the room.

"I don't know. I just feel icky."

"Brie, get a cool wash rag and some aspirins." I hurry to the bathroom, bringing back what she asked for. I help Alex sit up so she can swallow the pills. Her face is flushed, making the dark circles under her eyes more apparent than ever. Grandma lays the cool cloth on her head and pushes the covers to the end of the bed.

"I'm cold," she whimpers.

"It's the fever, honey. When you've cooled down, you can have the covers back."

"Is she going to be alright?"

"She'll be fine; I'll stay with her for a while. You better get to school before you're late."

"Call me if you need me to bring anything home."

"We'll be just fine." Grandma rubs Alex's arm.

With backpack in hand, I head downstairs and out the back door. I've been late to school most of the week, and today it's going to be close.

At my locker, as I'm taking out books, I'm grabbed from behind. I turn around to see Josh's smiling face. "You're back," I say.

He squeezes me. "And not soon enough."

"From all your texts, I thought you were having a good time."

"Um . . . that's what you got from them?" His head tilts to the side. "I should've added emoji's, 'cause fun doesn't exist in the backseat when you're with two year old twin sisters who get car sick."

I laugh, "Yeah that would suck."

"It sounds like things are better for you."

I nod. "You were right, it must've been stress."

Josh grabs my hand as the school bell rings. "What are you doing later?"

"No plans, why?"

"I get off work at nine. Want to hang out?"

"Sure." I smile.

"See you at lunch."

My first class is Social Studies, and it's not my favorite. My senior year, I should have all my required classes done, but no. Too many electives in the prior years left me scrambling to get caught up. As an average student, I hope my grades are good enough to get into a decent college.

Jill leans over and whispers, "Hey, I hear you and Josh are going to Appleton?"

"Yeah, it's going to be great to get away from here for a while."

"What're you going to do there?"

"Shop, eat, whatever." I shrug.

"Sounds like fun."

"Why don't you and Eric come with us?" I ask.

"What time you leaving?"

"Around eight."

"I'll see if Eric wants to go."

The morning goes by at a snail's pace. Two movies and one test later, it's finally lunchtime.

Josh sits next to Eric and Jill in the cafeteria. When I see him my stomach flutters. Josh scoots over so I can sit down. I press my leg firmly against his. Out of the corner of my eye, I see him smile. "They're going with us tomorrow," he says.

"Nice, we'll have so much fun," I say. "What are you guys doing tonight?"

"It's our anniversary; we've been dating for three years." Jill says.

Eric eyes widen, "Uh . . . yeah that's right."

Josh engages Jill, "What did Eric get you? Three years — I bet it's something special." He nudges me.

"That's a surprise for later." Eric shoots Josh a look of horror.

"I can't wait," Jill giggles.

WITH THE SCHOOL day finally at an end, I stop by the store to pick up a pint of chocolate ice cream. If anything can make Alex feel better, it's this.

My heart guns into overdrive when the ambulance parked alongside the house comes into view. Screeching to a halt next to the ambulance, I jump from the car and hurry to get inside. I think for sure it's Alex, but Dad is on the kitchen floor, lying in a pool of blood. Alex is wrapped in a blanket, standing next to Grandma, crying.

"What's going on?"

"Oh, Brie, it was horrible. A dog attacked him," Alex cries.

"It's just a good thing Dan was here. He scared it off and helped your father inside," Grandma, notes in a shaky voice.

Tears fill my eyes when Dad's blood covered face comes into view. The paramedics work hard to stop the bleeding from the gaping wounds in his arms. "Dad?" I try to get close, but Dan holds me back.

"He's going to be alright— just let them do their job," Dan says.

Dad moans when they tighten the bandages around his arm.

"Are the dogs still out there?" I ask.

"Police went after them. They'll find them, don't worry," Dan assures me.

"How many more are there?"

"Don't know, but I'm going to stay over for a few nights. Thought I'd sleep in the barn, just in case any more of them damn things come back. Hopefully I can kill 'em."

The paramedics carry Dad out on a stretcher. We follow behind. I look over at Grandma. "I'm going to the hospital with them."

Grandma nods. "Call us the minute you know anything, all right?"

Following close behind the ambulance, it makes me feel better that no emergency lights are required. The injuries can't be as bad as I'd thought.

Once inside the hospital, I'm asked to stay in the waiting room until the tests are done. It surprises me when Jill comes through the door and over to me. "Alex told me what happened when I dropped off the shirt I borrowed." She sits in the chair next to me. "How's your dad?"

"Haven't seen him yet."

"I'm so sorry. Is there anything I can do?"

"No. But we might have to postpone the trip." I say.

"Don't worry about that, we can go anytime." She looks down at her phone. "Eric said that if you need anything to let him know."

"Tell him thanks."

Then, my phone beeps. Josh: I just heard. you ok?

Me: yes

Josh: how's your dad?

Me: don't know yet

Josh: you want me to come up there?

Me: aren't you working?

Josh: yeah, but I can leave.

Me: No, Jill here's

Josh: <u>keep me posted</u>

Me: <u>k</u>

"Aren't you going out for your anniversary?" I ask.

"Eric had to do something first, so he's picking me up at six."

I chuckle silently, thinking about Eric frantically shopping for something special to give to her tonight.

Jill digs through her purse for some change. "Want a soda?"

"Sure."

She comes back with two sodas and two bags of chips, handing one of each to me. "We might be here awhile."

"Thanks."

"Your Dad's tough, don't look so worried."

I can't help but think the worst—no matter how hard I try not to. "They sure are slow." I sigh.

"Have you got your dress for the dance yet?" Jill asks.

"I can't think about that now."

"Sure you can, look at these." She leans over to scan through the pictures she has downloaded onto her phone. "I think you'd look good in this one."

"Way too much bling for me. Besides, I don't know if I'm going."

"What!" Jill gasps. "You can't be serious. Josh is a great dancer."

"Even if I were to go, I'm sure it wouldn't be with him."

"Why."

"Well for one thing, he's not my boyfriend. And for another, he hasn't asked."

There's a gleam in her eyes. "But you're not opposed to going with him, are you?"

A nurse comes through the double doors. "Brie?" she questions.

I jump to my feet. "I'm right here."

Jill gives me a quick hug, "I'm leaving, but text if you need something."

I nod. "Have fun tonight."

I follow the nurse back; I'm prepared for the worst, but relieved when I see him. "Hi, Dad, how are you feeling?"

"Pretty sore right now, but I'll be just fine. No broken bones, just a few stitches. I'll be better in no time." His face is swollen and bruised from the dog bite on his cheek, and his arm is bandaged from the elbow all the way down to his hand.

Pointing at his arm, I cringe. "Just a few stitches?"

"Just a scratch, don't worry." He winks.

I call Grandma with an update, then text Josh, telling him that I'm too tired to hang out tonight and we'll have to postpone our trip. I chuckle when he texts back with sixteen different sad emojis.

Finally, the nurse comes back with discharge papers. She explains that he'll have to undergo rabies shots. I'm pretty sure that will be horrible, but Dad doesn't even react to the thought. He chuckles, looking at me. I'm sure I have a ghastly look on my face.

"It's not that bad," he whispers.

"Yeah, right."

Dad won't ride in the wheelchair, no matter how hard the nurse insists. With my arm around his waist, I help him out to the car. He rests his head against the seat.

Our family sure is having a string of bad luck. Or maybe it's good luck? Both Dad and I have made it out of a terrible situation without life-threatening injuries. The ride home is quiet. Other than the fact that I'm the one driving and Dad's the one injured, it's eerie how similar this night is to last Friday.

I park close to the house, then hurry around to help

Dad out of the car and up the stairs. Dan is sitting at the kitchen table. "You look better than I thought you would," he says, pulling out a chair for Dad.

"Yeah, well, I feel like shit. Did you hear whether or not they got those bastards?"

"Haven't heard yet, but as soon as the officer finds out, I'm sure he'll let us know."

"I'm going to check on Alex. Do you need anything?" I ask.

"No, I'm fine."

"I'm not going tomorrow."

"Thanks, honey."

I overhear Dad telling Dan that he won't let him spend the night in the barn by himself. I'm pretty sure Dad has made up his mind to stay out there too.

The upstairs is quiet. Grandma is already asleep, even though it's only eight. Hopefully, she isn't getting sick, too. Alex is asleep in my bed. It comforts me that her forehead is cool to the touch—obviously it was just a twenty-four-hour thing. I change into a pair of pajama pants and T-shirt before heading downstairs to get something to eat.

"How's Alex?" Dad asks when I enter the kitchen.

"She's fine, the fever's gone." I yawn.

"Good . . . what're you doing?"

"Thought I would warm up dinner, do you want some?" I pull the roast out of the refrigerator.

"No, but thanks, honey,"

I make a plate, grab a Coke, and go back to my room. I sit at my desk, eating, while searching the internet. It's hard to keep my eyes open. I'm exhausted. On my way to the bathroom, a strange noise comes from behind the attic door. I'm at a standstill, waiting to hear it again. A light flashes through the keyhole. It scares me to think the craziness is starting up again. I hurry back to my bedroom and curl up under the covers.

Footsteps resonate in the hall, then the bedroom door slowly opens, letting in the hall light. To my relief, Dad peeks in.

"I want you to go tomorrow."

"I can go another time."

"No, I insist—and besides, you could use a break." He lays money on my dresser. Dad didn't want me to work outside of the farm. When Mom was sick, I still had chores and school; he said I had enough to worry about.

"Are you sure?"

"I am. Now, get some sleep. I'll be in the barn if you need me." He holds up his cell phone.

"Wow, you're really going to use it?"

Dad never carries his phone too often. He always said that if people wanted to talk to him, they needed to do it face to face. "I figure, with the way things have been going, I better start keeping it close."

"Thanks, Dad."

He winks before closing my door.

I text Josh: <u>still want to go tomorrow?</u>

Almost immediately, he texts back: <u>absolutely</u>

Me: <u>good I'm in</u>

Josh: <u>be there at 8</u> ☺

TWELVE

Appleton

I hurry out the door at the sound of Josh's car in the driveway. "Where're Eric and Jill?" I ask.

"Eric's sick, and Jill texted me this morning."

"She could've still come."

Josh shrugs. "I told her that. She didn't want to. So where do you want to go first?"

"Let's go to the mall. I want to look for some shoes and get Alex those pretzel bites she likes."

"The mall it is."

"I want to thank you again."

"For what?"

"Being right about the whole stress thing, it's been almost a week and nothing strange has happened." I chalked up last night's incident to my imagination and decided against telling him.

"Told you."

"You never did tell me if you like the college."

"I guess it was all right," he sighs.

"Just all right? This was your second trip there."

"Dad likes the school," he glances over at me. "Don't know if I want to move that far away though."

I smile, then look out the window. This week without him, made me realize how much I'm going to miss him. I secretly hope that he picks University of Madison. It's close enough that we could still hangout occasionally on weekends.

IT'S nine-thirty by the time we get to the mall. We stop by the food court before heading to my favorite shoe store. I try on several pair before settling on a pair of flats. Josh finds a pair of boots—probably the more practical choice for this time of year. However, the flats are just too cute to pass up.

The electronic store is Josh's pick. I sit in the massage chair while he flies the remote-control helicopter around the store. Occasionally he gets it too close to the other shoppers, making them duck. His laughter ricochets throughout as he flies the helicopter too close to a mannequin, knocking off its hand. It doesn't take long for him to get kicked out.

We leave the mall for the historic part of town to where Toni's Pizzeria is located. A wide variety of shops line the streets, from luxury boutiques to souvenir shops to specialty foods. This place is as touristy as it gets, and it's always busy. Today is no exception. We're forced to park several blocks away, but with the great weather we're still having, we're okay to walk a-ways. Josh comes around to my side of the car, opening the door for me.

"Let me help you out, my lady."

"You're so weird." I take his hand, but when he pulls me close, my stomach feels as though it has just collided with my heart.

He must notice the look on my face. "What's wrong?"

"Just hungry," I quickly answer.

The pizza is just how I'd remembered it: crisp crust, with a hot, tangy sauce, and just the right amount of toppings. It's without a doubt the best around. With the first bite, the cheese sticks to the roof of my mouth, burning it on contact. I immediately drop the pizza onto my plate, grab for my Coke and suck it down, trying to cool the burning sensation.

"You okay?"

With watery eyes, I cringe. "I hate when that happens." I make sure the pizza has sufficiently cooled before taking another bite.

"Where we going next?" Josh asks.

"The antique store—you know . . . for Mom."

"I knew that." He smiles.

Antiques stores were Mom's treasure troves. Her eyes would light up when she entered. The last time I visited the area was with her. She had wanted to find something special for Grandma's birthday. We had so much fun searching through junk, trying to find a gem.

The door chimes sound, and light illuminates the dust particles that take flight as we enter the store. An over-abundance of odds and ends is stuffed in two large display windows, denying the room of much needed light. A single light bulb hangs from a brown cord in the middle of the shop. The place is a cluttered mess and the air is sweetly nauseating.

"This place stinks," Josh whispers.

"I'll look quick."

Glassware, old dolls, cigar boxes, picture frames encrusted with sea shells, a puffer fish inflated and dried are just a few things stuffed on dust covered shelves. A blue and green, satin vintage dress, suspended from a wire hanger, claims my attention. "This is beautiful." I hold it up to my body. "What do you think, Josh?"

"It's not really my taste."

"I'm talking about me, dork."

Josh reaches over me. "Oh, no, now *this* is cool." He picks up a stuffed squirrel.

"No, it's not."

He swings the squirrel by its tail, almost hitting me in the head with it. "Gimme a kiss." He holds the mangy looking thing up to me.

I toss the dress aside and grab for the washboard to cover my face. "Stop it."

"Come on—just one kiss."

"You're acting ridiculous." Turning my back to him, I look through some books.

"Does this bother you?" He lays the squirrel on my shoulder.

"Will you knock it off?"

He grabs me from behind, turning me to face him and, yes, he still has the squirrel. "Look, he's sad." Josh tries to mimic the squirrel's expression.

I laugh. "He looks just like you."

"This will make a great gift."

"You can't be serious. Who in their right mind would want that?"

"You never know." His brows flutter.

I suddenly realize that I'll be un-wrapping a stuffed squirrel at some point in my life. "Seriously, there's something wrong with you."

He laughs as he shifts his attention to a display of war memorabilia. I make my way to the back counter to look at jewelry, hoping to find something for Alex. Leaning forward onto the glass case, my necklace falls out of my shirt, revealing itself. An old woman comes over and starts interrogating me.

"Where'd you get that?" She gasps, bringing her hand up to her face. Every finger is adorned with fascinating rings. I can't help but stare.

"Pardon me, get what?"

"That thing there?"

I look behind me, expecting to see Josh.

"Talking about that thing round your neck." She pushes her braided, steel-grey hair away from her pale, gaunt face and moves closer to me. The smell of incense secretes from her skin and the deep lines embedded into her face, along with her stained teeth, make her look ancient.

"My necklace?" I question.

She points at me, making the bangles around her wrist rattle. "Why you wearing it?"

"I found it."

"Where? Who'd have that hideous thing?"

"I like it."

"Oh, Lord, child, don't you know what that means?"

"It's just a necklace."

Her decorated fingers hold tight to a pen. She uses the pen to turn the pendant around, never actually touching it herself. When she looks at the inscription, fear flashes in her clouded blue eyes.

"What is it?" I ask. She doesn't answer. Instead, she turns, disappearing through the heavy dark curtains that hang from the door frame.

"What was that all about?" Josh asks, coming over to me.

"I don't know. She said something about my necklace and then left."

"Maybe we better get out of here."

"You got that right."

We start to leave, but the strange woman reappears, carrying a huge book.

"You need come see this, don't be scared." She reaches a hand out to me.

I'm reluctant at first, but the intensity in her eyes makes me stay.

"I have a feeling this isn't going to be good," Josh says.

The old woman flips the pages, releasing a musty odor that makes me sneeze. She slaps her hand down on the page and spins the book in my direction. "Read!" she demands.

"'The emblem of the Moray clan is said to have the power of the devil locked inside it. Two ropes are intertwined around two Aluben stones. The ropes signify one's destiny. Two black stones symbolize the eyes of Satan. Together, they heighten the metabolic process of the quarter-blood, forcing one to face up to their true self, calling on the entity of darkness to surround the wearer, assuring that evil will prevail.'"

Wide-eyed, I stare in disbelief at the picture in the book. It looks just like my necklace. "There has to be some kind of mistake. This can't be right."

"Take it off."

"*No!* I have to keep it on, it makes me feel better."

"Better? Never better, make things bad."

"You're lying."

"Look here, child, you know what that inscription says?"

"No."

"*Totus malum.* Means, 'All things evil.'"

"You're wrong."

She points. "That thing is bad."

"Can you explain to me, then, why I feel better when it's on?"

"Keeping all good away, given your soul time to die."

"Come on, Brie, let's leave." Josh says.

"You might think you're safe, but you're not. People you love will die. You need to learn how to stop it." She shakes her head. "Might be too late already."

"You don't know what you're talking about," I say. "It's just a necklace."

"The ones around you will suffer first. Terrible things will happen to them. Mark my words—when that thing there is strong enough, everyone in contact with you will fall." She stands with her arms raised and starts to chant in a strange language.

I turn away. "I won't listen to any more of this."

She chants louder as we leave the store.

"She's just a crazy woman," Josh says.

A tangle of emotions keeps me quiet. Josh stops me. A troubling gaze crosses his face. "What are you thinking?"

"I don't know."

"Think you should take the necklace off?"

"I can't."

"Why not?"

I look away. "It's complicated." My anxiety has stopped and so have the visions. If I take it off, I'm scared they'll come back. I step around him and off the curb, right in front of an oncoming car. The driver honks, waking me from my thoughts.

My fear is for Josh. I push him toward the curb. He trips, falling backward onto the sidewalk. The world goes silent and time seems to slow while I watch in horror as the car comes straight toward me. A plume of smoke gently rises into the air from the tires, which are locked up tight, but no noise can be heard. Unable to move, I close my eyes, waiting for the inevitable.

Then I hear my name, and I look up to see the world back to normal. The car has come to a stop only inches from me.

"Oh my God, Brie, you okay!?" Josh grabs for me.

"Yeah, the car didn't touch me." I'm in disbelief myself.

A crowd gathers around me; the frantic driver rushes to my side. "I'm so sorry, I didn't see you."

"I'm fine—I think."

Josh examines my arms and legs. "Does anything hurt?"

"I said I'm fine." Then, noticing the blood trickling down Josh's arm, I grab onto him. "You're bleeding."

"It's just a scratch," he says, still looking me over.

The driver is insistent that I go to the hospital. The noise and chaos is too much. I scream, *"The car didn't touch me! I'm fine!"*

The driver, finally satisfied that I'm not hurt, gets back into his car. The crowd disperses.

"You're the one who needs medical attention," I say, holding onto his arm.

"It's nothing."

"I'll be the judge of that." Taking his hand, I lead him inside the nearest store and toward the women's restroom.

Josh stops firm. "I'm not going in there."

"You baby." I enter the men's restroom without hesitation, grab a paper towel, and dab it on the wound. Josh flinches. "Hold still."

Wiping away the blood, it becomes clear that the injury is a minor one.

"See, I told you it was just a scratch," he says.

"It still needs to be cleaned."

A man comes through the door. "You do realize where you're at?" Josh smirks.

"Oh, crap." We hurry out of the store to see the old woman standing in front of her shop. Her eyes pierce through me. My stomach knots up.

Josh points toward the park. "You want to check out the art walk?"

"I kinda want to go home, if that's alright with you?"

"No problem."

Clutching onto the pendant, which is fastened around my neck, I stare out the window. Josh reaches over for my hand, but I move it away. "Hey, don't look so worried. I'm with you, no matter what."

THIRTEEN

Evolving

We pull up in front of my house and park. "Why are you so scared to take off the necklace?" Josh asks.

"You realize I haven't seen the stranger since I put it on." I admit.

"You don't think that's a coincidence?"

"No. I can't explain how it feels, but there's definitely a connection. I just know it."

"What're you going to do?" For the first time, there's a glimmer of affirmation in his eyes. "I need to find out the truth." Our gaze continues as a different kind of warmth slides through me.

"This is messed up." He sighs.

"The messed-up part is she said my family and friends will suffer." I hold the necklace away from my chest to look at it. "Since I put this on, Alex gets sick, Dad gets attacked —and even you almost get hit by a car."

Josh eye's the necklace. "But Alex was only sick for a day, wasn't she? And I was never in any danger, remember? You were in the path of the car. As far as your dad, that could've happened to anyone, and he's okay."

I know he's trying to make me feel better, but at this point I've already made up my mind that there's a direct correlation between the necklace and everything that has happened.

"You want me to come in with you?" he asks.

I shake my head, "I need to be alone so I can figure this out."

"Text me later . . . Let me know if you find anything."

I lean in to give him a kiss on the cheek but instead our lips meet, and the kiss lingers. He pulls me close. My stomach tumbles, making my body tingle.

Backing away, I get lost within his dark eyes. Before he can say anything, I place my fingers up to his mouth, lightly touching his lips. I open the car door and get out. "I'll text you." I say as I run up the porch steps. The smell of his cologne on my shirt makes my heart flutter. I take a deep breath and open the front door.

"*Dad!*" I shout, entering into the living room.

"He's not here," Alex answers. She's lying on the floor in front of the television.

"Where is he?"

"Don't know, just said he would be back later."

I'm sure it's going to be another drunken night. I remove the necklace from around my neck, place it on the end table, and lay on the floor next to Alex.

"What've you been doing all day?" I ask.

"Nothing."

"How you feeling?" I move her hair behind her ear.

"Good." She looks up, wide-eyed. "Can we go to the lake tomorrow?"

"I'm not ready to go back there just yet, if that's okay with you."

"I guess," she says, with a disappointing sigh.

"We can go do something else, though. Where's Grandma?"

"Said she had a headache and went to bed."

Grandma seems to go to bed earlier and earlier. Pretty soon she'll stay in there all day. Pulling the bag with the pretzels out of my purse, I hold it out to her. "Got you this from the mall."

She opens it up and takes a big bite. With a full mouth, she mumbles, "This is so good."

"Better not eat too much. Don't wanna get sick."

"I won't."

"I've got some homework to get done. Want to hang out in my room while I study?"

"It's Saturday. Why're you doing it now?" she whines.

"I don't like to wait 'til the last minute." I turn off the television and lock the front door, leaving the living room light on for Dad.

"I don't have any homework. What am I supposed to do?"

"Read."

Her shoulders droop as she follows me up the stairs to my room. "Why don't you call Amy to see what you missed in class yesterday?"

"'Cause I don't wanna." She collapses face-down onto my bed, letting out a heavy sigh.

I toss her a few books from my desk. "Why don't you look at these? I think you'll like them."

She keeps her face buried in the comforter. "Don't wanna read."

"Then just lay there."

"Fine, I will."

It's hard to concentrate on the essay that is due on Monday with visions of the old woman from the antique store stuck in my head. Her words were clear. *People you love die first.* An hour later, and making little progress on the essay, it's time for a break.

"So, what do you think about . . ." I start to say, when I notice that Alex is fast asleep. I take a pillow from the end of the bed and put it under her head before heading downstairs for a drink.

Passing by the end table, I stop to pick up the necklace. How can something so beautiful be so evil? Running my fingers over the inscription, I whisper, "Totus malum."

A crash from upstairs quickly compels me back up the stairs. I'm seized with panic when I reach the top and see the attic door standing wide open. My heart rate accelerates while my mind replays the horror of seeing the ghostly image again. But the necklace in my hand, the old woman's words in my head, and the knowledge that Mom was part of this give me the determination to resume my search. I summon up the courage and walk through the attic door. The lantern is still where I'd left it a few days earlier. With no other light available, I take hold of it, close the door and make my way up the stairs.

I lay the necklace on an old rattan chair before heading over to where I'd left off. A bag filled with brochures, postcards, and pictures from our family trip out west a few years ago. That was one vacation I'll never forget. I'd often wondered where this bag had ended up.

A metal padlocked box becomes my next focus; things rattle around inside. I try to pick the lock with a roofing nail. After an unsuccessful try, I toss the nail aside. I'll take it to the tool shed in the morning.

Kicking a roll of bubble wrap to the side causes me to lose my footing and fall over an odd-shaped cardboard box and land with a thud on the floor. Grandma had to have heard the noise. Now, to think of an excuse for being up here before I'm confronted. But she doesn't come.

Back on my feet, I remove the magazines piled on top of a box. Several tightly packed canvases are inside. Using my leg to push against the box while tugging on a canvas, one pops out. A painting of our farm in the winter, the snow in the picture seems to glisten when the light from the lantern hits it.

The next one is just as good: our pasture in the spring. Cows are placed throughout, and numerous clusters of yellow daffodils give the picture a splash of vivid color. I notice this one has been signed, squinting while I hold it close to read the signature. "Beatrice Bishop—No way, Grandma?" She never told me that she was an artist. And a good one, too.

There's even a portrait of my mom when she was young. It's so lifelike, her eyes seem to follow me. *Why would Grandma quit painting? For that matter, why wouldn't she tell anyone of her talent?*

There are twelve paintings in all; each one telling a different story. This is going to be hard to keep to myself. I stack the paintings up against the wall before throwing the empty box on top of the junk I've already looked through.

It's then that a dresser shoved in the corner catches my eye. I pick up the lantern, step over several boxes, and move a coat rack out of the way in order to get to it. The dresser is painted white. A blanket draped over the mirror hides the top from view. Pulling the cover off sends a cloud of dust into the air, making me cough. When the dust settles, the beauty of the dresser is exposed. Scrolls of flowers etched into the wood cascade down along the side of a mirror. Moving my fingers down the wood and across the top of the dresser, my hand brushes against something carved into the wood. *Beth.* This must've been Mom's dresser when she was young.

Staring at my reflection in the beveled glass, a ghostly

figure appears behind me. I quickly twist around, but the space is empty. Facing the mirror again, I'm momentarily robbed of breath. Once again, the silhouette of a man appears. Fear keeps me still, until the apparition drifts out of the reflected view, giving me back the ability to move.

Part of me wants to run, but my need to figure this out makes me stay. I refrain from looking into the mirror and focus solely on the dresser. All the drawers are empty. *Of course . . . it can't be that easy.*

The bottom drawer sticks. I push against it with both hands, it shuts hard. Something thumps inside. Pulling it open again, I see that the board in the bottom has split. The light from the lantern reflects on an object through the crack. Wedging my finger into the crack, the wood pops out, disclosing a secret compartment.

A black book with gold trim titled *'Boundless'* is inside. The book is old and tattered. Flipping through it, I stop on a marked page.

A chant to summon the dead is highlighted, along with instructions on how to open the gates of hell. While I can't bring myself to read the words, the heading is enough to freak me out. *How creepy is this?* Handwritten notes fill the page. It's the same strange writing that is on the necklace. The old woman pops into my head. She can read this. I lay the book on the floor, then reach inside for the small leather bag.

It's embellished with the same rope design as my necklace. Dumping the contents into my hand, two black stones fall out. I jump up to retrieve the necklace. The stones are an exact match.

My anticipation grows as I make my way back to the dresser. The papers are just within reach when footsteps resonate behind me. My heart races while I whirl around to see Grandma standing there with hands on her hips. Relieved to see her and not a ghost, I let out a sigh.

"What're you doing up here?" she asks.

"Couldn't sleep." I close the drawer with my leg. Thank goodness. There's so much disarray between us she can't see what I'm doing.

"You don't need to be up here." Her head dips in the direction of the dresser. "What do you got there?"

Come on, Brie . . . think of something. And, with that, I have a story. "Sorry, Grandma. I just remembered the trip we took. You know the one out west?"

"Yeah." Her brows tighten. "What about it?"

"I wanted to put together a scrapbook. Thought the pictures from that trip would be perfect to put in there." I rush over to where I'd laid the bag. "And look what I found."

"Is that all you wanted up here?"

"Yeah."

"This floor isn't safe; your dad had to put plywood over a few broken boards. You shouldn't come up here anymore without telling someone, and especially at night."

"Okay." I nod.

"Come on, it's late. You need to get some sleep." Grandma motions for me to go first.

"What're you doing up so late?" I ask.

"Couldn't sleep."

Well, no wonder. You go to bed so dang early, I think to myself. "Goodnight," I say before going into my room.

Alex is stretched out on the bed. I plop down at my desk, lay the bag down, and struggle to work on my essay while I wait for Grandma to fall asleep.

The minutes tick by slowly. I search the internet for a book resembling the one in the attic but nothing even comes close.

Once I'm sure she's asleep, I tiptoe across the hall toward the attic door, but the knob won't turn. No matter how hard I try, it won't budge.

The sound of Dad's truck roars down the driveway, and I hurry back to my room.

FOURTEEN

Exposed

"Hey, Brie, you awake?"

"Yes, Alex."

"We're going to church . . . right?"

"Give me a few minutes."

She jumps from the bed. "Okay, but I'll be back," she taunts before skipping out of the room.

My phone beeps. I grab it off the nightstand.

Josh: did you find anything out last night?

Me: no

Josh: what r u doing today?

Me: church. then idk

Josh: you ok?

Me: yes

Josh: I'll stop by later

Me: k

I'M NOT in any hurry to leave. Grandma usually goes grocery shopping on Sunday mornings. She says it's the best time with everyone in church. She practically has the store to herself. I'm still lying in bed when Grandma comes into my room.

"Aren't you going to church?" she asks. "It sounds like Alex is getting ready."

"Yeah, we are . . . I thought you would be gone to the store."

"I bought enough groceries last Saturday for two weeks. I think that's the way to shop from now on."

I'm disappointed. I'm sure Alex would help me look through the attic if we were alone.

Grandma straightens the top of my desk, then picks up the bag I'd found last night. "That was a fun trip," she says, pulling out a few pictures.

"It was."

Grandma opens the top desk drawer, as if searching for something. "Whatchya lookin' for?" I ask.

"Nothing." She shuts the drawer and comes over to sit next to me on the bed.

"Is something wrong?"

"I just want you to know how proud I am of you." She takes my hand in hers.

"Okay . . ."

She sits there, staring at me like she has more to say.

"I better get dressed." I try to move away, but she holds firm to my hand.

"What happened to your bracelet?" she asks.

Oh great. I forgot it in the attic. "I must've left it downstairs."

"You get dressed. I'll have breakfast ready." She pats my hand and stands to leave. "Brie, I do love you."

"I love you, too."

She leaves the room. With more determination than ever, I quickly dress, then bolt to the attic door. Just as my fingers touch the handle, the floor creaks behind me.

Whirling around, I gasp. "Holy crap, Alex, you scared the shit out of me."

"What're you doing?" she asks. "Why do you want to go in there?"

"I thought I heard something."

"Like what?"

"I don't know. Just . . . come on."

Breakfast is waiting for us in the kitchen. We eat fast, rinse our plates, and head out the door. Dad is driving the tractor down to the pasture. I'm curious as to how he keeps going with the little bit of sleep he seems to be getting.

"Brie, do you think Dad's changed?" Alex is watching him, too.

"He's just sad, I guess."

"He's scaring me," Alex confesses. "I don't even want to be around him."

That takes me by surprise. "What do you mean?"

"He yells at me all the time. The other day I saw him burning some of Mom's stuff. I asked him what he was doing, and he told me it was none of my business."

"Are you sure it was Mom's things he was burning?"

"Yes, 'cause when he left, I went out to the fire and found some pictures that weren't all the way burnt. I took them to my room."

Excitement stirs inside me. "Who were the pictures of?"

"Mostly Mom, but with people I don't know."

Could these be the photos Grandma spoke of, the ones of my real dad? "Where are they now?"

"Under my mattress. I didn't want Dad to find out I took them."

I stop the car at the end of our driveway.

"What're you doing?"

"Alex, you know those detective books you like?"

"Yeah . . ."

"How would you like to become a detective yourself?" I exude enthusiasm. "That would be fun, right?"

"What're we detecting?" Her eyes narrow.

"I'll tell you, but first I need for you to do me a big favor. Okay?"

"Like what?"

"I need you to act like you're sick again, can you do that?"

"If I'm sick, Grandma won't let me go anywhere."

"I promise, if you help me with this, I'll take you to the movies next Friday and let you buy whatever you want there."

She shakes her head. "Not good enough."

"Okay, how about I do your chores all week, and I'll still take you to the movies Friday."

"So, let me get this straight. You'll do all my chores all week long *and* take me to the movies?"

"Yes." Nothing like adding to my already-full schedule. But, at this point, I'd promise her anything to get back to the house.

"Deal." She smiles.

That's all she had to say. A U-turn at the end of our driveway and we're heading back toward the house.

"How sick do I have to be?"

"Sick enough to make Grandma believe you need to stay in bed."

"Wait—I have to stay in bed all day? You didn't tell me that."

"You can make a miraculous recovery as soon as I get what I need out of the attic."

"What's in the attic?"

"Like I said, I'll explain everything, but first you need to get sick. And fast." Alex starts to get out of the car.

"Wait until I help you out, just in case Grandma's around. We need to be believable."

Alex doesn't get sick often, but when she does like the other day, she's usually helpless.

With my arm around her, we walk up the porch steps and through the back door. Grandma is nowhere in sight. We head up the staircase. Alex leans against me with most of her weight and works on fake tears. At the top of the stairs, my legs wobble when I notice the attic door standing wide open.

Abruptly, I release her. She falls, hitting her head hard on the wall before landing in a heap on the floor. *"Shit."* I quickly help her up.

"Why'd you do that?" she cries. Fake tears are no longer needed, and she holds onto her head.

"I'm so sorry, Bug."

"No, you're not!" she screams, running to her bedroom.

I run after her. "I didn't mean to let go of you like that."

She lies across her bed, crying into her pillow. "Let me see your head." She fights against me as I try to roll her over. "Come on, Bug, let me take a look." She holds tight to the pillow that covers her face. "Listen, we don't have to do this." Pulling at the pillow, she finally lets go. She does have a huge red mark on her forehead.

"But what's in the attic?" she sniffs.

"Found some cool jewelry and a pair of boots you might like."

"You did?"

"Yep." Alex loves jewelry as much as I love shoes. "But I need to get up there before Grandma finds them."

"Okay . . ." she sniffs again.

Grandma's probably found the items in the dresser by

now, but just in case she hasn't, I decide to see what part of the attic she's in before yelling her name.

To my relief, she is looking in a different area than where I'd been. "Hey, Grandma."

She grabs her chest. "Good God, you scared me."

"I yelled for you. Didn't you hear me?"

"No. Why are you home?"

"Alex isn't feeling well again. I didn't think it would be a good idea to have her around all those people."

Grandma comes over to me. "I better have a look."

"What were you looking for?"

"Canning jars," she blurts out.

We store the jars in the barn, and she knows that. I stay close to her as we leave the attic, making sure she doesn't lock the door. She shuts the door and heads for Alex's room.

Alex is doing a good job moaning, and with the real tears, it's definitely believable. "What's wrong?" Grandma asks, placing her hand on Alex's forehead, and then her cheeks.

"My stomach hurts."

"You're a little flushed. No fever, though. That's good. Maybe you just need a little more rest." Grandma goes over to the dresser and takes out a pair of pajamas. "Let's get these on and get you under the covers." She hands Alex the pajamas.

"I'll go get you something to settle your stomach."

I wink at Alex as Grandma covers her up.

"Are you going to church, Brie?" Grandma asks.

"No, I thought I'd get the rest of my homework done."

"When you're done, you need to get outside and help. You've got to do Alex's chores today, too."

"I will."

I go to my room and wait for Grandma to go downstairs before hurrying back to Alex. "You get those pictures. I'm going to get the stuff upstairs."

The attic floor squeaks beneath my feet as I rush to the dresser, scoop up the papers, and grab the book, the bag with the stones, and the boots. I shove the bracelets and necklace into my pocket before swiftly making my way back down the attic stairs. I quietly close the door and slip into my room when I hear Grandma coming up the stairs.

Grandma is attentive when you're sick. Maybe this wasn't such a good idea after all. Grandma stays with Alex for an extended period of time. Then finally, Alex yawns loudly. Not long after that, Grandma comes into the hallway. "You get some sleep, honey, and I'll check on you in a little bit."

"Okay, Grandma."

A few seconds later, I'm in Alex's room. She's already up, retrieving the pictures from underneath her mattress.

"Good job. How many times have you practiced being sick?" I laugh.

We lay our findings on the floor. Alex hands me the pictures she saved from the fire. The edges are charred and torn, but the images are still visible. Mom is in all of them, mostly with girls I don't know. They must've been her friends from school, considering how all of them seem to be the same age. There is one of Mom with Grandpa. They're standing in front of a car. They look as if they're laughing.

"Mom sure was pretty, wasn't she?" Alex says, staring at the photo.

"Yes, she was."

"What happened to Grandpa? I don't remember."

"He was burnt in an accident. It happened before I was born, but I remember Mom telling me that he almost died in that fire."

"Oh, yeah, that's right. What'd you think he would look like without all those scars all over his face?"

"I don't know. I've only seen pictures of him like this."

There are five photographs in all. *Why would Dad burn pictures of Mom?*

Alex opens the book from the attic and starts reading from it. "'Evil is born from the blood of those who have fallen.'"

"Give me that," I yank it out of her hands.

"Why'd you do that?"

"Sorry, it just sounded creepy."

Alex picks up the papers from the floor. "This looks like Mom's writing." She holds them out to me.

"That is Mom's writing. But what language is it?" I thumb through the pages of the book and a photo falls out.

Alex grabs it first. "Who is this?" She hands me the picture. I'm sure I turn white. There in the photo is the face of the stranger who is haunting me.

"What is it, Brie?"

"Nothing." I can't take my eyes off him.

"Come on, Brie, that's not fair, I'm supposed to be helping you." She tries to swipe it out of my hand, but I hold onto it tight. "If you don't show me, I'm telling Grandma about it."

I show her the picture. "Do you know him?" she asks.

"No, but I'm going to find out who it is."

"Why?"

I pull the bracelet out of my pocket and give it to her. "Look at this."

"That's so pretty."

"And look at these." I hand her the boots. "If you're interested, there's more jewelry and clothes like this up in the attic." I clasp the bracelet around her wrist.

"Next time, I want to go up there with you."

117

Footsteps come from the staircase. Everything gets pushed under the bed. Alex jumps into bed, covers up, and starts to moan. I rush to her side.

"Don't play it up too good. You might be stuck in here all day." I say, taking the book from her nightstand and opening it to a random page.

"How's she doing?" Grandma asks.

"She's doing better."

"Your homework done?"

"Almost. Alex wanted me to read to her."

"I'll take care of Alex."

"Can I get up now?" Alex pushes off the covers.

"Not so fast," Grandma says, feeling her head again.

"But I'm hungry."

"Where'd you get this?" Grandma asks, holding onto Alex's hand.

It never dawned on me that it might be Grandma's bracelet. "I found it in the sack I took from the attic. You know, the one that had the pictures from our trip." I say.

"This was my mother's. I wondered where it ended up." Grandma says.

"Do you want it back?" Alex starts to take it off.

"No, you keep it." Grandma pats Alex's hand. "Besides, it looks good on you."

"Thanks, Grandma."

"Maybe it wouldn't hurt for you to come downstairs for a little while."

That's all it takes for Alex to grab her robe, slide her feet into her slippers, and head over to Grandma.

"Come on, sweetie, I'll make you something to eat. Brie, you come downstairs, too."

"I will, I just want to turn off my computer."

"Don't take too long. You have a lot of chores to do."

"I won't."

With them downstairs, I hurry back to Alex's room, gather up all of our findings, and take them back to my room. I stuff everything into my desk drawer—everything except the picture of the stranger.

Alex is sitting at the kitchen table eating a biscuit. Grandma rummages through the freezer. "Hey, Grandma, I also found this picture in the bag with my vacation photos. Do you know who this is?"

She walks past me with her hands full and glances at the picture. "Why, that handsome man is your grandfather."

I gasp. "That's Grandpa?"

"Yes, before the accident that scarred him so badly." She sets down the food, wipes her hands on her apron, and comes over to me.

"I thought he was burnt when he was a kid. In this picture, he looks a lot older. Why hadn't I ever seen pictures of him like this before?" I question.

"The fire destroyed almost everything." She takes the photo. "And the ones that were left . . . well, let's just say those pictures were hard for him to look at, so he got rid of them." Grandma sighs. "Not that I could blame him."

We were told he had an accident when he was young, but we were never told anything else. And we didn't ask. I don't want to sound insensitive with my next question, but it's imperative to find out. So, without giving much thought as to the way it comes across, I ask, "Was Grandpa a bad guy?"

The silence in the room makes me hot. Both Alex and Grandma stare at me like I'm crazy.

"I mean, was he nice?"

"And why would you ask that?" Grandma looks dumbfounded.

"I mean . . ." I gulp. "I just wanted to know, did he love his family?" No matter what I say, it comes out wrong.

"That's a horrible thing to ask. Of course he loved his family. He almost gave his life to save me, not to mention what he did for your mother. And you . . . he loved you very much." Grandma's face turns a bright pink, her voice sharpens with anger. "I can't believe you'd ask that."

"I'm sorry. I didn't mean anything by it. I just want to remember him."

"Remember him by asking me if he was evil?"

"I never said evil, I just meant . . . Oh, forget it."

Her eyes follow me as I make my way out the door. "You need to stop with the nonsense," Grandma scolds.

Nothing makes sense anymore. Grandpa and I were so close. Why would he want to hurt me? All the uncertainties and fear I'd experienced over the past few weeks comes rushing back. I need time alone to think.

Dad yells my name, but I ignore him and head down the driveway, walk through the yard, and disappear into the woods.

FIFTEEN

Falling

I've spent more time roaming these woods than anywhere else. Being out here alone seems to help clear my head.

Following along the bank of the creek while listening to the rush of the water, I try to piece together the fragments of my life that are falling apart.

Why did Grandpa want to hurt me? Why did I have to know about a father who didn't want me? And why was Grandma so adamant about me knowing? Then there's the necklace, the old women, the book…it's all just too much.

I make my way to my favorite spot, a small inlet where the water is crystal clear. A natural spring feeds the small pool. Even though the creek is rough and fast-flowing, being so close to the river, this area is quiet and serene. The east-facing bluff opens to a small cave that hovers over part of the water.

Josh and I stumbled onto this place ten years ago while mushroom hunting with my dad. We quickly claimed this area as our own. We've spent countless days here—swimming, exploring the cave, or just hanging out.

A big, flat rock that protrudes from the bank is where

I've sat many times to let the water soothe me. Removing my shoes and socks, I roll up my pants and dip my feet into the cool water. Leaning back onto my forearms while closing my eyes, I try to clear my head. It's difficult to think about everything that has happened, let alone believe any of it. I convince myself that learning more of my past will only add to the turmoil; it's time to let it go. I need things back to the way they were, when I at least knew who I was. When my life felt right.

"Yep, that's what I'll do," I say aloud, reassuring myself of my decision.

"And what's that?" A voice from behind makes me jump.

Hastily turning around, I breathe a sigh of relief. "One of these times you're going to scare me, and I'm just going to fall over dead."

Josh laughs. "That's impossible. Besides, I know what will bring you back from the dead."

"And what's that?"

He sits next to me, runs his hand down the side of my face and then leans in to whisper, "I know CPR."

"Real funny." I push him away.

He grabs onto me, hugging me tight. "You know you still love me."

"I used to." I wriggle out of his arms. "I'm not so sure anymore."

"What're you doing out here anyway?"

"Just thinking." Our eyes meet. "What are you doing here?"

"Told you I'd stop by."

"How'd you know where to find me?"

"Your dad said you took off to the woods." He nudges me. "I knew where you'd be, it's been awhile since I've been here, though."

"It's been months."

"You *do* keep track of me," he teases.

"No I don't." I scoff. "I just meant, you know, it's been awhile."

Amusement twinkles in his eyes. "Admit it." He nudges me again.

"Fine." I look down. "I don't know what I'd do without you right now."

"Are you sure you're okay?"

"I'm fine." I give him toothy grin.

"Yeah, 'cause that doesn't look fake."

"It just seems like my life is spiraling out of control. I mean, every day something new comes up."

"You mean there's more?"

"A lot more. I didn't want to tell you because, in reality, I didn't want to believe it myself." I tell him about my real dad, what I found in the attic, the stranger being my grandfather, and my mom's letter. He listens without saying a word as I reveal everything, including those moments of confusion and anxiety when the necklace is out of my possession.

"It looks like we have a mystery on our hands," he says without hesitation.

It comforts me that there's no skepticism in his voice. "We?" I ask.

"There's obviously something going on." He slips his arm around me. "And besides, you don't think I'd let you have all the fun figuring this out on your own, do you?"

The past melts away and so does the fear of losing him. In actuality, he has always been there for me. I just had to let him back in. I smile, feeling a sudden need to kiss him.

"I know we joke a lot, but you have to know how much you mean to me." He sweeps my hair to the side of my face. "I'd do anything for you."

For the first time, I admit to myself what I knew all along, there's no one else I'd rather be with. Grabbing onto his shirt, I pull him into me.

Our lips meet.

The kiss leaves me wanting him more than ever before. His forehead rests against mine. "Wow, what was that for?" he whispers.

"For just being you."

"Sometimes you're strange. I mean that in a good way."

"Of course you do."

His heart beats with the same intensity as mine. Nothing else matters to me right now. I'm safe. But then, the old women's warning about hurting the people around me shoots into my mind. I push away from his embrace. "You have to promise that if you ever feel like you're in danger, you'll leave."

"Nothing's going to happen."

"I'm serious."

"I am, too—nothing bad is going to happen."

The idea that he might be right bounces around in my head. First hope sets in, then reality, and then the truth comes to light. He kisses me again, distracting me from my thoughts and arousing something wonderful in me.

I whisper against his lips. "I better get home."

He takes hold of my hand and pulls me to my feet. "Yeah, your dad was pretty mad when I talked to him."

I slip on my shoes and shove my socks into my pocket.

"It's going to be alright," he tries to assure me once again.

Wide-eyed, I acknowledge with a slow, incredulous nod.

Once the farm comes into view, he slows his pace. "So, what's next?" he asks.

"I guess the first thing is that I need to find out what those papers say."

He cringes. "You talking about that old woman at the antique store?"

"She knew what the inscription on the necklace meant, so maybe she can read the notes in the book or the papers I found . . . unless you have a better idea?"

"I wish I did, cause she's creepy."

"I found her interesting. I don't know why you think she's creepy."

"I don't know, maybe the fact that she's two hundred years old and still breathing."

"She is not."

"You don't know that. I'm sure she's at least that old, if not older." He shudders.

"Then she ought to know something about all this." I feel my pocket, making sure the necklace is still inside.

"Do you want to go there now?"

"It's Sunday, I'm sure it's closed. Besides, I have to apologize to Grandma and get *all* my chores done. Then maybe Dad will let me go tomorrow night."

"I don't work today. I can stay and help."

"Any other day, that would be great, but with hurting Grandma's feelings, ignoring my dad, oh, yeah, and making Alex lie . . . " I'm sure she's told Grandma the plan I'd concocted by now. "I think it's best that I do them on my own."

I walk with Josh to his car. "Why aren't you driving your pretty plum truck?"

"I don't want everyone getting jealous just yet."

"Ah . . . that's what you're telling yourself now." I laugh.

"Really, it needed a little more work than I thought." He smiles. "But don't worry, you'll get to ride in it first."

"I might be busy that day."

Humor flashes in his eyes as he sweeps me into his arms. "You're not getting out of it that easy."

I point to the front window. "The house has eyes." Alex is peering out at us. "Really, I have to go."

He lightly kisses my lips. "'Til tomorrow, then."

"You're so weird." I grin. "I'll call you later tonight."

"Okay."

UP THE PORCH STEPS, I trip on the last stair and fall forward, catching myself on a chair before I hit the ground. Hoping that no one saw, I quickly regain my balance and then notice Dad sitting in the porch swing.

"You feeling better?" he asks.

My smile fades with the seriousness of his tone. "Yeah, just fine," I say, pushing my hair out of my face and pulling at my sleeve.

"You care to sit with me for a while?" I'm sure he isn't asking. When I make my way over to him, he briefly stops the swing to let me sit down. He presses his foot against the wood floor, moving the swing.

"We have been through a lot in the past few weeks," he says, looking straight ahead.

"Yes, we have."

"How're you holding up?"

"I'm good, but I *am* worried about *you*, Dad."

"You know, your mother meant the world to me. I'm not sure what to do without her." His eyes water, but I don't want him to cry.

"She meant the world to me too."

"I know I haven't been here much lately, and I'm sorry. I just don't . . ." His voice cracks. "I know you have a lot of questions, but hurting your grandmother is just mean."

"I didn't mean to hurt her. I just wanted some answers."

"Asking if your grandpa was evil is not a question that needs to be asked."

"I never said evil. I asked if he was bad."

"And why would you ask that?" He looks at me with the same disappointment I've seen numerous times in the past few weeks.

"You know, Brie, I'm beginning to think you might need to talk to someone."

"That's it—I'm nuts."

"You've been through a lot. Counseling might do you good."

"*Me!* What about you and the things you've been doing? I know about those pictures you burnt of Mom. What else did you throw away that maybe her daughters would've liked to have?"

"*That* is none of your business."

My stomach trembles as anger explodes inside of me. The need to hurt him comes out of nowhere, scaring me to death. "*I've got chores to do!*" I scream.

"I think you're stepping over the line," he scolds.

"You mean the *same* one you've crossed?" I don't wait for him to respond; jumping from the porch, I run to the barn, grab the pitchfork, and take my aggravation out on a bale of hay.

Hay is scattered all around before my rage subsides. I throw the pitchfork aside and collapse in the mess.

What's going on? Laying my head in my hands, I sob.

IT'S late afternoon before I'm able to compose myself and get up. Any other time, Dad would've come out to see what was taking me so long, but not tonight.

With the rake in hand, the mess I'd created gets cleaned up before scraping out the stalls. The air is chilly, which makes chores easier for some reason.

By the time the stalls are cleaned, the barn cats are fed and watered along with the chickens and two bucket calves, all the eggs are collected, and the bedding is taken off the clothesline, I'm exhausted. I still have an essay and dinner with the family to look forward to.

A hot shower does nothing to revive me, but at least the anger has quieted. Maybe I *am* going crazy. That would explain a lot. I take a deep breath and make my way to the kitchen. All eyes are on me as I take a seat at the table.

"I'm sorry if I upset you today, Grandma. I know Grandpa loved us. I guess it just came out wrong," I say, hoping to diffuse the tension.

"It's okay, honey. Sometimes we all say things we don't mean."

It's easy to get Grandma's forgiveness. Dad, on the other hand, isn't as easy to forgive. "I'm sorry Dad,"

He locks me in with a serious gaze. "I won't have you talking to your Grandmother like that again."

"I didn't mean it. Can we just say I actually *did* go temporarily insane?"

"I still think counseling might help."

Grandma chimes in, "We've all been a little on edge, not just Brie. Let's see how the next few weeks go before we start airing our dirty laundry to a stranger."

"Maybe you're right," Dad says.

Thank goodness that's all it takes. Counseling is the last thing I need. "Where's Alex?"

Grandma answers, "Aunt Edna took her out to dinner."

"Is she feeling better?" I ask.

"I don't believe she was too sick today." Grandma says. "Should be back by seven."

It's hard to keep from bringing up the things that I'd found. But I'm more scared that talking about it might make things worse.

The rest of evening goes without any other mishaps. I clean up the kitchen before going to my room.

My phone beeps.

Josh: how'd it go?

Me: it sucked

Josh: ?

Me: chores

Josh: we on for Appleton?

Me: I didn't ask tonight. I'll talk to Dad in the morning. letting things cool off just a little

Josh: good idea

I lay my phone on my desk and take out the things I'd hid in the drawer earlier. I want so badly to understand, but, I'm not sure where to begin.

I open the window wide and stare up at the stars. "Mom, if you're out there, can you help me out just a little bit? I'm not sure what I'm supposed to do. And well, to be honest, I'm scared."

Lightning illuminates the distant sky and the air is heavy with the sweet smell of rain. The quiet makes me feel very much alone. The only person who seems to make things better is Josh and I'm sure I'll mess that up sooner or later. Apprehension makes me second guess everything about my life.

Come on, Brie, get it together.

SIXTEEN

Progressing

_____

The sun shines through the window, waking me up. To my surprise, I'm still at my desk. Slowly, sitting upright in my chair, I wipe my eyes with the sleeve of my shirt. I must've rested my head on the open books and dozed off.

Squeezing the back of my neck to relieve the stiffness, I notice a neatly typed paper lying in front of me. It's my essay. Even though I don't remember writing it, it's done and it's not bad either.

I glance at the clock—seven. "Great, I'm going to be late *again.*" I leap from the chair, but my legs are having no part of it. I fall forward onto the floor. "*Crap!*" I scream, grabbing for my legs. The numbness slowly recedes, allowing me the ability to stand.

Now, with only seconds to spare, I quickly dress and run down the stairs. Grandma and Alex are in the kitchen.

"You look good today," Grandma says, setting down a plate of eggs and toast.

"I feel great, just a little stiff from sleeping at my desk all night." I glance over at Alex. "Where were you last night?"

"Slept with Grandma."

"Why?"

"You said I had too."

"I did?"

"Yes." She rolls her eyes up.

The subject gets dropped, and I gobble up breakfast like I haven't eaten in days.

"All those extra chores must be good for you," Grandma says. "Would you like more?"

"No thanks, gotta run." I grab another piece of toast before going to get my books. The necklace is lying on my bedroom floor; it must've fallen out of my pocket when I changed into my pajamas last night. I'm hesitant at first, but against my better judgment, I fasten it around my neck. I feel so much better when it's on. I just want to feel normal.

Alex is already in the car. "Can we pick up Miranda?"

"I guess."

I push the speed limit to pick up Miranda and drop them off before the first bell rings. The crossing guard is standing on the corner—always a good sign that we're not late.

"I can't pick you up tonight, so don't miss the bus . . . Okay?"

"I won't." The two of them disappear inside.

I pull out into the flow of traffic when, suddenly, the car next to me swerves into my lane. I veer left and into the path of a second car. I slam on my breaks as another car comes from a side street and slams into the side of the oncoming car before it smashes into me. I'm able to swerve around them. The vehicles come to a crumbled stop.

I jump from my car. Mrs. Daily, who lives two farms over from us, is the one driving the t-boned car. In a way, she saved me from the crash. The airbags are deployed and she is slumped over. Blood oozes down the side of her face. The area explodes into chaos.

I'm not sure if I'm being pushed back, or if I retreat on my own. Wanting to distance myself from the accident, I make my way over to the curb and sit down. The look of Mrs. Daily's face won't leave my mind.

Within minutes a fire truck, police car, and ambulance are on the scene. A police officer sits down next to me. "Can you tell me what you saw?"

"I swerved and then this car just came out of nowhere. And then Mrs. Daily got hit." It's all still kind of a blur in my head.

"Are you alright?"

"Yeah, I think so."

"Maybe we should have the paramedics check you over, just to be safe."

"I'm not hurt, but how's Mrs. Daily?"

"Who?" he asks.

"The woman in the silver car, is she okay?"

"I don't know." He's lying, I'm sure of it.

"Can I leave now?"

"We should probably call your parents."

I shake my head. "Nothing happened to me or my car. I just want to leave."

"It's not easy seeing someone in a bad situation. Are you sure I can't call someone for you?"

"I need to get to school."

"Okay, give us just a few more minutes and we should have you out of here."

It's hard to watch the paramedics place Mrs. Daily into the ambulance. She is the same age as my mom. I think briefly about her three children and husband. What if she doesn't make it?

A few minutes later, the officer comes back to me. "If you're sure you're okay, you can leave."

"I'm fine."

He walks with me to my car and opens the driver's side door. I drive away without looking back.

In the school parking lot, Josh is leaning against his car. I park and get out. The sudden stop during the accident propelled my books, papers, and backpack to the floorboard. I make my way around to the passenger side to organize them. I don't hear him come up behind me, but I know he's there. Stuffing books and paper back into my backpack before turning toward him.

He smiles as his hand brushes against my cheek. "Hi."

"Hello."

"You're late," he says.

"Car accident."

His tone becomes serious. "What? Where?"

"By the elementary school. It was Mrs. Daily." I can still see her face.

"Is she okay?"

I shrug. "Don't know."

"Did you get hurt?"

"No, I'm fine. It was awful though."

"That sucks," he takes his hand in mine. "You sure you're okay?"

"Yeah."

We walk together to my locker. All the apprehension I felt last night melts away when his lips lightly touch mine. "Try not to worry; I'm sure Mrs. Daily will be fine." Josh always seems to know what to say.

"I hope so . . . I'll see you at lunch," I say.

· · ·

THE MORNING GOES FAST. Even though I'd eaten a big breakfast, I'm starving by lunch. Josh, Jill, and Eric are already at the table when I walk into the cafeteria. I barely sit down when Jill blurts out, "Have you seen the new guy?"

"No," I say with a mouthful of potatoes.

"Oh, Brie, you're so oblivious to your surroundings." She slides her lunch tray over to Eric, and then applies a generous amount of glittery red lip gloss. "You would know if you had seen him. He is absolutely gorgeous."

"Wow . . . you hungry?" Eric teases.

Ignoring him, I shove a piece of bread into my mouth.

"Give her a break," Josh says.

That's when I notice him eyeing me, too. I huff. "You two amaze me. Why don't you pay attention to how much *you* eat?"

"Don't look now, but here he comes." Jill says. We all look up. "Do you have to be so obvious?" she whispers, gawking at him, too.

"I bet a girl with an appetite wouldn't bother him," I quickly point out.

"Again, joking!" Josh says, "But what's so special about him anyway?"

Jill taunts, "I don't know, maybe the perfect body or his gorgeous smile or his beautiful eyes or –"

Eric stops Jill in mid-sentence. "Okay, okay, we get it, why don't you just run up there and throw yourself at him."

I laugh. "Are you jealous?"

"No."

Jill snickers, drifting closer to Eric. "I'll take that as a yes," she says.

. . .

I WALK with Josh to his locker. "I'm thinking that we could go to Appleton Saturday, if that works for you," I say.

"Yeah, the weekend would give us more time."

"Besides, I have Alex's chores to do."

"Is she sick?"

"No," I roll my eyes. "Long story."

His eyes move away from me. "Don't look now, but Mister Newbie is coming this way."

He stops beside me. "Do you know where this class is?" he asks, holding his schedule out to me.

I glance at it. "That's the class I'm going to right now."

"Then you won't mind if I follow you, I hope."

"No, not at all." Turning back to Josh, I grin. "I'll see you in math."

"Yeah." He scowls.

"By the way, my name is Blake." He extends his hand out to me. Shaking his hand, I'm amused with the formality of his actions.

"I'm Brie."

"Nice to meet you, Brie."

We walk into our creative writing class to a slew of stares. Blake is introduced to the class and then told to take a seat at the empty desk next to mine.

"At least I know someone," he says, leaning my way.

"Like you haven't met several people willing to show you around," I joke. But I'm sure any girl would have been happy to help him out.

He smiles, exposing perfect, white teeth. "No one like you."

"I bet you say that a lot."

"Now, what makes you say that?"

"Just a guess."

"You would be wrong," he says matter-of-factly.

I grin and turn my attention to Mrs. Shoemaker.

Jessie, the girl who sits next to me, tries to engage Blake into a conversation. After being told three times to be quiet by Mrs. Shoemaker, I'm the one asked to move.

"But it wasn't me," I argue.

She stands, pointing to a chair in the front row, next to creepy Wayne.

"Next time, I'll ask you to leave," Mrs. Shoemaker says.

"Okay, class, I have a short film for you. You'd better pay attention—there will be a quiz afterward."

The subtle glow from the film is enough light for me to see Blake staring at me from across the room. He smiles when our eyes meet. I quickly turn my attention back to the screen.

When the bell rings, I jump up, grab my books, and head for the door. Mrs. Shoemaker bellows my name, "Brie, I'd like to talk to you!"

"Ugh . . ." I slowly turn.

Blake is standing next to her desk. "Could you come here?"

I have a feeling that she's going to ask me to do something I don't want to do.

"Brie, you probably understand the works of Edgar Allan Poe better than anyone else in this class. Since we are halfway through with the assignment, I was hoping that you could help Blake catch up."

"Hmm . . . well . . ." I want to scream, *Find someone else!* My life's hectic enough right now.

"Thank you," Mrs. Shoemaker says, not giving me a chance to decline. She hands Blake the packet we're working on, and then we leave the classroom together.

"I do appreciate this," he says.

"Yeah, no problem," I push out a heavy breath. "So, I guess we should meet for a few minutes to look it over."

"Whatever works for you."

"Why don't we meet in the cafeteria right after school? I don't have a lot of time tonight, but it shouldn't take long."

"Okay, then—the cafeteria." He nods with a subtle shift of his demeanor. "I'll see you then."

An eerie feeling stirs in the pit of my stomach. I quickly turn away and walk down the hallway toward the math rooms.

Josh is already sitting at his desk. I make my way over to him. "So, how's the newbie?" he asks.

I moan, "Wonderful."

"You sound mad."

I whisper, "Mrs. Shoemaker thinks I need to help him get caught up."

"That sucks."

"Yeah, and with everything else I have to do." Josh seems to find humor in my frustration. "What's so funny?"

"You—I thought you would've liked to be close to the newbie."

"Will you quit calling him that? His name is Blake, and, no, I don't need any more stress in my life."

"You want me to come over and help you tonight?" he asks.

I accept his offer immediately. "Yes, I do."

His eyes widen. "Seriously?"

"What, you didn't mean it?"

"Of course I did. You'll be done with chores in no time."

When Josh helps me around the farm, it takes longer to get things done, but it's more fun. "Good, you'll also have to stay for dinner, which, by the way, we have to make."

"It's a good thing I can cook, then." His brows flutter. "I'll just follow you home."

I groan. "I have to meet Blake first."

Josh shrugs. "I'll wait."

Mr. Grey taps a ruler on his desk to quiet the class. "I have posted three equations on the board . . ."

Thank goodness the class goes by fast. Josh walks with me to the cafeteria to sit and wait for Blake. Twenty minutes later, there's still no sign of him.

Josh smirks. "I think you've been stood up."

"Good, like I care." It's odd, though, he didn't seem like that kind of guy. "We better get going. You have a lot of work to do." I chuckle, thinking of the worst jobs to give him. We leave the cafeteria and head down the hallway. The hairs on the back of my neck stand when a shadowy figure appears behind the frosted window in one of the open classroom doors. I glance at Josh, but he doesn't seem to notice—he's still rattling on about how easy the night is going to be. When I look back at the door, the figure is gone.

While getting into my car, Mrs. Daily enters my thoughts. For a brief moment, I think about Mom. A car horn cuts through my thoughts. I look up to see Josh motioning for me to pull out. He follows me home.

Alex is walking down our driveway. I pull up alongside her and roll down my window. "Hey, Bug, how was school?"

She gets in. "It was good."

"Told you it'd get better."

She turns her attention to the car behind us. "Why's Josh here?"

"He's helping me out tonight."

Alex heads inside while I wait for Josh. "I'll go get us something to drink. If you want, you can start over there." Smiling, I point to the chicken pen.

"Nah, I'll wait for you. We're in this together."

I head up the porch steps and through the back door

for sodas. Grandma has her neck stretched tall, looking out the window. "Is that Josh?"

"Yep." I grab two Cokes out of the fridge. "Did you hear about Mrs. Daily?"

"Yes, I got a call just before noon." Grandma shakes her head. "So sad."

"Is she . . ." I gulp, "Dead?"

"Oh no, she's in pretty bad shape, but she's strong."

"Thank God." I sigh. "I'll be outside doing chores if you need me."

"Okay, honey."

Josh is making his way to the chicken coop. He swings around once I catch up to him, grabbing me around my waist. "We're alone." He kisses me.

"We're never going to get chores done," I whisper against his lips.

"Sure we will."

I hold the Coke up to his chest. "Here, this will cool you down." He rubs his hand over mine as he takes the Coke. "Come on." I pull at his shirt sleeve.

We start by collecting the eggs. Josh opens the pen. "Hey, did I ever tell you I can hypnotize a chicken?"

"Of course you can," I taunt.

"I'll show you." With his arms outstretched, he moves his body from side to side. "The first trick is catching one." He starts clucking, forcing the chickens into a corner.

"This oughta be good." I laugh.

He lunges for one. Feathers are a-flying as the chickens scramble in all directions. It's hilarious to watch. He hastily reaches out, grabbing hold of a chicken's leg. She squabbles and flaps her wings. Josh jumps around, trying to get her under control. Then, to my surprise, he turns around holding her calmly in his arms.

"Nice." I clap.

"Now, watch this." He gently lays the bird on the ground and flips her onto her side. Holding her down with one hand, he takes his other hand and gradually moves his fingers back and forth an inch away from the chicken's head. It's remarkable--the chicken never moves. Even when he takes his hand off of her, the dang bird just lies there, like it's dead.

Alex walks up. In a soft voice, she asks, "What's he doing?"

"He's the chicken whisperer."

Josh is concentrating on the bird; I take an egg from the basket and throw it at him. It hits his shoulder, making him jump. "Holy shit! Why'd you do that?" The bird comes alive, flapping its wings.

"I'm saving the bird." I laugh. Alex and I hurry out of the coop, into the barn and duck behind the door. Peeking through a crack in the wood, we wait for just the right moment, then leap out and yell, "Gotcha!"

He jumps, then lunges for me. Grabbing me around the waist, he lifts me into the air. "You mean I've got you."

"Okay, okay, let me go."

"Not until you tell me how great I am."

"Fine, you're great."

His arms stay wrapped tightly around my waist as he sets me back onto my feet. "Kiss me and I'll let you go."

"*Ew* . . ." Alex sneers.

We laugh, looking over to see her mortified expression

"One day you won't think it's so horrible," I say.

"Yes, I will."

"I'll remind you of that when you're older."

"Not happening," she reassures me.

I chuckle and hand a shovel to Josh. "Here, your greatness, you can clean that up." I point to the piles of poo in the stall.

"Oh, sure, give me *that* job."

"I'm giving you the easy job." I take a rope, tether it around the calf's neck, and lead it out of the stall. Even though Alex doesn't have to help, she leashes the other calf.

"So how'd you do it? How'd you get that chicken to just lay there?" Alex asks.

"It's all about repetition and never breaking eye contact. It's supposed to work even on people."

I roll my eyes. "You better start shoveling or we'll never get done."

First scoop, he gags. "How much can these things shit?"

"You'd be surprised. I didn't think things like that bothered you."

"This is just nasty."

Alex chuckles. "He's kind of a wimp."

I laugh. "Did you hear that, wimpy?"

Alex and I move aside as a shovel full of poo comes flying our way.

"Now who's the wimp?" Josh asks.

It's six-thirty before the outside chores are done. We make our way into the kitchen to wash up before starting dinner. Alex goes into the living room to watch TV.

"What're we making?" Josh asks, looking through the fridge.

"Enchiladas." I take the ground beef out of the sink. "I'll start the meat if you want to chop the tomatoes and shred the lettuce."

"Aye-aye, captain," he says.

I plop the hamburger in the skillet and start chopping the onion. "When we're done, I'll show you the stuff I found in the attic."

"Have you had a chance to ask your dad any more questions?"

"No, he's been acting weird."

"Weird, as in . . . ?"

"Just different." I look over at him. "What the heck are you doing to the tomatoes?"

"Choppin' them up."

"More like mutilating them."

He scrutinizes the pile of mashed tomatoes in front of him. "We'll just call it salsa."

With dinner in the oven and the table set, we go up to my room.

"Here they are." I hand him the papers.

"Wow, this is wild." His eyes float over the pages. "What language do you think this is?"

"I don't know." I hold the book 'Boundless' out to him, "Look at this, it's got all kinds of disturbing stuff in it."

He flips through it, "This *is* creepy." He turns the book sideways. "Hey, do you recognize any of these names? Osborne, Carrell, English, Hawks . . ." He stops and holds the book out to me, pointing. "Look here."

"Bishop," I whisper, and then notice the name alongside it. "Proctor. Both my grandparents' families are listed."

Josh lets out a long breath. "This can't be good."

"You're just realizing that now?"

He reads the last name. "Williams. Hey, remember Mike Williams?"

"Yeah, didn't his dad get a job somewhere out east a few years ago?"

"I don't know about that, but the rumor was that his older brother went insane."

"I don't remember that."

"That's because they wanted everyone to believe his dad was transferred. My mom was his nurse. Wasn't supposed to talk about it, but I overheard her telling Dad that he was completely out of control."

"That's not true."

"Believe what you want, but I'm telling you . . . it's true." He continues to flip through the book.

"What could all seven names have in common?" I ask.

Josh dumps the stones from the pouch into his hand. "We'll figure it out." He closes his hand around the rocks. He shrieks, throwing the stones across the room. "Crap, those things just burnt my hand." He holds his hand out to me, sure enough, in the palm of his hand is two red circles.

I go over and pick the stones up.

"I wouldn't do that if I were you," Josh says, still rubbing his hand.

I hold my closed fist out to him. "I don't feel anything."

His eyes widen, "Hey, Brie, look at your necklace."

Glancing down, I see that it has turned a vibrant red, with black streaks swirling throughout.

"Brie, look at your hand."

Light shines through the spaces between my fingers. I open my clenched fist to see that these stones have also come to life with swirling, vivid colors. The longer they are in my hand, the wilder the movements in the stones become. Then, ever so slowly, the air around me explodes with the same colors as the stones. Josh fades into a clouded sea of black as cries of "Help" echo around me.

Releasing the stones, I watch them gradually fall from my hand and roll in slow motion across the floor. The cries quiet to a soft hum.

The color dissipates when the stones come to rest against my oak baseboard, and the stones in my necklace are black once again.

The light in the room flickers, bringing the space quickly back to normal.

Josh hurries to my side. "Is your hand okay?" He takes my hand in his.

"I'm fine, but weren't the colors bizarre?"

"What?" His brows rise.

"The colors those things gave off."

"Still don't know what you're talking about." There's a puzzled note in his voice.

"Whatever," I snap, pulling my hand away.

"Geez, okay." He makes his way across the room to pick up the bag. He tosses it over to me. "You can pick them up, but I'm not."

I'm cautious as I gather up the stones and shove them into the bag. To my relief, nothing happens. "I think we need to get to Appleton soon," I say, dropping down to sit next to Josh on the floor.

"That I'll agree with. Maybe that lady can shed some light on all this stuff." Then he smirks. "Or maybe we're in an alternate dimension and being studied by aliens."

"I'd say someone's been watching too much sci-fi."

He grabs onto me and laughs. "I just saw a show on it."

I cuddle close to him. "Then all of this isn't real?"

He kisses me. "Okay, you win." Josh's phone rings, and we jump. A startling laugh escapes both of us. "Hey, Mom," he answers. "Right now?" By the expression on his face he isn't enjoying the conversation.

I pull a bag out of my closet and drop the stones, book, papers, and necklace inside.

"Ugh . . . parents," he says shoving his phone into his pocket.

"What's wrong?"

"Mom just said Dad needs to talk to me."

"Uh-oh, what'd you do now?"

"I'm pretty much perfect so . . ." his brows rise and a faint smile touches the corner of his lips.

"Oh no," I gasp. "We *are* in an alternate dimension." I snort out a laugh.

He jumps to his feet and within seconds he has a hold on me. "You're not getting away from me that easy."

I wrap my arms around his neck, loving the familiar warmth of his body next to mine. "And now I have to eat your cooking alone?"

"You'll want me to cook all the time after you taste my masterpiece."

"You can cook anytime. I hate to do it."

"See. We are perfect together." His lips lightly touch mine.

The thought of losing him shoots into my mind, causing a rush of quiet anxiety to flare. I back away, needing to distract my thoughts before the panic strengthens.

"You okay?" he asks.

I shake my head. "Yeah," I lie, trying to keep the anxiety at bay. "I've got to check the enchiladas."

He follows me down the stairs and into the kitchen. Grandma has already pulled the pan out of the oven. "I was just going to do that," I say, breathing a little easier as the sudden onset of anxiety decreases.

"It looks good," Grandma says. "I steamed some broccoli."

"Gross," I glance at the bowl, "Broccoli doesn't go with enchiladas."

"What vegetable did you want?" Grandma asks.

"None."

Josh laughs. "Dang it, I'm going to miss the broccoli enchiladas."

"You're not staying, Josh?" Grandma asks.

"I can't."

"Well hang on." Grandma rummages through the cabinet, pulling out a plastic container. "You can take some home."

Wide-eyed, I flash Josh a smile, "Make sure to put extra broccoli in there, Grandma. It's his favorite."

"It's okay, Ms. B, I can . . ." Too late, as she already has the container ready to go and holds it out to him. "Thanks," he murmurs.

"Anytime darling."

I chuckle as Josh follows me out onto the porch. He grabs hold of my hand. "I'm not eating this," he says.

"You'll hurt her feelings."

"She won't know."

I raise my brows. "I'll tell her."

It's amazing how good he can make me feel, even with everything that's going on. He holds me close as we walk to his car. "Maybe we should go to Appleton tomorrow," he says.

"I have a huge test in creative writing. I should probably be there."

"Is it the test or the newbie?"

I look up at him and smile. "Wouldn't you like to know?"

I melt into him as he kisses me. Withdrawing slightly, he whispers, "I guess I got my answer."

"Yeah . . ." I grin. "It's the newbie."

SEVENTEEN

Lost

———

My phone beeps, waking me up. I roll over and grab for it.

Josh: meet me at school early

Me: ? what's up

Josh: tell you in person

Me: k – 7:45?

Josh: k

JOSH IS ALREADY in the school parking lot. It's obvious from the look on his face that something's wrong. I park next to him and hurry to get out of my car.

"What's going on?" I ask.

"Only the worst thing ever." He sighs. "My dad . . ."

Before he can finish, Blake yells my name, "Brie." He waves as he walks toward us.

"Ignore him, Josh, What's going on with your dad?"

Blake boldly interrupts, "What happened to you last night? I waited."

"What?" I huff, "I waited for twenty minutes in the cafeteria."

"The cafeteria? Oh . . . I'm so dumb, I thought you said to meet in the library." His eyes flash. "I'm sorry."

"I don't have time for this now." I turn my attention back to Josh.

"Wait, Brie, I just have one question."

Exhaling noisily to substantiate my annoyance, I whirl around to tell him to get lost, but when our eyes meet, I'm totally captivated by him.

"Could you just take a look at what I have done so far and tell me what you think." A smile flickers across his face.

Josh butts in. "Look, man, she already said she was busy, leave her alone."

Blake seems to infiltrate my thoughts. "Are you sure?" he challenges. "Just this once."

I stammer, "I guess . . . I mean . . . I did promise." I look back a Josh, but Blake is still inside my head. "It's the least I could do, just until he can find someone else." I can't believe what's coming out of my mouth.

"So what I have to say isn't important?" Josh says, his anguish seems to diminish Blake's hold on me.

I'm reaching out to Josh when Blake places his hand on my shoulder. My will is no longer my own. I look over my shoulder and into Blake's eyes. "You got time now? It won't take long." he says.

I take a step toward Blake. Conflict ignites inside of me. *What am I saying? I don't want to go with him.*

Josh stops me. "Really, Brie."

"We'll talk later." I say.

"No," his voice trembles. "It's not important."

Blake breaks the moment. "If this isn't a good time . . ." The intensity of his touch is so strong that I have no choice but to go with him. My chest tightens. I want to run to Josh. But I can't stop myself from walking away with Blake, leaving Josh standing there alone.

"Is that your boyfriend?" Blake asks.

"Yes."

"I hope I didn't interrupt. I just wanted to get some of the worksheets done before class." His voice is soft and inviting.

"No problem." We head for the cafeteria. "We'll only have about fifteen minutes to go over the assignment."

"That'll be enough time."

"Okay, so how much do you know about this?" I open the book on Edgar Allan Poe and pull out my worksheet. "Do you have your paper?"

"I left it in my locker. I can just look at yours." He slides close to me. Our legs touch. An odd excitement races through me. I want to move my leg away, but I don't.

"Let's start here." I point to the first question: Edgar Allan Poe's birth and contribution to the world.

Without looking down at the paper, he recites. "Edgar Poe, born in Boston on January 19, 1809, was an American author and poet, among other things. He was considered part of the American romantic movement." The intensity in his eyes creates a feeling of avidity deep inside of me.

I try to look away, but I can't. "You really don't need help with this, do you?"

"Of course I do."

"You learn fast, then." I chuckle nervously.

"Great teacher, I would say. And I enjoy the company." He touches my hand.

My heartbeat elevates. Needing to divert the disconcerting excitement that's coursing through me, I move my hand away and ask, "So, where are you from?"

"New Jersey. And you—have you always lived here?"

"Yes, always."

"What do you do around here for fun?"

"Not a whole lot."

"Maybe we could get together sometime. You could show me around." He pulls his phone out of his pocket. "Can I call you?"

"Sure." My voice squeaks. It's wrong. I know it. But again, I just can't help myself and give him my number.

He plucks a pen from my backpack and writes his number on my worksheet. "Just in case." He smiles.

"I better get going." I gather up my things and stuff it all into my bag. "I'll see you in class." His hand brushes against my bare arm, making me tremble.

I hurry out of the cafeteria and down the hall. I see Josh talking to Eric by the front door. Class is about to start, but when Josh leaves the building, I panic and follow him out. I catch up to him just before he gets to his car.

"Hey, Josh wait."

It hits me hard to see the emotional hurt in his eyes when he turns around. Guilt trickles through me. "I'm sorry, I don't know what happened. I guess I felt bad for not helping after I said I would."

"You can say no, sometimes." He gets into his car.

"Where're you going?"

"I've got to get out of here."

"What about school?"

"It doesn't matter." He gazes up at me.

"Why?"

"I say I have something important to tell you, and you walk away." A heavy sigh escapes him. "I'd never do that to you."

Ever-increasing confusion and total regret dominates

my thoughts. There's nothing I can say to make it better. I touch his arm. "I'm really sorry."

His gaze shifts away from me as he remains silent.

"Look at me?" I ask, but he keeps his head down. I hurry around to the passenger side of the car and jump in. "I'm not going anywhere until you talk to me."

For a second he simply stares at me, before asking, "What are we, Brie?"

"What do you mean?"

He shrugs. "If it's that easy for you to walk away…"

"It's not," I grab for his hand and squeeze it tight, "You're my best friend—there's nothing that can make me feel any worse than I do right now."

He whispers, "Maybe I'm overreacting—I'm just mad."

"Mad about Blake?"

"No . . . mad that my dad's been transferred out of state."

"You're joking, right?"

"We're moving to Texas at the end of the month."

"What? You can't be for real. That's only a couple weeks away."

"That's what I said. I did everything I could to try to convince him to let me stay, but he said it was the opportunity of a lifetime. That it would be good for all of us."

"That's not fair. Did you tell him you could stay with Eric, or, for that matter, me? Grandma loves you. She would let you move in."

"I've already tried all that; Dad's not budging on this one."

Butterflies take flight in my stomach. *Okay, calm down. He's not moving to Siberia—it's Texas. At least he'll still be in the States.*

"Hey, Brie, don't worry. We can talk every day, and I still plan on helping you solve the mystery before I leave."

I lean over to grab onto him, breathing in his cologne. "What will I do without you?"

"I'll always be here when you need me."

"You can't leave."

"What'd you say to us getting out of here?"

"Okay." I sigh.

"You want to go to Appleton?"

"I didn't bring the papers with me."

"How about the lake, then?"

"Sure." I'm a little apprehensive, not having been back there since the accident, but I know I'm safe with Josh. Both of us are silent on the way. I guess we both know what the other is thinking.

He parks so we can sit on the hood of the car and look out at the water. The lake shimmers when the sun breaks through low clouds. The familiar sense of peace the lake usually makes me feel is dismissed by the thought of Josh leaving. My heart flutters when he looks into my eyes. He traces the side of my face, then kisses me softly. "You okay?" he whispers.

"I don't know."

"We need to get to that antique shop before I leave."

"Definitely," I sigh. "I need you there with me."

"Oh, so you *do* need me."

"I'll always need you. Don't you know that by now?"

"This is all a bunch of crap. I'm going to keep trying to convince Dad to let me stay, and maybe Mom will help."

"But what if it doesn't work?" A deep sense of loss overcomes me.

"I plan on coming back over Christmas break, spring break, and any other time I can."

"Your parents aren't going to go for that."

"I'll just tell them that I can't leave my girl alone too long."

"Your girl." I do like the sound of that.

"You know, Brie, we . . ."

Suddenly Josh's voice succumbs to a ringing in my ears. An upsurge of heat radiates through me. I take a deep breath, but the air isn't finding its way to my lungs. That's when I see the stranger levitating just about the water's edge. My throat constricts and the world around me disappears.

∞ ∞ ∞

SLOWLY THE DARKNESS MELTS AWAY, leaving me in a haze. Josh is talking, and we're walking along the lakeshore. Looking back, I see the car is parked a few hundred feet away from where we are.

"You know what I mean, right?" Josh says.

"What?"

"What'd you think?"

"I--I don't know."

"What's wrong, Brie?"

"I feel weird." I pull my phone out of my pocket; I'm shocked to see that two hours have passed.

Josh stops in front of me. "Are you sure you're okay?"

It's almost impossible to quiet the conflict inside of my head.

"Brie." He shakes my arms. "What's wrong?"

"I'm a little dizzy," I sputter, "and sick to my stomach."

"Are you hungry?"

Slowly nodding, I say, "Yeah, that's it, I'm just hungry."

"Okay." He takes hold of my hand and leads me back to the car. "I know a place not too far from here." He opens the car door; I get in while I try to evoke a memory of the last two hours. "So, you never did answer my question."

I'm clueless as how to answer and stay silent.

"Never mind." He says. Closing the door he heads around to the driver's side.

We take the back roads—not that anyone would see us, but just in case. The town is small enough that everyone knows who you are. "There's a café about thirty minutes away. Want to go there?"

"That's fine." I turn up the radio to drown out my thoughts, and I try to convince myself that it's low blood sugar making me feel this way.

"Is there something you're not telling me?" Josh asks.

"No."

The cool air coming through the window helps.

I'M glad the café isn't busy. Josh sits across from me in the back booth. "So, what sounds good?" he asks, looking over the menu.

As my hunger grows, my anxiety increases. "Anything right now—I'm starving."

"I think the cheeseburger basket and strawberry malt sounds good."

"I'll have the same."

Josh orders for both of us and asks the waitress for some crackers. I wolf them down, and they do seem to make me feel a little better.

Josh reaches across the table and takes hold of my hand. "I like this—being with you."

"I like it, too."

"You know we can't go back to school until it's over."

"What do you have in mind, then?"

"We could go to the park."

"Okay."

The waitress comes over with our food. It looks as good as it smells. Josh picks off his pickle, onions, and lettuce.

"Why do you order everything when you take half of it off?"

"Easier."

"Easier for who?"

The unease dissipates the more I eat, reassuring me that what I'd thought previously is correct: low blood sugar.

"Are you feeling any better?" Josh asks.

"A lot better."

The thought of him leaving crosses my mind, but with it being our senior year, we can survive it. We both have college dreams that will take us on separate journeys for a while. Just a little bump in the road is all.

The waitress places the bill on the table. "Is there anything else I can get for you?"

"No, we're good," Josh snatches it up. "You ready to go?"

"I'm going to use the bathroom first."

"I'll wait outside."

I glance in the mirror to make sure food isn't stuck in my teeth, then wash my hands, comb through my hair with my fingers, and brush a few crumbs off my shirt.

Josh is leaning against the car. He sees me and opens the passenger door. "My lady." He motions for me to get inside.

"You're so weird."

It's midday by the time we get to the park. The place is

deserted. "Want to go for a walk?" he asks, pulling off the road. "It looks like rain."

"That doesn't bother me." I grab a jacket from the backseat.

"Me either." He takes my hand in his, and we head for the trail. It feels as if we're a million miles away from Kiel and a million miles away from the madness that has become my life. I never want this moment to end.

I climb onto a log that had fallen across the path. Josh jumps across it with no problem. My shoelace catches on the bark, causing me to tumble face-first toward the ground. I'm in his arms within seconds.

"Holy crap, that was close." I laugh, holding onto him.

"I'm just irresistible," he laughs while he yanks my shoelace free and sets my feet on the ground. "Hey, look over there." He points to a pavilion not far from the path.

Pushing him back, I run for it. Before I make it to the picnic table, he grabs me mid-step; my feet come up off the ground as he whirls me around.

"Okay, okay, stop." I laugh, trying to wiggle free.

He turns me to face him. I wrap my arms around his neck. For the next few minutes, the only noise is our breathing, our lips coming together and parting, and the occasional moan of delight. His lips find their way to my neck, sending goose-bumps down my arms.

I sigh. "What do we do next?"

"I'm going to try talking Mom and Dad into letting me stay, but just in case it doesn't work out, are you going to be okay here? I mean, with everything that's going on?"

"I think so."

"You know, you can always come to Texas for a visit."

Heat radiates throughout me at the thought of him leaving. I silently try to reassure myself that it'll be all right, but the more we talk about it, the hotter I get.

My head spins as the heat rages inside. Desperately, I tug my jacket off to relieve the heat.

"What is it?" he asks.

My vision is obscured by flecks of black, which grow so fast I'm blinded in a matter of seconds. Without uttering a sound, I slip into the murkiness of the unknown.

EIGHTEEN

Defeated

An icy current rolls through me as little black flecks disperse from my view, giving me back my sight. I'm lying on a blanket next to Josh. He's propped up on one arm with his other hand on my bare skin underneath my shirt. My heart-rate skyrockets.

"What do you think; you think it's a good idea?" Josh asks.

Scared to speak for fear I'll lose my reality again, I don't answer. Anxiety coils around my body, squeezing me breathless. My throat constricts, forcing me to hastily sit up.

"Brie, what's wrong?"

"I— just—I just—need space." My breath wavers while trying to suck in air. I drop my head into my hands, and tears fill my eyes.

"Brie, look at me."

"No."

His hand touches the side of my face, making me look at him. "What is it?"

That's when the sun, sinking into the west, catches my

eye—not at all where it should be for early afternoon.

Hastily, I pull the phone from my pocket. "Six-thirty . . . how can that be?"

"That's what I said, but you insisted we stay. I wasn't going to argue."

"That's crazy!" I jump to my feet and start walking. "I have to get home."

"Okay, but you're going in the wrong direction."

I spin around to see Josh pointing the opposite way. "The car's over there."

"Will you hurry?" I'm already halfway to the car before he snatches up the blanket and makes his way over to me.

"Why're you acting this way?"

"I just want to go home."

He stops me. "We will, but first, what's going on?"

My thoughts are overshadowed by fear, I can't explain this to him. I can't even make sense of it myself. "I just can't believe I stayed out here so long."

"I'll come home with you to explain what happened."

"And what *did* happen?"

"Uh . . . what do you mean?"

"Between us."

"Still don't know what you're talking about."

I point to the blanket. "What was that about?"

He looks bewildered. "I have no idea what you mean."

"Just forget it—I need to get home."

He throws the blanket into the backseat. I turn to face the window, believing now that I've really gone crazy.

"Brie, look at me?"

"No . . . I just need to get home."

"First you need to look at me."

"I can't." My voice is a little more than a hoarse whisper now, "Josh, please."

"Fine, we'll leave."

. . .

WE PULL into the vacant school lot. My phone's been ringing nonstop since we left the park. I don't dare answer it until I've come up with an excuse not only for being late, but also for skipping school. I'm sure the office has called Dad.

"You sure you don't want me to follow you home?"

"Yeah, but thanks."

"Call me later."

"I will if I'm not dead."

On the way home, I become lost in a mental maze of all the insane things that have happened. Is this what it feels like to be derailed from reality? Crossing in and out of consciousness while the world goes on normally around you, and no one notices your struggle?

I park by the barn, and I try to steady my trembling body as I make my way toward the house. Unsure of what to say or how to act when confronted, I decide to wait until Dad asks. In reality, there's no punishment he can give me that will be worse than the hell I'm already living in.

When I'm a few steps from the porch, my vision becomes obscured once again. Then a sudden sharp pain in my stomach drops me to my Knees. Even with my arms wrapped tightly around my waist, the pain intensifies.

∞ ∞ ∞

I'M STANDING in my room with my pajamas on. Alex is lying in my bed. The clock reads: nine-thirty. *How can that be? How did I get here?*

"You comin' to bed?" Alex asks.

My whole body warms with terror. "What happened tonight?"

"What do you mean?"

"I mean, how'd I get here?" I ask.

"What?"

"Is Dad mad?"

Her brows draw together. "Why would he be mad?"

Fire blazes in my stomach and my legs become jelly like. "What'd he say when I got home?"

"Nothing." She rolls over and closes her eyes.

"Alex, listen to me. I need you to tell me what happened tonight." Rage hisses through me, pushing out my fear. I rush toward her, grabbing onto her arm. She flinches. "Just tell me," I say through clenched teeth.

"You're hurting me. Let me go!" she shrieks, digging her fingernails into my skin and trying to free herself. "*Dad! Grandma!*" Alex cries, "Brie, stop it!"

When I realize what I'm doing, I throw my hands into the air and back away. "Oh, my God, Alex. I'm so sorry."

Red blobs dot her arms. "Go away." She jumps from the bed and runs out of the room.

Anger once again explodes inside of me and quickly rages out of control. I run for the bathroom and lock myself inside. Scared beyond belief, I fill my hands with cold water and splash my face again and again until water trickles down my arms and legs, collecting into a pool on the floor.

Inhaling three big breaths, I open my eyes to look into the mirror. But it's not me. A woman with a likeness to me is staring back. I slam my fist against the mirror to rid it of the illusion—but the face remains.

Stop it! Tears of agony roll down my cheeks. I melt into the puddle of water on the floor. My clothes and hair are dripping wet. I bring my knees up to my chest and wrap my arms around my bent legs. I curl up in a ball and sob.

MY SOBS FRAGMENT into irritating hiccups and goose-bumps cover my skin. The hostility eases. I sniff back the tears while I reach up for toilet paper to wipe my face. It sticks to my wet fingers. I yank off the whole roll and toss it aside. I use my shirtsleeve to wipe my face instead. I pull myself up to take a peek in the mirror, and thankfully it's me.

It takes the last of my strength to scatter towels onto the floor to sop up the water, and I throw them into the tub. Taking out another towel, I wrap it around my shoulders. Exhaustion has a firm grip on me now, but before going to my room, I need to make sure Alex is okay. Standing outside Grandma's room to think of the right words, I hear Alex talking.

"Grandma, I can't sleep."

"You need to try."

"What's wrong with Brie?"

"She'll be fine, don't worry," Grandma says.

"She was so mean—What'd I do?"

"It's not you, Sweetie. I promise."

"You think she'll be better in the morning?" There's a hint of sadness in her voice.

"Yes I do. Now, you need to go to sleep."

No matter what I say, it won't take away what I've done. I quietly slip into my room and shut the door.

Dry clothes halt the goose bumps, but not the pain. My cell phone rings, scaring the crap out of me. It's Josh.

"Well, how'd it go with your dad? Are you grounded forever?"

"No."

"What happened?"

"I don't know . . . I can't talk right now. I'll tell you tomorrow." I hang up without giving him a chance to speak.

Stress. It has to be stress. I just need to go to bed and get a good night's sleep. Tomorrow will be a better day . . . I hope.

My stomach growls, but I'm sure I've eaten. Actually . . . I'm not sure, I'm not sure of anything. When the hunger becomes too much to ignore, I get up and head downstairs to the kitchen.

I'm nauseated, but that doesn't stop me from devouring two bowls of cereal. Before leaving the kitchen, I grab a soda and a package of graham crackers. I'm still so hungry. Great, I'm not only going crazy, but at this rate, I'll be huge, too. I stuff a cracker in my mouth and head upstairs.

I'd hoped to talk to Dad, but his room is empty. Grandma and Alex are now asleep. I stop at the attic door, thinking that maybe the picture that Grandma spoke of—the one of my biological dad—is up there somewhere.

Lack of energy stops me from entering. Back in my room, I set the crackers and soda on the nightstand. I take the bag with the things from the attic to my bed and begin to search through them again.

I thumb through the book 'Boundless,' reading a few sentences out loud. "Malevolence has no bounds or limits. It's in us all and stems from an inherent need to delve into the deepest and darkest parts of one's self. Though it is dangerous and painful to realize one's primal fear, the journey can be well worth it. Practices of sorcery draw on assumed malevolent powers.'"

With Mom's letter and the obvious lying in front of me,

the only conclusion that makes any sense is my real dad must've been involved in something bad.

I shove the book into my backpack and then finish off the entire package of crackers while I read through the letters again. It's all right here, but I don't get it.

Frustrated, I lay the pages on the floor next to my bed and then fasten the necklace around my neck. I hear the old woman's warning loud and clear in my head. The false sense of peace: this thing can make you feel, but I'd do anything to get rid of my anxiety. Even if it's only for a little while. And more than that, I pray that it can keep me from fading into the darkness. Even though that sounds ridiculous, it can't hurt—or, at least, I think it can't.

NINETEEN

Knowledge

Nightmares wake me several times through the night. Each time, it takes a little longer to calm down and fall back to sleep.

The sound of my alarm rouses me from another horrible dream. As soon as my eyes open, the dream is pushed out of my head. Since I'm scared to death to face the day, I just want to stay home. But then I think about the old woman from the antique store. I have to get there today.

The morning goes slow. Even getting dressed seems to zap what little energy I have. My insides tremble as I head downstairs. I'm never going to explain last night, so there's no sense in putting off the inevitable. Taking a deep breath I enter the kitchen.

"Good morning, darling." Grandma greets me with a smile. "Hope your day goes better today than yesterday." She hands me a plate of food.

"Uh…yeah, so do I." I wait for more questions to follow, but they don't. I sit next to Alex. "Hey, Bug, I'm sorry about last night. I didn't mean to hurt you."

Her brow rises. "Huh?"

I squeeze her tight. "I love you so much, don't ever forget that."

"Are you okay?" she squints.

"I don't know. I mean—yeah, I think."

Grandma pours me a glass of orange juice. "I still can't believe what you went through." She touches my shoulder. "You'll be fine once it gets fixed. How'd you get out of that anyway?"

With no idea what's she's talking about, I shrug and stuff my mouth with toast and eggs to avoid answering.

"You eat up, now." She picks up the laundry basket and pushes through the back door.

"I'm leaving a little early do you still want a ride?"

Alex nods.

"Go get ready, and I'll clean up." I take the plates to the sink.

Dad comes through the door. "Hey, Brie, how're you feeling?"

Cautiously, I answer, "Good . . ."

He comes over and kisses my cheek. "Things will turn around, don't worry. Oh, and your friend seems nice."

"Friend?" I question.

"Yeah, it was nice of him to help you out last night."

What is he talking about?

He says nothing else as he makes his way over to fill his coffee cup. I leave the kitchen doubly confused.

Alex meets me halfway up the stairs with my backpack in hand. "I grabbed this for you." She holds it out to me. "If we leave now, can we pick up Miranda?"

"I guess." I follow her down the stairs and into the kitchen.

"Hey, Dad, I might be a little late tonight."

"Why's that?"

"Mr. Grey is letting me retake a test that I missed."

"I'll let your Grandmother know, but try not to be too late."

"Okay."

Now to pick Alex's brain a little on the way to school. "I'm sorry about last night, is your arm okay?"

"What?" She looks down at her arm. "What's wrong with it?"

"Okay, forget that. Can you tell me why I was late getting home last night?"

"You were late? Does Dad know?"

"Alex, you're not listening." I try to keep the tone of my voice soft. "Just tell me what was said last night."

"When?"

Not sure if she's trying to be funny or if she truly has no idea what I'm talking about.

With wide-eyes she asks, "You okay, Brie?"

"Just forget it." I turn up the radio.

Before dropping her and Miranda off at school, I remind them again to take the bus home. With all my bases covered, Appleton becomes my focus.

Josh is getting out of his car as I pull up next to him and park. "Hey, got a sec?"

He jumps in the passenger side of my car.

"You look tired," he says.

"I'm fine. But I need to know what happened last night. I'm talking about from the time we were sitting on the picnic table, 'til the time we left."

"Nothing much, we just talked. Why?"

"I don't remember any of it."

His brows knit together. "You forgot?"

"No, I didn't forget. I was never there."

"Yes, you were."

"No, you're not getting it. I can't remember hours at a time."

He falls back against the seat. "So everything you said to me yesterday was a lie?"

"I didn't lie, I just don't know what I said."

"Oh." He nods. "I get it. Here comes the commitment issue."

"That's not it. Will you just *listen to me*!?" I scream.

"I'm trying, but you're not making *any* sense!"

"Ugh . . ." I exhale noisily. "This has nothing to do with how I feel about you. I love you. This is about me. I'm going insane and you're the only person I trust."

He smiles. "Oh, so you do love me?"

I roll my eyes. "That's the only thing you got out of that? I tell you I'm nuts, and you don't care?"

"Of course I care."

"Josh, please, I'm scared. I need your help."

Point made; his smile fades. "You're serious."

"I am."

"What d'you want me to do?"

"How do you feel about going to Appleton right now?"

He nods. "Okay, freaky lady here we come. But I get to drive."

"I hoped you'd say that."

Inside his car he leans my way. "By the way, I love you, too," he says, bringing a short-lived smile to my face.

Josh pulls out of the parking lot as I take the book out of my backpack. "I was reading this last night. You should hear some of the creepy stuff in here." I flip through the pages and gasp, "Oh crap!"

"What?"

"The papers, they're not in here, I must've left them at home. We have to get them."

A quick U-turn and we're on our way. A few blocks away from my driveway, Josh steers the car off the pavement and into the tall grass on the side of the road. He maneuvers his way through the trees and parks. "You think this will work?"

The street is barely visible through the dense brush. "It's like you've done this before."

"Just good driving skills," he says with pride.

We walk through the woods, keeping hidden until we can figure out where Dad is. The sound of the tractor in the lower pasture gives us his location.

"We need to find out where Grandma's at," I say, pointing to the kitchen window. "I bet she's in there."

"One way to find out." Josh takes off running toward the house. I stay close behind. We make our way to the window just as the back door slams shut.

"Someone's coming." My heart races as we hurry to the other side of the house, and I peek around the corner to see Grandma carrying a large box out to her car. She places it in the passenger side of her vehicle before hurrying around to the driver's side.

Her car speeds down the driveway. We race up the porch, through the back door. Josh stops at the bottom of the stairs. "I'll keep a lookout."

"It'll only take me a sec." I rush up to my room and over to where I'd laid the papers on the floor, but they're not there. Even after searching under the bed, in the night-stand, and then in the closet, I come up empty handed. Josh yells up the stairs.

"What's taking you so long?"

"I can't find them."

He comes into the room.

"They were right there." I point at my bed.

"Did you look under the bed?"

"Yes." I'm looking through my dresser when Josh comes up behind me.

"Hey, look!" He smirks, holding the pages in his hand.

"Where were they?"

"Right where I said they'd be, under the bed."

"Whatever." I grab the papers and take off down the stairs.

Dad's truck roars down the driveway as we reach the bottom of the stairs. We run for the door. But before we can make it out of the house, he comes up the porch steps. I motion to get back to the living room. Dad comes through the door just as we dive behind the couch.

"Great," Josh whispers.

I whisper, "He never stays inside long." I'm kind of surprised when he comes into the living room, turns on the TV, and sits down.

"How's this going to work?" Josh mouths.

I shrug and answer inaudibly. "He'll leave soon . . . I think."

Josh's wide eyes and funny expression almost makes me laugh. I clasp my hand over my mouth. Just then, Dad's cell phone rings.

"Yeah, I'll be right there," he says.

I give Josh a thumbs-up as Dad heads for the kitchen. The back door slams.

We run out the front door and toward the woods. Concealed once again in the woods, our tension turns to laughter.

Now on the road, I pull the book from the bag. "I tried to match the writing from my mom's letter to the passages in the book."

"Did you figure any of it out?"

"No, but these two items definitely go together."

Josh pulls into a gas station to fill up. He goes inside to

pay and comes back with two cokes and candy bars. "Thought you might be hungry."

"Thanks." Just being with him makes me feel better. "You want to hear some of the creepy spells in the book?"

"Heck yeah." He turns off the radio.

"The first one here is a spell to gain powers."

"That would be a good one to start with."

"It goes like this. 'The secrets we hid in the night, the oldest of gods are invoked here, the great work of magic is sought, in the night and in this hour, I call upon the ancient power. Bring your powers to we sisters three, we want the power, give us power.'"

He scoffs. "That didn't sound like much."

"How about this one? It's a stay awake chant, 'God and Goddess, hear my call and understand that should I fall asleep, I'll feel like never waking. This spell is yours, mine for the taking. All I ask is to stay awake, to not sleep 'til the next moon wake. And as I call your spirits forth, with harm to none, especially me, as I will, so mote be.'"

"Aren't there any cool ones?"

"Like what?"

"I don't know, maybe one to turn things into gold."

"Get real. There's nothing in here like that. Now, do you want to hear more or not?"

"Yeah, go ahead." He smirks. "I don't want you getting scared reading them to yourself."

"I think you're the chicken, remember."

"I'm only afraid of the things that I should be."

"Yeah, like little old ladies," I laugh.

I continue reading the spells and chants, but not the incantations. They're way too disturbing.

"This one's bizarre; it says, 'Exhilarating power penetrates the chosen one's soul with every death they cause.'"

With raised brows, I question, "What do you think that means?"

"It sounds as freakish as everything else you've read."

"Okay, fine, I'll move on."

The hour and a half ride seems like minutes. The small snack we had didn't do much to quiet my hunger. I'm so hungry that by the time we get to Appleton, my stomach hurts. "Let's eat something before we go to the antique shop."

"You want something fast, or do you want to go to Toni's?"

I glance at my phone. "In order to get back before school lets out, we'll have to make it quick. Look there's a drive-thru."

I order the biggest sandwich they have, and large fries. Josh has the same. We park up the street from the antique store to eat our lunch and summon courage to face the old woman again.

"You ready?" I ask.

"I guess." He looks nervous.

"Don't be scared, I'll hold your hand."

Josh squeezes my arm as the door chimes sound.

"I'll be right there," a voice comes from the back room.

"I was hoping there would be other people in here," Josh whispers.

"Yeah, me, too."

A framed photo of the old women and two small children sets on the counter. They're all smiling in the photo. I point to it, "See Josh, she's a real person."

"It's fake."

"Is not."

The old woman appears from behind the heavy curtains. Once she catches a glimpse of us, she slows her pace. "So . . . what brings you back?"

"I was hoping you could help me."

"Help with what?" She keeps her distance.

"With this." I hold the papers out to her. "I was hoping you could read these."

She squints and tilts her head to the side as she approaches "First, you wearing the stones?"

I gulp, I *did* put on the necklace. I don't need to answer. She reaches for the chain around my neck, lifting the pendant from my shirt.

"Can't help," she grumbles, letting the chain fall from her hand, she turns to walk away.

"Please, I don't know what's going on." She stops but doesn't turn around. "I know what you said about the pendant, but when I don't wear it, I see things. I hear voices, I lose time, I feel horrible. If it's so evil, then why do I feel better when it's on?" I let go of Josh's hand and take a few steps toward her. "Tell me what to do. I need you."

She takes a breath. "Take it off . . . I'll be back."

Josh keeps his eyes on the heavy curtains that she disappears through. I remove the necklace from around my neck. She comes back carrying a small ornate box and opens it. "Put it in here." She closes the box, setting it on the counter. "Come," she says, leading the way into the back room. I glance over my shoulder at Josh, to make sure he's following.

The room is a hodgepodge of endless piles. Large arrays of lit candles are arranged around the space. Books and cobwebs line the shelves. I'm sure this place hasn't been cleaned in years; a noticeable coating of dust covers everything in sight.

We follow her to a small table. On top is the book she'd shown me a few weeks earlier. Next to it is a wooden bowl carved to look like a feather, and several crystals are scattered about. A white candle covered in soot is propped up against the bowl.

She opens the book, chanting ever so softly. "I'll take the papers." Her hand stretches out to me. She places them in the wooden bowl, setting three crystals on top.

Next, she picks up the candle and lights the wick. She reads from the book. "Brighten the area with the purity of the light. Protect us from evil that surrounds the wearer." She blows out the candle. "Cleanse the air with the smoke."

She lays the candle in the dish and picks up the papers. Taking a seat in the chair next to the table, she points to a small couch. "Sit."

The cushions are not visible through all the clutter spread out on top of them.

"Don't be shy."

We move to the couch and scoot over as much of the mess as we can. I jump, letting out a scream and grabbing onto Josh, when a black cat appears from under the clutter.

"Told you, I'm not the only one that gets freaked out," he whispers.

We manage to make enough room for the two of us to sit. Although I'm practically sitting on top of him, I'm not going to move. I still have a tight hold on my bag.

"Now then, tell me, what you're gonna do with the knowledge?"

I don't know how to answer. If I say the wrong thing, will she ask us to leave? "What do you mean?" I ask.

"With knowledge comes responsibility. You accept this?"

I shrug. "Yeah, I suppose."

"I need more than that." Her haunting eyes seem to burn through me. She nods slightly.

I mimic her nod. "I accept it," I say, without hesitation.

"Okay, let me see what you have." She reads the papers to herself first. When she's done, she lays the pages in her lap and folds her hands on top of them.

"Am I going crazy?"

"You're not crazy, these papers is a cry for help."

"Help for what?"

"No . . . not help for, but rather from, you see, the person writing this was cursed." Her nonchalant tone makes me believe she's joking.

Josh chimes in, "Okay, really, you want us to believe that?"

"Believe what you want, but it's all here."

I glower at Josh, letting him know to just be quiet.

"If you don't believe . . . than leave." She rises out of her chair.

"I believe you," I blurt out. Leaving is not an option.

She exhales and sits back down. "The person writing this had powers—strong powers. You know who this was?"

"It's my mom's handwriting."

"Then that's why you feel better with the stones. You carry the curse. But more important . . . you carry the power."

"*What!*" Josh says. "That's ridiculous."

"The curse is eating your soul. Gobbling it up 'til there's nothing left." Her voice begins to fade.

I reach for Josh while struggling to keep reality from diminishing. But within seconds, the darkness takes me.

TWENTY

No Way Out

My name comes to me as the fog gradually lifts. Josh and the old woman are inches away from my face.

"You with us?" the old woman asks.

"What happened? Did I pass out?"

Looking horrified, Josh answers, "Uh—no."

"It's worse than I thought." She waves her hand in the air. "You better go home."

"I can't until I know what those say." I eye the papers she still has in her hands.

"He knows." She nods at Josh and hands me the pages.

He keeps his attention focused on her. "Come on, let's get out of here." Josh grabs onto my hand.

"Not until you tell me."

"I'll tell you in the car."

"*No!*" I scream and yank my hand away. "I'm not leaving."

"You are," Josh orders. Grabbing onto my arm, he pulls me to my feet.

"You can't tell me what to do." I spin around him to face the old woman, but she's gone. "What the . . ." I falter when the clutter around me begins to vibrate—softly at first, but it rapidly intensifies.

"We gotta go!"

All at once, as if a fan has been turned on, the mess around us takes to the air, scattering in all directions. The letter gets shoved in my bag as we bolt out of the back room. Books fly from their resting places on the shelves. We duck as objects narrowly miss our heads. Total chaos erupts.

With a firm hold on my hand, Josh guides me through the mess. The whirlwind chases us through the store. I've no idea how we make it to the front of the store without getting clobbered, but we do. Josh swiftly opens the door, shoves me out first, and then follows. He slams the door shut just as a plate smashes against the glass.

"Come on, let's get out of here."

"Oh, my God, my necklace. I forgot to grab it from the box."

Josh doesn't slow his pace as he responds. "You're wearing it."

Sure enough, it's fastened around my neck. "How'd that happen?"

Josh keeps walking.

"Will you answer me!?" I stop dead in my tracks. "What did she tell you?" He turns around. The color fades from his face. "It can't be that bad, just tell me."

"She's an old, creepy woman, who doesn't know what she's talking about."

A loud explosion rocks the area. Turning around, I see the antique store engulfed in flames. Hastily, Josh grabs onto me and moves me toward the car.

Neither of us says a word as we scramble to get out of there. Josh doesn't take the time to buckle his seatbelt as he accelerates slowly, heading in the opposite direction of everyone else.

"Did you get hurt?" Josh asks.

I scan my arms and legs. "No, what about you?"

"I'm fine."

"What happened?" The fire reflects in the mirror outside my window.

"I don't know. I just hope no one saw us coming out of there."

"Do you think the old woman is all right?"

"I'm sure she can take care of herself."

Once we're on the highway, I open the bag and pull out the letter. "Now, you have to tell me what she said about this."

"You know, Brie, I'm not sure that woman was the one to ask."

"Why?"

"It just seems a little too ridiculous."

"Ridiculous or not, I want to know." He stays quiet. "Fine, but if you don't tell me, I'll go back there. I won't stop until I have the answers."

"That would just get both of us in trouble. You know, we're probably suspects."

"I don't care. You don't know how I feel." My voice cracks.

"Okay, don't get upset."

"That's easy for you to say. You're not the one going crazy." Tears threaten as I try to swallow the lump growing in my throat.

"Just don't freak out." He glances over at me.

"I can handle it, whatever it is."

"And you can't take everything she said seriously." The alarming tone of his voice adds to my dismay.

"Just tell me."

"First thing was . . . she said whoever wrote that letter was trying to escape."

"Escape from what?"

"Herself . . . like she had two personalities. As soon as she would feel herself slipping from reality, she would write down her thoughts, hoping to remember the time she would lose. Unfortunately, most of the pages are written in gibberish."

"So she couldn't make out any of it? Nothing at all?"

"She was able to read a few things." His grip on the steering wheel tightens. "Like how she couldn't remember hours at time." He eyes the necklace around my neck. "That is . . . until she was given a necklace and told that as long as she wore it, she would remember."

"Oh, God."

"But she also wrote how her friends and family suffered when she had it on. That's why the old woman had you take it off. She said that whoever was cursed would fade into darkness if the power of the stones was taken away from them."

My dismay turns to terror.

"Are you okay?"

I don't answer. I think about the moments that I had lost, wondering now if the stones were in my possession at the time.

"Brie." He startles me.

"Yeah . . ."

"It's gonna be okay." He reaches over for my hand, but I move it away.

"Did she say anything else?"

"There was one more thing . . . Your mom wrote that she hoped whoever found the pages would forgive her for the vulnerable situation she put the others in with her decision to take her own life."

"My mom *didn't* kill herself!" I'm infuriated by the thought.

"I know that, calm down."

"Then why'd you say it."

"I'm telling you what she wrote; this has nothing to do with me."

"Who are the others?"

He shrugs. "That was it, that's all she could read."

"What good is any of this, then? You have to be leaving something out."

"There's not much more. You started going a little crazy in there, screaming for everyone to leave you alone. You looked pretty freaky."

"Did she say anything about the curse?"

"Just that it dates back hundreds of years, and that all who were cursed died or lost their way. The only ones that had any chance to fight this were the descendants of the ones who were first cursed." Josh's forehead wrinkles as he affirms my fears. "Yes, Brie, she confirmed that your family is part of this."

"So you're saying my ancestors are to blame? What were they?"

"She wouldn't tell me. Said both her and I were in danger for even being associated with you. Also said you would have to start paying attention to the people around you—that this will tell you how fast the curse is progressing."

My thoughts quickly turn to Alex. "What's going to happen to them?"

"I don't know. She was pretty much on edge the whole time, told me not to mention this to anyone. Even said telling you would put me in more danger than I already am."

"And you're not scared?"

He glances at me. "Scared of what? I mean, I understand you're going through . . . well, *something*. But there's no proof."

"What about the letter? The stones? The weird stuff that's happened?"

"I don't believe in curses."

"How do you explain what happened back there? Things were flying all over the place and then the fire?"

"You saw that room. It was a mess. And with all the candles she had lit . . . and who knows, maybe there was an earthquake or something." He shrugs.

"Earthquake . . . are you kidding?"

"Maybe that's reaching, but I'm sure it can be explained." He touches my leg. "Your mom didn't die from a curse. Up until the cancer, she lived a normal life. Whatever this is must be something temporary."

"You're right, my mom was an amazing person and was loved by everyone. Maybe if I keep the necklace on, I can wait it out."

Josh lets out a heavy sigh, which sends another warm rush of panic to surge through me. "Okay, now what aren't you telling me?"

"That old woman was pretty scared of the necklace. Made *me* put it back on you."

I hold the necklace away from my chest to stare at the stones. "How can this scare anyone?"

"She said the stones actually absorb the life from the people around you, killing them slowly. This is what gives this thing its power. As long as you keep the stones on, the curse stays dormant in you until it has reached its full power from those around you. Then the good in you will die . . . and . . . you'll be one of them."

I shudder. "What are they? What will I become?"

"She said only you can solve that part."

The tone of his voice assures me that, even though he says he's not scared . . . he is. Josh places both his hands back on the steering wheel and stares straight ahead.

"Maybe it's good that you're moving away."

"Dammit, Brie, I said I would help you, and I plan on keeping my promise."

"Yeah . . . okay." I turn to look out the window. Neither of us seems to know what to do next and an awkward silence descends.

My thoughts turn to my Mom, wondering how she managed to live through all this. The rest of the ride I agonize over everything that has happened and everything to come.

THE ONLY CAR in the school lot is mine. Josh pulls up alongside it and stops. "I wish she had more answers for you. I wish I had more for you."

"You just being here helps."

He touches my cheek. "It's going to be okay." His lips meet mine. I close my eyes, loving the feel of his touch.

He withdraws, and I look up at him. "I don't know what I would do without you."

"You're never going to find out." He sweeps my hair to the side. "So, what's the next step?"

"Grandma has to know something."

"Give me a call later and let me know what happens." He leans in, kissing me again. "I'm here for you," he whispers.

"I know."

TWENTY-ONE

Defiance

There's a brand new, black Dodge Charger parked in our driveway. It's got to be one of Dad's friends, as there's no way any of my friends could afford that.

Grandma's car is gone. Maybe this is the advantage I need. With Dad occupied and Grandma gone, I'll only have Alex to avoid. I'm worried about being too close to my family with the necklace on. The only plan I've come up with to protect them is to break my promise to Alex and leave. It's going to be hard, but there's no other way.

My plan falls apart. When walking through the back-door, I'm brought to a standstill. There, sitting at the table with Dad, is Blake.

"Hey, Brie, how was school?" Dad's voice is weird.

"Fine," I answer, glaring at Blake.

"I better leave you two alone so you can get your homework done." Dad stands to leave. "It was nice to see you again, Blake."

"You, too, Mr. Birlow," Blake nods.

"Please, call me John."

"Wait . . . Where're Grandma and Alex?" I ask.

Dad heads for the door as he answers. "They went shopping, said something about school supplies." He closes the door behind him.

I turn toward Blake. "What are you doing here?"

He points at the stack of books on the table. "You said you would help me get caught up. Besides, I missed you in school today." His eyes spark.

"I told you, I don't have time."

"Oh, but I think you do." His disposition changes as he stands to face me. "You think it's that easy to get away from me?"

"What're you talking about?" I back away.

"We're the same, Brie. The sooner you stop fighting the inevitable, the better you'll feel."

"I have no idea what you're talking about."

"Your future has already been decided for you. There's no stopping it." His casual gestures and the way he seems to look right through me amplify my panic.

"That's a lie. You don't even know me."

"I know far more than you think. Oh, by the way, how was your family last night? They seemed to be concerned with your whereabouts, that is, until I explained everything to them."

"You did not."

He laughs. "I guess you could say I'm here *now* to make sure nothing or no one gets in your way." He walks over to me, lifting the necklace from around my neck. "You've already learned that denying this is not an option."

"Why don't you tell me what's going on, then, if you know so much?"

"All in good time," he whispers. "But you need to understand that no one can give you what you're looking for except you. So you might as well let it happen." A self-satisfying smirk rolls across his face. "But know this, I wouldn't be here if it was still dormant."

"What?"

"One day soon I'll never have to leave you."

"Get out!" I start for the door. "*Dad!*" I shout through the screen door.

"Be careful who you get involved." His hot breath on my neck makes me cringe. "I would hate for your family to lose everything like the old woman at the antique shop." He runs his fingers through my hair. "That's right," he mutters. "There's only one ending for those who interfere." He whips me around to face him. "Wow . . . how fast those old buildings can go up in flames."

It feels as if the oxygen has been sucked out of the room.

"Don't look so shocked."

"You . . . you couldn't have done that."

"Let's just say I'm good at making things look like accidents. Now, you don't want to see what kind of accidents might happen to the ones you love."

"You wouldn't."

"You don't know me, but you will. Until then, I suggest you quit fighting what you can't." His cold fingers glide down the side of my face and wrap around my neck. "Everyone you confide in will fall first." My mind quickly turns to Josh. I don't say his name out loud, but Blake knows.

"No," he mocks. "Even he can't help you." He squeezes my neck ever so softly. "We will be good together."

"Go to hell." I stand defiant against his threat.

His grip tightens, taking away my breath all together. "Be careful, you never know when I'll show up again."

I gasp when he releases me and walks out onto the

porch. For a moment, paralyzing fear keeps me still. His words echo in my head. Out of the corner of my eye, I watch him saunter to his car, afraid to move until his tail-lights disappear down the driveway.

The ringing of my cell phone startles me. I take a few long breaths before pulling it out of my pocket. It's Josh. I want to tell him. But, thinking about the antique shop, I'm scared that Blake will hold true to his promise. I ignore his call.

I step out onto the porch to look around at the place I'd always called home. Two barn cats are playing in the thick wisteria vines that have taken over part of a fence bordering the pasture. Dad is barely visible, on the tractor, pulling a large, round hay bale down to the cows.

With tears in my eyes, I go to my room to pack. I'll leave after everyone is asleep. There's no way I can take the car. It will be too easy to track, so I'll have to pack light.

I dig my duffel bag out of the closet and start with a few basic items. I silence my phone before laying it on my dresser. Josh keeps calling, but I can't put him in any more danger than he already is. If I don't answer, then I won't be tempted to tell him.

The picture of my family gets tucked safely inside my bag, to remind me of why this is necessary. Hesitant to include the information that started it all, I hold onto the book, questioning my mom's ability to stay sane.

I think briefly about Blake's warning, but Grandma's family is part of this. So, technically, she is already involved.

Although I anticipate she can help, I'll be ready to leave just in case she can't. The bag gets shoved under my bed, and I nervously wait for her to return.

Suddenly, my name comes to me as a distortion of light moves from the hallway and into my room. The beat of my heart intensifies. I hear my name again. A cold sensation brushes against me, then my necklace heats up against my chest. I work up the courage to yank the necklace away, breaking the clasp. As it falls from my hand and onto the bed, a bright light appears in the hallway. I make my way across the room and into the hall, coming face to face with the apparition.

"I know who you are." I sigh. "Grandpa?"

The look in his eyes assures me that I'm right.

"Why do you want to hurt me?" He holds his arm out in the direction of the attic. "Am I evil?" He holds his position. "Please answer me," His stance is unyielding. I glance at the attic door. "You want me to go up there?"

His steadfast position validates his answer. I start for the attic, remembering all the untouched clutter, and I'm instantly overwhelmed. Not sure how long I'll have before my world starts to fade, I hurry. With Grandpa beside me, I ascend to the top of the stairs.

Grandpa moves in front of me. His attention is focused on the adjacent corner of the attic. I follow his gaze to the boxes stacked up in the corner.

I pick up one box at a time while looking back at him. Each box I hold up, he stands still. But then I pick up the small, metal box I'd set aside weeks earlier because I hadn't been able to pick the lock. Grandpa's eyes follow it around.

"This must be it." Excitement billows inside while I look down at it. "Okay, now what?" I glance back to Grandpa, but his ghostly image is gone.

I bolt to the stairs, needing to get to the tool shed fast. In the hallway, lightheadedness comes on strong, and little black specs obscure my vision. "The necklace . . . it will keep me here." Without delay, I grab it and shove it into my pocket before bolting down the stairs.

My whole body quivers, remembering Blake's words:

'You'll never know when I'll show up.' I slow down to scan the area before sprinting across the yard toward the shed.

Once inside, I close the door and head over to the workbench. With a chisel and hammer in hand, I break the lock. My heart pounds as I open the lid.

The first thing I take out is a picture of my mom standing next to a stranger. They're holding on to each other. It's obvious that this is my real dad, Sean. Picking up a broken piece of mirror tile from one of the shelves, I look at my reflection and then back at the photo. Grandma was right. I do look like him.

I then take out a newspaper clipping. Sean is pictured in the article. The headline reads, 'Missing Person.' I read the article out loud.

"'Twenty-one-year-old Sean Merit was last seen on January 2nd. He left his home at approximately six p.m. to meet friends. He never made it to his destination. An extensive search was headed up by friends and family of Sean. Local authorities found his car parked a few miles outside of town on Highway 67. If you have any information regarding the whereabouts of Sean, please contact your local authorities.'"

January 2nd. That was about the same time my mom was in the hospital. Why wouldn't Grandma tell me about this?

The next thing I take from the box is a book, titled, 'The Truth Behind the Salem Witch Trials.' Flipping through the book, I open to the page where a piece of paper has been tucked inside. The words, 'Morey Clan,' are scrawled across the top of the page. The sentence below it reads, 'A small demonic clan of witches that lived near Salem in the 1700's unintentionally drew attention to the very thing they were trying to hide.' The rest of the page tells how this group of witches stumbled onto the early settlers and tried to increase their numbers by using children to implant their powers into, as true evil cannot breed on its own. But the children weren't strong enough to live through this process.

When so many children became ill with strange and unexplainable symptoms, the people thought for sure they had been cursed, setting into motion the Witch Trials. It was then that the leader of the clan came up with the idea that if they could instill their powers into the unborn, then the evil would be part of that child. So, when the time was right, the evil would awaken and take over the child's soul.

Highlighted at the bottom of the page is the name Proctor. The paragraph below that that reads. '1692, Elizabeth Proctor was convicted of witchcraft and sentenced to be hanged until dead. Her execution was put on hold when it became evident that she was with child.'

"Proctor . . . my grandma's maiden name."

Handwritten notes alongside the paragraph read:

'Elizabeth Proctor, unborn child first victim.'

'Bridget Bishop, second victim.'

'Two sets of stones, keeps the curse alive.'

'Possession of the soul must be done slow.'

A piece of paper slides out of the book. I reach down for it when the shed door flies open, crashing against the wall. My hand smacks hard against the metal box as I whirl around to see Josh standing in the doorway. *"Dammit!"* I yell, "You scared the crap out of me."

"Are you all right?" He hurries over to my side, grabbing onto me.

"What're you doing here?" My hand throbs.

"You texted me."

"I *did* not."

"Stop yelling, you did too . . . look." He holds his phone out to show me the text.

I need your help—hurry I'm in the tool shed.

"I never sent that." I feel my pockets for my phone, but realize I was in such a hurry to get to the shed, I left it in my room. "I don't even have my phone."

"Then who does?"

"I don't know." Just then, it hits me. "Blake," I mumble.

Josh questions, "What's he got to do with this?"

"You have to leave." I shove him toward the door. "I don't need your help."

"What the hell's going on?"

I have to keep him safe, no matter what the cost. "I have to be honest with you."

"Honest about what?"

I meet his gaze, take a deep breath and confess a lie, "I'm not in love with you."

The betrayed expression on his face rips through me like a knife. "I don't believe you," he says.

"I'm sorry, I didn't mean for it to happen . . . it just did."

"When did you figure this out Brie? Just a few hours ago you couldn't get close enough to me . . . and now . . . What the hell?"

"Blake," I convincingly say.

"Oh, so it is Blake. What, is he hiding around here?" Josh spins around me to search the shed.

"No, he's gone."

"So he was here."

I nod. "When I got home, he was waiting for me . . . and I just knew when I saw him . . ."

"You just met him." Sorrow builds in his eyes.

"I can't explain how he makes me feel . . . it's like nothing I've felt before."

"After everything we've been through together, that

means nothing to you?" His eyes gloss over with tears. "You can't be serious."

I gulp down a sob and deliberately hurt him even more. "That's why I was hesitant to date you. I wanted to feel more. I tried, but I can't deny how I feel for Blake." He reaches out to me, but I back away. "Moving to Texas will be good for you."

"If you walk away Brie, this is it. I'm not coming back. *Ever.*"

My thoughts fall into an endless repeating loop. *Leave. Leave now. Leave before you can't.* I turn away to hide the sadness in my eyes.

"You're really serious?" he asks in disbelief. "Tell me . . . Did you ever love me?"

"I love you as a brother . . . nothing more." Tears of regret blur my vision.

"Why did you wait to tell me, if you knew all along." He forces me to look at him. As I stare into his eyes, a sob constricts my throat, cutting off my words.

"You just needed my help, didn't you?" he asks.

I just stand there, not admitting to it or denying it.

"Oh wait, it makes sense now. You really didn't care that I had something important to tell you at school, you just wanted to be alone with Blake." He runs his hand over his face. "Say something."

"I'm sorry," I whisper.

His jaw clenches, and his eyes flare with disbelief. "You had me fooled." He bolts by me. "I never want to see you again." Tears saturate his voice.

Anguish and grief consume me as he leaves. The sound of his car roars down the driveway, taking all of my heart with it.

I run for the house, through the kitchen door, and up the stairs. Fear looms before me, thinking Blake's in my room. I wipe my eyes, not wanting him to see my pain. But to my surprise, I'm alone.

My phone is still on my dresser. I make a quick search through the texts, but there are none to Josh from me. My phone beeps with a new text.

It simply reads: don't try to run. I will find you.

With cell phone in hand, I rush over to my backpack and take out the worksheet that Blake had written his number on and compare the numbers. My heart sinks when they match. My mind turns to Josh.

Tears break through once again. I try to convince myself that it's for the best he's gone. I think about the danger my family is in now. My only chance to protect them and survive is knowledge. I have to learn fast.

TWENTY-TWO

Vanished

———————

I'm sitting at the kitchen table when Grandma and Alex come through the back door. I try to keep my eagerness at bay. I've learned that the only way to keep others safe is to not get them involved. I look over at Alex and can't bear the thought of anything happening to her.

"Hey, Brie, look what Grandma bought me." She holds up a paisley-print shirt.

"That's cute. Where'd you guys go?"

"Had a few errands to run. Thought it would be nice to have company," Grandma says. She reaches into a bag, pulling out a pair of gloves and a scarf. "I noticed your gloves from last year had seen better days and thought maybe you would like these." She hands me the set.

"Thanks, Grandma."

"Is something wrong?" Grandma asks—maybe because my eyes never waver from hers. "Did you eat?"

"I'm fine."

"I think you have something on your mind?" Grandma nods. "Don't you?"

"Yeah."

Alex stares at me as I lift the metal box up from the floor and set it on the table.

Grandma brings her hand to her mouth as her eyes roll over the box. "Where'd you get that, honey?"

"In the attic."

"What is it?" Alex asks, coming over to me.

"Alex, you need to get changed for bed," Grandma says, directing her into the living room.

"But I'm not tired."

"I'm not asking. You need to do as you're told."

"You coming, Brie?" she asks.

"I'll be there in a minute, Bug."

With Alex out of the room, my attention turns to Grandma. "I have so many questions."

"I know you do." She sits across from me and then reaches out to take hold of my hand—the one with mom's ring. She rubs her hand across the diamonds. "This was your mom's wedding ring from Sean. She often told me that it belonged to you."

"Did he ever love my mom?"

"Yes, he did, and he was always there for her."

Her reply surprises me. "I thought you didn't know him."

"There is so much I have to tell you."

"Does it have to do with the things in here?"

"You have the right to know." She opens the box, taking out the picture of Sean along with the newspaper clipping. She glares at the photo for the longest time. "As you've probably already figured out, this is your real dad." She hands me the picture. "You do look like him." She smiles.

Her trembling hands hold onto the newspaper clipping, "This was such an awful tragedy."

"Tragedy . . . in that he left?" I question.

"What I'm about to tell you can never leave this room." Her eyes water. "You need to promise me."

"I need to know for myself."

She starts to speak several times, but then stops before saying a word.

"Grandma, please."

She lets out a heavy sigh. "It all happened shortly after your parents were married. Your mom had been going through some pretty bad times. But I had no idea until I saw for myself. She was out of control. Sean, along with Grandpa, had convinced her that she needed to come home and get help."

"Are you telling me this disappearance was planned by him to get away from her?"

She looks down at the paper in her hands. "No . . . He loved your mother very much. He would never have left." Her eyes meet mine.

"Then what happened?"

"Your mom would go through periods of time where she couldn't remember."

"Where is he?" An alarming sensation sweeps over me.

"You have to know it wasn't your mom's fault. She had no idea what she was doing. You need to believe that." Grandma takes a napkin from the table and wipes her eyes. "I didn't know what else to do. If the authorities found out, your mom would have been locked away. So I did what I thought I had to in order to protect her." She twists the napkin.

I place my hand on hers. "What did you do?"

"Don't hate me." She wipes away another tear as she talks. "Your mom and Sean had an argument. She had completely lost her mind. She was screaming something about how she needed to end it before anyone else got hurt. They were out back. Your mom was fighting mad. He had a tight hold on her but she broke free from him.

"Running to the car, she locked herself inside. Your grandpa went out to try and help. Sean was in front of the car, trying to stop her. She accelerated as if she wanted to kill him." She pauses to blow her nose. "By the time your grandpa got out there, Sean was lying in the driveway. And your mom was driving away."

"*What!?* You expect me to believe that?"

"It happened so fast, we didn't have time to think. Grandpa went after your mom. A few miles from here, her car slid off the road. It flipped several times before coming to a rest on its roof in the ditch full of water. It took Grandpa several minutes before he freed her from the wreck. She wasn't breathing. He performed CPR on her until the ambulance got there. He thought for sure she was gone."

"What about Sean? You didn't even try to help him?"

"Oh, Brie. It was obvious that there was nothing that could've been done. It was awful, just awful."

"But you didn't even try?"

"I couldn't move. I'd never seen anything like that before . . . I can't talk about it." Tears run down her cheeks as she moves to the other side of the room. "Your Grandpa came back to the farm, telling me what had happened to your mom, and that I needed to get to the hospital. I panicked, thinking that I was going to lose my only daughter. He said I needed to put Sean out of my head, for Beth's sake. Made me promise not to mention this to anyone . . . I left without knowing what he was going to do, and I kept my promise to him."

"Wait a minute, you're telling me that my mom killed my real dad?" Pictures of Mom emerge in my mind.

"You're lying . . . Mom would never do something so awful."

With her back still to me, she sighs, "She was just so mean."

"Even if I were to believe that, which I don't, wouldn't there be something on his death?"

"We never told anyone."

I spring from my chair to pace back and forth. "So you just let everyone believe that he was a terrible person—someone who just left without any consideration for his family?"

"It wasn't that way. Guilt ate at me for years, and it still does. But when your mom was released from the hospital, she was different. Back to the loving person she had been when she was in high school. It wasn't long after that we found out she was pregnant."

"But how could she live with what she did?"

Grandma trembles slightly. "She didn't know. The only people that knew were Grandpa and me. We promised each other that we would take it to our graves. Grandpa had told your mom that Sean didn't want anything to do with her or the family and left while she was in the hospital."

"But didn't she try to find him when I was born?"

Grandma shakes her head. "Grandpa convinced your mom that the anxiety and depression she had went through was because of the marriage. She was so scared of feeling that way again that she left it alone."

"Why are you telling me this now? Why do I have to know?"

"Your grandfather was adamant that I tell you about Sean. Said you needed to know what you were up against." She wipes away a tear. "He also said this would set you on the course to finding your truth."

"What's that mean?"

"He said it was a puzzle only you could solve."

I pull the necklace from my pocket. "Does this have anything to do with it?"

She nods. "Oh, Brie, I wish I could tell you more. I'm not sure what this all means. I do know the necklace kept your mom with us, but when she wasn't wearing it, she would forget. I went through the same thing when I was eighteen, only I had a pouch with stones in it. I'm not sure where your mom got the necklace."

"Grandma, where's my dad?"

Tears drip from her chin. "Grandpa buried him out back under the oak tree . . . Brie, I never forgot about him. I just didn't know what to do."

I often wondered why Grandma had a patch of wildflowers so far from the house. She makes sure to throw seeds out there every year.

Sickened by the thought, I can't stay in the same room with her and head for the door.

"Brie, please don't. I'm so sorry."

"You don't need to say any more." My heart aches for the loss of someone I never met. From the back porch, the top of the majestic oak tree can be seen, standing defiant against the night sky. There's a crisp chill in the air, but I'm not cold. I run toward the tree and make my way through the brush until the patch of wildflowers comes into view. Even though a thin layer of frost blankets the area, some of the flowers still hold onto their pale colors.

"How can this be?" I sigh, falling to my knees amid the intertwined clusters of dying weeds. The picture of him is vivid in my mind. I imagine how he would have been as a father if he hadn't been cheated out of life. I'm angry that he had not been given a decent burial, just tossed away as if his existence didn't matter. I lay on the ground, reliving the horror of Sean's final moments in my head.

"This just can't be true."

"Oh, you're sad." Blake's sarcastic voice roars from behind me.

With my back to him, I quickly sit up and wipe away the tears. "You don't have anything else to do?"

"Um—let me think—*No!*"

There's no way out. The house is too far. Even if I yell, no one will hear me.

He grabs onto me before I have a chance to stand and slams my body against the tree. I'm no match for him. He presses his body up against mine. "So, what're you going to do now?" He laughs.

I try to wiggle free from his grasp, which only seems to amuse him. "What's this prove? That you're stronger than me? Do you feel like a tough guy?" I keep my voice steady.

"You *are* a tough one." He comes close to my face. His lips fiercely collide with mine, ramming my head against the bark of the tree. Suddenly, a need for him awakens inside of me, making me dizzy. Not wanting to accept this, I struggle harder to free myself from his hold. He slowly moves back and glares into my eyes. "I wish I could stick around longer. This is fun to watch."

"Go to hell."

"You can't resist me."

Out of nowhere, Blake's body goes limp, falling to the ground. Behind him, holding a large piece of wood, is Grandma.

"Thank God you're here." The words barely slip from my lips when I'm yanked backward by my hair. I scream in pain as Blake wraps his arm around my neck. Taking his hand from my hair, he latches onto my wrist and forces my arm up the middle of my back. The swift movement doesn't give me time to react.

"What'd you want!?" Grandma screams.

"Nothing from you," Blake calmly states.

The forcefulness of his hold around my neck renders me breathless. I try to wedge my free hand under his arm to relieve the pressure from my throat.

"If it were up to me, I would have already killed them," he whispers in my ear. "But it doesn't work that way. You see, you have to do it in order to gain the strength that you'll need to stand by me." He squeezes me tighter. "When that happens, I'll be able to stay here forever—not just for a few hours at a time. Together we'll be invincible."

Grandma moves closer. "Let's just calm down . . . Let her go and we can talk."

"Back off if you don't want anything to happen to her."

Grandma holds her position. "What do you want?"

Blake moves back, taking me with him. "I want you to leave."

"Let her go and no one has to know about this."

"I'll tell you what, you start walking away and I won't break her arm." The tone of his voice assures me that he's serious. Lightheadedness blurs my vision. My arm throbs, then slowly goes numb.

"Just don't hurt her," Grandma pleads as she backs away.

"You know it's because of you this is happening. If you had let your daughter accept this from the beginning, your granddaughter wouldn't be in this position now."

"I don't know what you are talking about!" Grandma screams.

"You will shortly." He takes his arm from around my neck. I gasp for air. "Try to stop it now," he says. Reaching into my pocket, he seizes the necklace, then pushes me to the ground. I land at Grandma's feet. She grabs onto me. It's then the area around Blake distorts and the trees seem to bow. "It might take longer without the stones, but it will be so worth the wait." He scoffs, then he's gone.

"What happened? Where'd he go?" I ask while frantically trying to stand.

Grandma helps me to my feet. "You okay, honey?"

"Where's Blake?" I circle around.

"I don't know," Grandma says.

"Grandma, do you know what's going to happen to me?"

"Let's not think about that right now. We need to get to the house."

"But what about the necklace? Without the stones, I won't remember."

She places a hand on both sides of my face. "Now you listen to me. You can beat this." Her voice is stern. "You can't let this thing win."

"I don't know if I have a choice." The weird feeling I had earlier consumes me. "Grandma, please help."

"I'm here for you, and I'll help you, I promise." She takes my arm in hers. Before we can make our way to the clearing, flecks of darkness grow around me. *The stones!*

"Grandma, I found . . ." But before I can finish, the world vanishes.

TWENTY-THREE

Reality

───────────

The haze clears, bringing me back to reality. I'm sitting in the attic with my mom's things scattered around me. The wind is howling outside, and a feather takes flight in the flow of air that found its way into this space.

I don't know what time it is or how long I've been up here. Moonlight shines through the porthole window, faintly lighting the room. I'm chilled, with only a light shirt and a pair of sweats on. The image in the full-sized mirror, which sits just a few feet away from me, is similar to the person I once knew, but it can't be me.

Even with the lack of light, my pale skin is visible in my reflection. I edge closer to the mirror, touching my cheeks. My hair is a mess of tangled curls. Even the color of my eyes seems to have darkened. Tears of unease stream down my face, and I drop my head into my hands. Immediately, I'm taken aback by how rough and sore my fingers are.

The attic door squeaks, then footsteps ascend the stairs. "Brie, honey, you up here?" Grandma asks. "There you are." She comes over to sit down next to me.

Waves of anxiety keep me silent. She places her hand

on my shoulder. "Is it really you?" she questions, as if she expects someone else to answer.

Though my mind is foggy with pain, I look up to see a sympathetic sadness in her eyes. "Yes." My voice quavers.

"You need to listen. I don't know how much time we have." Urgency sounds in her voice.

"Am I dying?" I whisper, thinking that death would be a welcome relief.

She pulls a small pouch from her pocket. The same pouch I had put in my escape bag under my bed. "You need to take these." She takes my hand in hers and dumps the stones into my palm.

The dreamlike blur that was clouding my thoughts slowly begins to lift. Pictures of Blake leap into my mind. "Blake?" I question. "Where is he?"

"He comes around for a few hours at a time." She sighs.

"Is he here now?"

She shakes her head. "I haven't seen him today."

I look down at the stones. "How'd you find these?"

"It wasn't easy. I tore this house apart trying to help you. I'm just sorry it took me so long."

"What do you mean so long? What day is it?"

Her eyes narrow. "It's Thursday," she whispers.

"Oh, my God, I've been gone for two days?"

"No, honey . . ." She pauses briefly. "You've been gone for over three weeks. Occasionally we'd see the real you, but those moments were few and far between."

"But . . ."

She stops me in mid-sentence as she folds my fingers around the stones and holds tight to my hand. "You need to let the power of the stones take over so you can stay focused."

Ever so gradually, the mental confusion and the haze

that blocks my memories begin to lift, bringing to mind short periods of time.

I'm horrified at the memory of Alex tumbling down the stairs, her lifeless body just lying there. Then my mind flashes to Dad in the barn, cleaning the stalls when I'm suddenly standing outside of the structure and watching it go up in flames. There's even a brief image of Josh covered in blood.

The fleeting but terrifying thoughts of the people I love feel endless. But none of the visions play out in their entirety, making me believe that I had somehow killed them all.

"What have I done? Where is everyone?"

Grandma is quick to respond. "Everyone's fine."

"But I remember horrible things."

"You're not remembering the past, you're seeing the future."

"What?"

"This is how it controls you—by giving you false memories to keep you confused. I'm telling you, everyone is alright. Alex is staying with Aunt Edna for a while, and your dad is here."

"What about Josh, where's he?"

"Josh is with his family in Texas. Now, Brie, you have to listen to me. I'm not sure I have the answers you need, but you have to trust that you can win." Her eyes fill with tears. "I can only hope that these stones will keep you here until it's over."

"Please," I cry, "tell me what you know."

Grandma attempts to run her fingers through my tangled hair. "Oh, sweetie, I'm so sorry." She takes a deep breath. "I had no idea how bad it was, not until I read the papers that your grandfather had put together."

"What're you talking about?"

"Stay right here. I have something to show you." She disappears down the stairs. I struggle to stay focused and hang on to my reality. It doesn't take her long to come back carrying the metal box.

She sits next to me, placing the box between us. I close my eyes while I strain to breathe. Even the weight of my shirt bothers me. I pull it away from my neck.

Grandma whispers, "You need to inhale deeply and slowly, holding your breath for a short time before exhaling."

I can't stop the panic.

"Brie, listen to my voice," she demands.

"It's hard, Grandma, it's really hard."

"I know, honey, but you need to let it consume you."

"I'm scared. I'm not sure what's going to happen if I let go."

"As soon as you stop struggling against it, you'll start feeling better. Then we can fight it."

"What if I hurt you? What if you're wrong? You don't know how this feels." I tremble, fighting against a power that has ignited inside of me.

"Brie, let go. You can do this." Her voice cracks. "Believe me, it will work."

I slow my breathing and inhale slowly to let the evil take me. Grandma's voice is steady as she talks me through the pain. After I inhale and exhale a dozen times, a calming sensation finally washes over me.

"That's it, honey, you're doing it."

I'm scared for her. I've been warned of the suffering those around me would endure if the evil inside of me was in control.

The pain subsides, replaced by a whoosh of air pulsating against my skin. The rush flows through me, mimicking the pace of my breaths. The black stones in my hand have come to life, swirling with colors and dancing to the rhythm of my heart.

I whisper, "It's working."

"We have to move fast," Grandma says, pulling a brown file organizer out of the box. "This is information that your grandpa worked on for months." She unties the ribbon wrapped around the folder and opens the flap. "Your grandfather loved you very much." She reads the writing on the inside of the flap. "'The pieces are here, they just need to be put together.'" She shows me the writing.

"Your grandfather wrote that. He spent months searching through family records, reading everything he could that was related to the witch trials. Even took off out East for a few weeks. I'm not sure what started his quest, but after you were born, it was like he was obsessed with this. He said it was important that he find out how to stop this before you came of age. I tried to help him, but he said it was too dangerous. That with knowing comes death. And that if he were to die, I needed to stay alive to give this to you."

"So the answers are inside here?" I lay my hand on the file.

"No . . . just the pieces." She nods. "One day, he came running into the kitchen with a piece of paper in his hand. He grabbed onto me, telling me that he had figured it out. Said that everything would be okay now and not to worry. The sad thing, though, was that I wasn't sure what I was supposed to be worrying about.

"He ran upstairs to put the paper in the file, but it never got finished. The authorities called it an accident, but your grandfather was more responsible with guns than that. They said it must have gone off accidentally, but I knew it was no accident."

"Grandpa was murdered!?"

"When I heard the noise, I ran upstairs and found him lying in our room, covered in blood. And the piece of paper he'd had in his hand was gone. I've added a few things to the file over the years. However, I knew it was going to be up to you. Your grandfather had made that very clear."

Grandma's hand begins to tremble as an invigorating sensation courses through me. This thing inside of me is feeding off her energy.

"If you can't figure this out, the horrible accidents you saw in your mind will come true." She puts everything back into the box and closes the lid. "That will be apparent to you when you read what's in here. You're smart, Brie. You can do this. Think hard about the information inside here."

"Grandma, can't you help me?" I plead.

"I don't know how." She moans. "The pieces are here, I just don't know how to put them together. But you're good at puzzles, always have been, just like your grandfather."

She takes me into her arms and, for a brief moment, I feel safe. Then I feel myself wanting to hurt her.

"I'm sorry," I say, pushing against her, she falls backward as I scramble to my feet. She reaches out to me, but I know I can't stay. "Tell me what I need to do!" I scream.

She slides the box in my direction. "Take this. I put everything that you have found and all the information from your grandfather inside."

The desire to hurt her is winning, scaring me. I quickly grab onto the box and head toward the stairs. "I love you, Grandma."

"I love you, too. But, Brie, remember, no matter how

incredible evil makes you feel, it's not real, and it won't last," she cries.

The only way she'll be safe is to put distance between us. Down the stairs, through the kitchen, stopping only briefly to shove my feet into a pair of boots, I grab a coat, then out the door.

The cold air stings my face. I can't believe it's snowing, at this rate, it won't take long for the frosty night to extinguish my energy.

Before entering the woods, I stop and set the box down to put on the coat. The stones in my hand will have to be kept close that much I *do* know. I shove them inside the pocket of the coat and zip it shut, picking up the box to continue on.

My breath clouds out before me as I sprint through the trees. The clear night sky gives me just enough light to maneuver around the underbrush without slowing my pace.

Along the creek, where a grove of pine trees is, will give me some protection from the elements while searching through the box. Dropping to my knees and praying that the answers will be easily revealed, I open the box.

The books on the Salem witch trials, I push to one side. Those obviously go together. The article on the disappearance of my dad and the pictures of him, I lay on top of the books. That, according to Grandma, was an accident. My grandparents' wedding picture is also inside, clipped to an article on a fire that destroyed the Bishop farm.

It happened six months after their wedding. It shows the remnants of what once was my grandfather's childhood home. The article told of the four people who died in the blaze, his mother, father, and two sisters. Both Grandpa and Grandma were in the house at the time of the fire, but they both survived. Upon reading further, it becomes clear that this was the incident that disfigured him. From the way the article reads, they were lucky to be alive, even with both of them in critical condition.

I think about my mom's plight and all she went through. She had defeated this and so had Grandma and Grandpa. But how?

Then Alex comes to mind. Will she be forced into the same situation if I fail? Determination pushes out the despair, and I focus again on the contents inside the box.

Seven folders each bear a different family name. They all sound familiar and then it dawns on me. These names are listed in the book 'Boundless.' Grabbing for it, I open to the page where they are written.

The first name listed is Osborne, so I pull that file first. Their family tree is drawn on the front of the folder, starting with Sarah, who lived in Salem Village in 1692. Three children are listed under her name. Joseph and James have been crossed through, and Abigail is circled in red.

James has two people listed under his name, and one is crossed off, while the other is circled. The records continue that way until present day. I open the Osbornes' folder and find copies of death records for all except those whose names are circled.

I pull out the folder on Bishop, Grandpa's side, to see the names of my ancestors. Our family tree is laid out just like the Osbornes', starting in Salem Village in 1692. Bridget Bishop tops the list, with names under hers crossed through and circled, until it comes to me and Alex.

Both our names are circled in red.

Grandma's family folder is next. Hers, too, ends with Alex's and my names circled in red. All seven folders are laid out exactly the same. It scares me to see that so many names have been circled, even though I'm not sure what it means.

With every word, I'm more lost and confused. Could all these names be associated? And if so, how is it possible that this has been going on for so long? Even as strong as my mom, my grandma, and my grandpa all were, they, too, had almost lost the battle. But before the evil could take over, something happened . . . But what?

Then, a familiar voice sends a disheartened chill through me.

TWENTY-FOUR

Deception

"What are you doing out here?" Blake questions.

I clench my fist and keep quiet. With no memory of the last few weeks, I'm uncertain how to respond.

"You have nothing to say?" He places his hands on my shoulders. "That's not like you, you're usually so happy to see me."

He pulls me to my feet and whips me around to face him. Our eyes meet. "I stopped by your house. Your grandmother said you threw a knife at her and ran out the door yelling my name." His hand brushes my cheek. "I know the hunger that's growing inside of you is overwhelming, but you have to wait to kill them until you're ready for this to work," he says, almost sympathetic. "Don't worry, Brie, I'm all yours. I'm not going anywhere."

Why would Grandma say that? Then, almost instantaneously, it comes to me. She is sending me a message, a message to hide the fact that I'm in control. So, as repulsive as it is to think about, I've got to come on to him.

His eyes narrow. "What, no comment?"

I swallow hard and force a smile. "I was wondering when you would find me."

He glances down at the box. "What's that?"

A warmth of panic rolls through me while I scramble for the right words. "Something the little bitch thought she could pull over on me," I say.

"Well, aren't you pleasant tonight?" He pulls me into his arms.

"It's the brisk air; you know what that does to me."

He presses his lips to mine. The assertive force in his kiss almost overpowers my ability to think rationally. But if he is the one in control, I'll lose. So I take charge, kissing him back, while forcing myself close to him.

I think of Josh, and how good it feels when I'm in his arms. That memory eases the deceptive passion that Blake is trying to inflict onto me. The more I think about the people I love, the more I can resist his evil desires.

Then it dawns on me. It's not physical strength that wins. It's the ones who stay true to themselves who prevail. My truth is the love for my family and friends. I'll use that to my advantage.

He moves his hand down the front of my coat, unzipping it. He slips it off my shoulders, letting it fall to the ground. I almost lose my nerve, thinking about the stones leaving my possession. I'm good at coming up with solutions, and I need one now more than ever—when it hits me. I withdraw slightly.

"Is something up?" he questions.

"No, but think about it. I'm still mortal. This body can't handle the cold like you. I need somewhere warm."

He laughs. "I guess I forgot. It's just I've waited a long time for you." I shiver when he touches my face. "There's something different in your eyes," he whispers.

"Maybe it's time." I reach for my jacket and quickly put it on, zipping it up around my neck.

"Maybe . . ." He pauses. His eyes seem to burn through me. He takes hold of my hand. "Take us to our favorite place."

Oh, shit, where's that? "Shouldn't I be getting home?" I say.

"And why's that?" He scowls.

The only explanation there is, is the very thing that scares me the most. "For this to work, don't I have to get rid of the ones that are closest to me first?"

"Yes." His lips curl into wicked smile. "You saying you feel strong enough?"

I pull him close. "I can't wait any longer."

He kisses me again. "I've been waiting to hear you say that. I'll walk you home."

With heavy heart, I glance down at the box and all its contents sitting among the pine needles as we walk away. Why couldn't I have found something in there to help me?

I'm unsure what my next course of action should be. Several scenarios play over in my head. But they all seem to have the same outcome—death.

Walking at a steady pace, he keeps a tight hold on my hand. I'm terrified to think what is about to happen. I stop a few times, convincing him that I need to catch my breath. When I stop for the last time, Blake questions my hesitation. "Don't tell me you're backing out?"

"Backing out of what?" I lean against a tree. He comes and places his hand on the tree above my head. He pushes against me.

"You must feel the inevitable by now. The burning desires to destroy those that don't understand." His fingers move down the side of my face. "The more you kill, the longer I'll be able to stay here with you." He smiles.

"When everyone you care about it gone, we'll be together forever and finally finish it."

"Finish what?" I hesitantly ask.

"You'll find out soon enough." He motions for me to lead the way. "Let's not put if off any longer . . . who's going to be first?" His emotionless tone is gut-wrenching. "Well?" he questions.

"Let's just see who we come to first." Deep, mournful sadness makes it hard to keep my angst hidden. We walk up the porch steps and into an empty kitchen.

Apprehension sits heavy in my chest as we make our way into the living room. I keep my pace casual with no hint of hesitation, as not to heighten suspicion. We make our way up the stairs toward the bedrooms.

I remember Grandma telling me that Alex is with Aunt Edna, and I'm thankful for that. With no sign of Dad, I'm confident that he's out on his nightly drinking binge, and again I'm thankful. When we head down the hall to Grandma's room, despair comes in waves as I know she always goes to bed early. But, to my surprise, her room is empty. A sigh of relief escapes me.

Blake takes me by the hand and leads me to my room. "Since we're out of the elements and you're ready for the next step, I say there's no stopping us." He stands next to my bed. Taking me into his arms, he kisses me.

Even though the feel of his body next to mine is alluring, I've got to keep a clear head. The only way to get through this is to think about the things that are my foundation. From the small triumphs, such as the elated feeling I had the first time I took the car out by myself and the rush of freedom it gave me. To the life-changing tragedies, and the unbearable heartache that is still fresh in my mind: when I had to say goodbye to my best friend, my mom. And all the moments in between, are who I am. And although some memories hurt beyond words, I won't give them up. Not for anyone or anything.

He caresses his way down my neck.

"Why me?" I sigh.

"Our numbers have grown. Now we need to find direction." I bite my lip to keep it from quivering as I stare into his rigid, cold eyes. "I've waited a long time for you; you can give me back what I need."

"Aren't there others that you could have chosen?" Not wanting it to sound like I'm probing for answers, I quickly recant, "I mean—how did I get to be so lucky?"

"You have the bloodline of two." He presses against me, making me lose my balance. With his arm firmly around my waist, he steadies me and eases me onto the bed. "And now the time has come to seal the fate of our future." He unzips my jacket once again. I reach in my pocket for the stones to keep them close. He leans in closer. I'm out of ideas and lose the ability to stay calm. Pain blazes through my hand as my fist connects with his jaw. There's shock in his face as he falls away.

I leap from the bed, rush out the door, and head down the stairs. Making it to the last step when I'm pushed from behind. I stumble over the last step, fumbling to the ground. The stones fall out of my hand. I fight against him, but with the stones out of my possession, I lose my fortitude, and the world around me slowly begins to fade.

He holds me down, looking more amused than anything else. "Well, well, Brie, nicely done. But what do you think this proves?"

"That my will is as strong as yours."

His boisterous laugh gives me chills. "You're as intolerable as your mother."

"So you *did* know my mom?"

"Let's just say if she hadn't been so difficult, she would be the one standing by my side."

"But she won."

"She's dead. How is that winning?"

His words anger me. "It's better than being with you." I mock his tone.

Clutching onto my arms, he jerks me to my feet, "You don't understand, but you will. Now you'll watch as I help you with your quest."

"My only quest is to get away from you."

"Oh, that's not possible. Besides, I know a whole lot more than you." He picks up the stones and shoves them into my pocket. "I wouldn't want you to miss this." He forces me out to the barn. "You'll forgive me when you feel the exhilaration you get from watching them die." He shoves me down into the corner of one of the stalls.

"I hate you!"

He snatches a rope from a hook and comes toward me. "Oh, Brie, you still don't get it."

The stones give me back my fight. I bolt to my feet and run past him. He grabs my hair, bringing me to a painful halt. He moves his leg in behind me, making me fall backward onto the ground.

Within seconds he's on top of me. I swing my fist in the direction of his head, landing a punch on the side of his face. He lists sideways but then quickly regains control and pins my arms beneath his legs.

"No matter what you do, I will never be with you!" I scream.

His eyes are wild, swirling with the same colors as the stones. "You don't have a choice." He ties my hands together, then grabs for my legs. I kick him, and he falls away from me. Somehow I get to my feet, but he tackles me, making me hit the ground with a thud, knocking the wind out of me.

Struggling for air, he ties my legs together. Now that I'm securely bound, he drags me back into the stall.

"You can't win."

"My mom did, and so can I." My voice breaks.

"I underestimated your mother, but I won't you." He disappears for a moment, coming back with a roll of duct tape. He wraps the tape around my hands several times, making it impossible for me to even move my fingers.

"It's sad to think you have to force me to be around you."

"This isn't for you," he scoffs. "This is for me."

"Whatever you're thinking, it'll never work."

"I've had enough for now." He slaps a piece of tape over my mouth.

He grabs my hair, forcing me to look at him. "Let me tell you a few things that are real. One: you have the blood of the Moray clan flowing through you. And even though you're trying to deny it, you can't. Two: with each death you cause, especially with the ones you love most, the stronger the immoral one inside of you will become. And, three: you will be mine real soon. That I can promise you." A shiver of disgust rolls through me at the thought of being with him.

He grabs my arm and drags me kicking and struggling toward the barn door. My eyes water from the dust that has been kicked up.

"Believe it or not, it doesn't matter how you kill them— as long as you're involved, you'll reap the benefits." He releases me. "I thought it was too good to be true when you told me you were ready."

He takes another rope from the hook, throwing it in my direction. Then takes one of the cans of kerosene from the shelf and begins pouring it all around the area, concentrating on the hay that is stacked up next to the barn door. Next, the three hay bales in the middle of the barn, is doused with kerosene.

He disappears into the tack room, coming back with several antique lanterns and setting them on top of the three bales. He then comes over to me. "Isn't this exciting?" he asks. Taking one end of the rope, he throws it up over the beam above the hay. It lands on the bales. He picks up the gas can and reaches for the lanterns. Removing the tops from three of them he fills them with gasoline, never replacing the lid. The lantern filled with kerosene, he ties to the rope.

I try with everything I have to get up and away but it's no use. He clutches onto my arm with one hand while grabbing onto the end of the rope with the other. He drags me over to a large stump that is positioned under a tree just a few yards away from the barn.

He throws the rope over the branch. "Another thing you might not know." He grins. "After your first kill, the desire for blood will be so strong that I won't even have to help you with the next. You'll be on your own. Well, just until your whole family is dead. Don't worry though; your other family will be waiting for you."

The rope is tied around my waist and arms before he goes back into the barn. With a flick of his wrist, he lights the wick of the lantern that is tied to the end of the rope. Sauntering back to me, he smiles. "This will be such a special moment for us."

I'm yanked to my feet so fast, my head spins, making me list sideways. With his arms around me, he lifts me effortlessly into the air, setting my feet on the stump.

"Now, hold still." The rope is looped around my neck several times until the lit lantern is lifted into the air. And then he ties a slip knot in the rope. "I made sure both barn doors were wide open. I wouldn't want to miss one minute of this," he whispers. "But just in case you still don't get it, let me enlighten you." He runs for the barn. "You watching?" He jerks a blanket into the air. Lying beneath it is my dad.

My screams are smothered by the tape. All I can do is watch in horror as Dad is dragged closer to the gas-soaked hay in the middle of the barn.

"You see, I figured I would cover all my bases this time. I knew you were getting close, so I took it upon myself to have plan B ready just in case." He brushes his hand against my arm. "Don't look so unhappy." He feigns sadness. "I'll stay with you until he's dead. Oh, and to make sure no one ruins this for us."

Now I understand. If I fall from the log, the rope will cause the lit lantern to come crashing down on the gas-soaked bales of hay, and I'll be the reason Dad dies.

Blake sits at the foot of the tree, never taking his eyes off me. "I could have done it fast, but what fun would that have been? Besides, you'll get tired soon. I only wish I could go back to my first kill, it was so exhilarating." He chuckles. "Just think, Brie, with the curse complete we will be invincible, and I will regain the preeminence I once had."

My brain races for ways out, but there are none. I can only pray that Dad will wake before I lose stability.

If I'm able to wait out the kerosene, maybe Dad would have a chance. Blake will have to refuel the can and, in that second, maybe something will come to mind. It's a long shot, but it's all I've got.

As the minutes tick slowly by, my legs begin to tremble. "Just think, Brie, there will be nothing and no one that can stop us. With my powers restored to their fullest, we will be indestructible."

My lower back and legs cramp, making me wobble a bit.

"Almost!" Blake taunts.

Then Dad moves. Relieved that he is indeed alive, I find newfound strength and stand rigid. Blake must have seen the glimmer of hope in my eyes. He kicks the stump out from under me. At first, the rope doesn't give way, leaving me hanging by my neck. It cuts into my throat, then without warning, releases, causing me to hit the ground hard.

An explosion shakes the area, irradiating the dark. The hay bales are engulfed in flames. The fight to free myself is unsuccessful, as the barn quickly fills with smoke. Another explosion sends a billowing cloud of black spiraling out of the barn. My heart breaks into a million tiny pieces at the thought of him burning.

Blake's hand is on me, turning my body over to face him. He takes hold of the tape that covers my mouth, yanking it off so fast that I'm sure remnants of my skin are stuck to the adhesive.

"Bastard!" I scream.

"Don't be like that. I'm doing this for us."

"I'll never be like you."

"As soon as you feel the rush, you'll thank me." He leans over me. Digging his fingers into my jaw, he presses his lips hard against mine. I sink my teeth into his lip until I can taste his blood.

He laughs as he withdraws. "I'm going to love making you mine."

"Never!"

"Wait. It'll hit you in a minute. As soon as you take it in, I'll go prepare the others."

My mind flashes to the passage in the book 'Boundless' and how with every death, a surge of satisfaction is felt.

Devastated with grief, but knowing that Grandma and Alex are still out there, I hold the pain in. Without further delay, I close my eyes and inhale deeply. It's then that the night air feels different on my skin, and being in Blake's arms is intoxicating. I tremble while trying to repress the disturbing sensation that is now rolling through me. I can't help myself and smile when my eyes meet his.

"You're on your way to the perpetual ecstasy of the underworld." He lifts me into a sitting position. "Take it all in and there will be no stopping you." He comes inches from my face. I lean against him. "Our powers will be endless," he says. He reaches into his pocket, takes out a knife, and cuts loose the bindings.

The battle raging inside of me keeps me silent, until pictures of my past play over and over in my head. The false sense of euphoria is diminished by the memories. Even though I'm back in control, the desire for him right now should be overwhelming. So taking hold of his shirt, I pull him close and press my lips against his mouth, hard. He backs away.

"All in good time, my love," he says, helping me to my feet. "But first you need to take care of a few things on your own. Then we will be rejoined."

Needing to know what part he plays in all this, I ask, "You mean *we* need to take care of some things?"

He laughs. "You don't need me for that. Besides, I must go join the clan and prepare for your homecoming."

"You're leaving?" I'm dying inside thinking about Dad, making my sorrow for him believable. "How long will I be without you?"

"Three days is all. Then we will reassemble our people

to finish what had been started so many years ago and avenge what was done to us."

"What if I need you?"

He tangles his hand up in my hair, forcing me close to him. "I'll let you in on a little secret. The longer you make your victims suffer, the more power you will receive."

"But you never answered my question, will you come back if I need you?"

"Don't worry, you're more than ready now. Besides, this is the time you'll gain most of your powers. And although I would like to stick around and watch, it doesn't work that way. With solitude comes supremacy. You need to dominate and organize your strength before you can direct the clan. I know you're ready." His kisses me fiercely. I taste his blood once again.

The sound of fire trucks roar in the distance. Without answering my question, he releases his hold on me and saunters toward the woods.

TWENTY-FIVE

Fighting Back

He disappears as the loud roar of the firetrucks make their way down our driveway. Flames engulf the barn, making it hard for me to breathe. Tears flow freely down my face.

The area explodes with people battling the blaze. A fireman comes over to me. "Hey, miss, are you all right?" he asks. "Is anyone inside the barn?"

In this moment I realize my nightmares are beginning. I close my eyes to block out the horror.

"Miss." He touches my arm. "Do you know if anyone's in there?"

"My dad." I sob.

He yells over his shoulder, "Joe, someone's in there!" He turns back to me. "Do you know how this started?"

I shake my head. Another set of headlights come down the driveway. The car stops and Grandma rushes to my side. "Oh, honey, let's get you inside." She doesn't seem to be affected by the blaze.

"Grandma . . ."

She hushes me.

Wrapping her arm around me, she moves me toward the porch. "We'll talk inside," she says softly.

"But Dad . . ."

"Brie, you need to compose yourself."

My legs wobble. "But, Grandma . . ."

"Shhh . . . Blake might be watching."

We walk up the porch steps, through the kitchen, up the stairs, and into her bedroom. She closes the door behind us and hurries over to the window to close the shades.

"What's going on?" I sigh, wiping away tears with my sleeve.

"You have to trust me. I need you to listen and do exactly as I say without asking any questions." She hands me a tissue from her dresser.

"But what about . . ." She stops me again.

"There's no time. You're being tested. Do you still have the stones?"

"Yes."

"Hang on to them tight, you'll need them soon." She goes over to her dresser and takes out the necklace that Blake had snatched from me a few weeks earlier. "Take this too; you'll need both sets to stop it."

"Grandma, please slow down. Dad . . ." My voice breaks.

She places her hands on the side of my face. "In order for this to work, you have to stay strong. I can't explain things to you now, but you must trust me that if you do as I say, it will all make sense." She pulls a tissue out of her pocket and wipes the blood from my lip. "This isn't going to be easy."

"Nothing makes sense."

"It will." She walks over to her closet, takes out a back-pack, and hands it to me. "Take this. I've put some things inside that I thought you might need. Now, you must get to the old shed, the one by the river." She glances into the hallway, then back to me. "But you need to stay within the trees so you're not seen. And, Brie, don't turn around, no matter what you hear."

She pushes me in the direction of the door. "Why?"

"Brie, you're our only chance." Her eyes are wide with fear. "You need to hurry while everyone's attention is on the barn. *Now go!*"

I'm down the stairs and almost to the front door when a commotion comes from upstairs. Hesitating briefly, but then remembering what Grandma said, I reach for the doorknob. I scan the area before running into the dark and toward the protection of the trees.

Even if I make it to the shed, what then? I have no idea what I'm supposed to do. If not for Alex, I'm sure I'd have given up by now. My first stop is the grove of pines where I'd left the box, but it's nowhere in sight. I search the entire area, but it's gone.

A rustle of footsteps sounds in the distance. I whirl around, trying to figure out which direction they're coming from. The footsteps grow closer, and Blake dominates my thoughts. My chest tightens with fear. I slink behind a bush to conceal myself. Every muscle stiffens and my pulse booms in my ears.

A twig snaps as a dark mass lunges at me. I gasp, "Just a deer." It takes everything I have to calm my adrenaline-fused mind and body.

A few minutes later, the bitter, robust wind pierces through me. The shed becomes top-priority. For the period of time it takes me to get there, my thoughts turn to the contents of the box and Grandma's logic for me to come out here. The insanity of it all makes my head spin.

The shed is just that: a small twelve-by-twelve enclosure. I'm not even sure why it's out here. Alex and I used it a time or two as a fort, but other than that, it stands empty. It's dark and gloomy. Cobwebs and dirt are the only things that occupy the space.

I throw my backpack to the floor and sit beside it, hoping that there's some kind of guidance inside. The flashlight is a welcoming sight. Even though it's nice not being in the dark, it does little to calm my nerves.

Without warning, the shed door flies open. I gasp, scrambling to my feet and bolting for the door. "I'm so sorry," I say, throwing myself into Josh's arms.

He squeezes me tight. "Don't be, I get it now."

All too soon, the danger we're in comes to the fore-front, so I push him away. "Why are you here?" I ask.

"I said I would help you." He reaches out to me.

"No, you can't be here, it's not safe." I move away from him.

"I know what I'm up against and I'm not leaving."

"You have no idea what's been going on, for that matter, neither do I."

"It's going to be okay, really it is."

"You don't know that. No one does."

"I have something for you." He disappears out the door and then returns, carrying the metal box.

"How'd you get that?"

"Your grandma let me in on some things."

"Then you know it's not safe for you to be here."

"I'm not leaving." He reaches out to me again. "Your dad, grandma, and I have been waiting to find you again. I knew you'd come back eventually."

"You've been here the whole time?"

He nods.

"Then you know about Dad." My voice wavers.

He nods again.

I stumble over my words. "So . . . you watched him? You just watched him die and without at least *trying* to help?"

"It wasn't like that. Your grandma called me when she found you in the attic. She told me that you were back. I got here as fast as I could."

"So you just watched?" I turn away.

"No! I couldn't find you at first. It wasn't until I saw the box and then two sets of footprints in the snow that I realized what was happening. By the time I got back to the farm, the barn was already on fire and you were in Blake's arms."

"So you just left me there, with him?"

"I thought for sure it was over, and that you were his."

"You weren't even going to try to stop me."

"I wanted to rip him apart, but I couldn't risk it. If I got killed, who would be left to search for you?"

"You would've come after me?"

He pulls me into his arms. "Don't you know by now that I'll never give up on you?"

I keep my head down, avoiding his gaze. "You have to leave."

He lifts up my chin, so I can look at him. "Not happening . . . your Grandma called me, told me she would send you here…If you were still with us." I can see the empathy in his eyes. "I about died when I thought I'd lost you."

"But, Josh, it's a long way from over," I say, as a sudden urge to hurt him creeps into my thoughts.

"Brie, it's not too late. You can fight this."

I'm sure he believes that, but I don't. "You need to get out of here—now!" Breaking free of his hold, I hurry to the corner of the shed.

"I'm not leaving."

"You don't understand. It's uncontrollable. This thing will start feeding off you, and I don't know how to stop it."

"Yes, you do. Think about all the things that mean something to you."

"I can't."

"You've done it before, I've seen it. Concentrate." His voice is unwavering, "Brie, remember the first time we met? We were, like, four?" He moves cautiously toward me. "You were the mean girl on the playground and I knew you were meant for me right then." He laughs. "Even when you made me cry."

"I can't do this." Anger grows inside of me.

"Remember when we found Gibson, and she had her kittens in the bottom drawer of your dresser?" He holds out his hand. I slap it away. "We got into so much trouble, bringing a stray cat into your room. She turned out to be the best cat ever."

The thought of Dad's final moments and the horrible desire to kill Josh clouds the memories he's trying to force me to remember.

"Brie." Josh reaches out for me again.

"I don't want you here."

"I'm not leaving."

"*Damn you!*"

He continues with the stories of the past. "Remember when we went skinny-dipping? I was the one who was scared, you weren't. I was the luckiest nine-year-old ever to have a best friend like you." His voice breaks. "Tell me, Brie, something that you remember about us when we were younger?"

Thoughts whizz around in my head, none of them good. "I don't remember anything."

"Sure you do. What about the week we camped in your backyard? Tell me about that."

"I can't—I'm scared."

He gently takes me into his arms. He trembles as his body heats up. I'm absorbing his energy and it feels good. His hold is firm.

"Tell me about that Brie, what did we do?"

At first, the memory is blocked, but the longer he keeps me in his arms, the clearer my vision becomes. "We took the tractor out."

"And where'd we drive it too?"

"We went to Mulligan's for ice cream."

"Yeah, like driving a tractor into town was a good idea . . . huh?"

The more we talk, the cooler Josh's body becomes and the desire to hurt him fades. Somewhat in control, I sigh. "Thank God you're here."

"I'll always be here." He takes a deep breath. "You need to keep hold of those memories, that's what keeps you strong."

"How do you know that?"

"The old woman at the antique shop said only the people with the strongest convictions and those who could hold on to their past could survive this curse and stay the person they were born to be."

"Did she have doubts about me?"

"That's why I couldn't tell you this before. With negative feelings, the evil controls you. But if you keep positive, then you control it."

"That's easier said than done."

"I told her that if anyone could do this it was you. I believe in you."

He kisses the top of my head. "We have a lot of work to do, though." He points to the box, "Your grandma and I both searched through the information in there, but we couldn't piece it all together. I guess the old woman from the antique store was right. I didn't tell you everything that she said, mostly because I didn't want to believe it."

"And now?"

"Let's just say I've learned a lot over the last few weeks." He lightly touches the side of my face. "Sometimes you have to believe, even when it's not logical."

"What else did she say?" A chill shivers through me.

"You cold?"

"Just a little." In actuality, I'm freezing.

"Come on." He gathers everything up.

"Where're we going?"

"I know a place not too far from here. It has a wood-burning stove. We'll look over all this there."

Following him out of the shed, he reassures me again. "We're going to figure this out."

We make our way to the road, but stay within the cover of the trees. I'm thankful yet worried that Josh is here. As we walk in the black of night, constant fear dominates my every thought. By the time we get to where we're going, my toes and fingers are numb.

Josh opens the door and gestures for me to go in. "Welcome to the Hilton," he says.

"What is this place?"

"My dad uses this place when he comes here fishing."

It wasn't much bigger than the shed we just left. But it does have a wood-burning stove, a small table with two chairs, and a cot in the corner. That's pretty much it.

"I'll grab some wood, if you want to wad up some newspapers over there and put them in the burner."

My hands hurt from the cold but that doesn't stop me from scrunching up a hefty pile of papers and cramming them into the burner. Josh comes back with kindling and laughs when he sees the amount of paper shoved inside the burner.

"Are you trying to burn the place down?" he says, removing some of the newspaper.

I think of Dad and my eyes water.

Josh must have realized what he had said as he makes his way over to me. "You have to think of only good right now. I'm sorry, I just didn't think."

"It's okay; I don't know how this is going to work anyway."

"It will."

"Do you even know what we're up against?"

"I do." He nods in the direction of the box. "The answers are in there . . . We just have to put it together."

I take the flashlight from my pack, pick up the box, and make my way over to the table to take out the contents. While searching through the documents, inexplicable thoughts sink me into new realities with ease. I try hard to battle back with the memories of my past; to lose control is not an option.

"We have to put together the things that belong with each other." My voice cracks. I quickly clear my throat and concentrate on the papers in front of me. I start where I had left off earlier, putting the files of the families to one side. The books get piled together, along with my grandpa's information.

With the fire blazing, Josh comes over with a battery-powered light. "I think this will work better than the flashlight." He sets it on the table, then picks up a book.

I skim through the book on the Salem witch trials. "This is where it started. We need to figure out what it is we're dealing with." The warmth from the wood-burner feels good, but it has also made me very sleepy. I yawn, and then realize I've read the same paragraph four times.

"Hey, listen to what's been highlighted." Josh says. "'Upon the death of their first victim, it is said that the cursed would be left alone for three days to complete the task and test their ability.'"

"Wait a minute—Blake did say something like that. He said that he'll be gone for three days, something about preparing the others."

"So this has to be right, then."

"You think Blake believes the evil is in control?"

"I don't think he would have left otherwise." Josh scans the rest of the page. "Oh, shit," he mumbles.

"What is it?"

"It says, 'On the third night of their solitude, under the light of the moon, all those that have gone before will congregate, to either welcome their newest member to the clan or . . .'" He looks up at me.

"Or what?"

"'To kill them if they fail to complete their task.'"

"What task?"

"It doesn't say. Did Blake say anything else?"

"No, not that I can . . . wait, he did say something about my family." I grab one of the family folders to look at their family tree. "Look, all names that are circled have arrows that point to family members that have been crossed off."

"Let me see that."

"You don't think . . ." Next, I take out their death records, matching up the names that are joined to the names that are circled. Then it hits me. "I know what the task is."

"What?"

"I have to kill my entire family."

"What're you talking about?"

"What's the strongest power?"

Josh shrugs.

"It's love." Spreading the papers out on the table so he

can see them. "Look at the name Beth, and then look at the death records on the ones that are linked to her. They all died within a few days of each other. And there is no death record on Beth."

"That can't be right." His brows draw together.

From the same family tree, I pull the names linked to Joshua. "Look, his name is circled, and, again, no death record on him. But the names linked to him all died within three days of each other."

Josh pulls another folder out. "No, wait, here's one that has been circled: Mary. But her family didn't die at the same time." He hands me the file.

I search through the documents, reading the information out loud. "Mary, born in 1912, and died in 1930, her death is listed as a bizarre accident. Isn't it obvious? She didn't complete the task and they killed her."

"Okay, even though it all looks bad. What about your mom, Grandma, and Grandpa? All their names were circled, and no evil took them over. And they survived."

"Then we have to be missing something." I slide three folders over to him. "You look through those, and I'll take these four. Look for the names that are circled where their family members survived. Whatever happened to my family must have happened to others."

It's hard to keep my eyes open. Even the urgency to find answers doesn't stop my eyes from closing. I yawn and rub my hands over my face, trying to wake myself up.

Josh closes his file and stands. Taking the files from me, he forces me to my feet. "I know this is bad, but at least we've just bought ourselves some time. It's late. I think you should try to get some rest."

"I can't sleep; I have too much to do." I push him away and sit back down.

"You're not going to figure this out if you're tired. You need to clear your head. We'll start fresh in the morning."

"That's easy for you to say. But the fact is that if I can't stop this, not only my family, but probably my friends, will all die. And even if I do stop this, it doesn't matter, because, again, we're all dead. So there's really no way out. Oh and the fact that I'll live forever as a demonic witch of some kind. I'd say that you're right, there's no need to panic." Intense anger grows inside. I throw a file across the table then bolt to my feet. *"It's hopeless!"*

Flames shoot out of the wood-burning stove, as if fueled by my anger. Josh grabs onto me. I dig my fingernails into his neck, drawing blood. He barks out my name, "Brie, stop!" He pries my hands off him and pushes me back. Blood drips onto his shirt.

I run for the door. Josh's arm is around me within seconds. *"This isn't going to work!"* I scream.

"Think about Alex. If you can't beat this, she has no chance."

"Alex," I whisper. "Oh my God, you're right." My body goes limp in his arms as the exhaustion wins.

"Come on, Brie, just give yourself a little break, that's all," he says, helping me over to the bed. "You take the cot. I'll sleep on the floor."

Eyeing the still bleeding scratches on his neck, I cry. "I'm so sorry, Josh."

"It's nothing."

Thoughts of Alex run through my head as I stretch out onto the small cot. Josh covers me up and kisses me on the cheek. "I'll be right here." He reassures me.

He closes the door on the wood burner, and then pulls a first aid kit out of an old footlocker. I watch with regret as he cleans his wounds. He looks over at me and smiles. "See, it's nothing."

I acknowledge with an uncertain smile.

He takes a sleeping bag down from the shelf and rolls it out onto the floor next to the cot, then lies down.

"I love you, Brie."

A knot in my throat makes it impossible to respond.

Silently, I pray for my dad. It seems the hole in my heart left by my mom's death has just gotten bigger with Dad's death—but the only way to save those around me is to push it out of my head, at least for now.

The thought of Mom and Dad back together again comforts me enough to let me doze off.

TWENTY-SIX

Pieces

―――――――――

I'm startled awake by a dream. Bounding from the cot as little twinges of anxiety roll through me, I get my feet tangled in the sleeping bag lying on the floor, and I'm brought down in a heap. It's then that the memory of the night floods my thoughts.

"Dammit!" I pick up the pillow and throw it to the other side of the shack. Suddenly, the realization that I'm alone hits me hard. The cell phone on the table beeps, and I bolt to my feet while thinking the worst. What if I've been gone longer than a night? What if something happened to Josh?

The date on my phone and the note lying beside it brings a sigh of relief. The note reads: *I won't be gone long. Went to get my car and something to eat. Don't worry, I will be back.*

A fleeting glimpse at the papers scattered about on the table is enough to make me feel sick. Not wanting to deal with that until Josh gets back, I grab my backpack from the chair and sit on the cot to rummage through it.

I'm relieved to pull out a bottle of water and don't waste any time guzzling it down. A sweatshirt, a pair of jeans, a pair of socks, another bottle of water, and two granola bars are now laid out on the cot. Immediately, I open a granola bar. *Thank you, Grandma.*

Now looking around the deserted space, my palms begin to sweat and my heart rate escalates. My mouth dries up, so swallowing the granola bar is almost painful.

My ability to stay calm is lost when pictures of Blake and my dad creep into my mind. Needing a distraction, I rush for the table, grab a paper, and read the words out loud. The stronger the feelings, the louder I read, until I'm screaming.

Josh comes through the door. "What's going on?"

I drop the paper and run over to him. He sets down the items in his hands as I fall into his arms. "Are you okay? I could hear you outside."

"Just hold me."

"It's all right, I won't let you go." He wipes away my tears. "What happened?"

"I don't know, all of a sudden I got so scared. I couldn't stop thinking about awful things."

"You're okay now?"

"Yeah, don't worry. I don't feel like hurting anyone." I try to pull away but he holds on to me tight.

"I didn't mean it like that." Our eyes meet. "There's nothing you can do to scare me off."

"Thanks, Josh."

"You better?"

I nod.

"You need to eat something." He picks up the bag and hands it to me then reaches down for the books. "There's donuts and juice in there."

With my anxiety quieted my stomach growls again. We sit at the table as Josh explains what he's found. "I've been studying these over the last few weeks." He flips through one of the books, opening it to a page where several sentences have been highlighted. "I marked all the pages that I thought might be what we're dealing with."

The book titled 'Myths and Legends of the Underworld.' I say, around a mouthful of doughnut.

"Most of the books could only explain a few things. This one has some good stuff in it." His finger glides over the page. "It states that seven sets of stones were forged with the powers of heaven and hell inside them and presented to the seven daughters of the Greek gods Atlas and Pleione as a gift. These stones had great powers and were to be guarded carefully, as they contained the balance between good and evil. All the sisters were consorts to gods and took their responsibility seriously, with the exception of one, Merope. She dishonored her family and was cast out of the heavens, but before she left, she stole the stones, upsetting the balance in them to evil and scattering them upon the earth."

"What's this got to do with me?"

"Apparently, anyone who comes upon these stones can use them toward their own desires. It states that these stones have been sought after for years, giving insight to the one that finds them."

"How come I've never heard this before?"

"Just listen, I think you'll find it interesting."

I cram another doughnut in my mouth.

"Remember the witch trials?"

I nod.

"Well, the stones gave the Moray Clan the power to curse the unborn. They didn't just have one set; they had two, giving them even stronger powers than most." He shows me a page in the book, and there, in full color, is a picture of my stones. "And if that's not enough to convince you, look at the page I marked here." He opens another book—'Witches of Salem'—and turns to the section on the accused. A sketch depicts one of the witch trials. And the weird thing is that the woman pictured is wearing the very necklace I have on.

I read the caption underneath the sketch. "'Salem Village in 1692. Bridget Bishop on trial for witchcraft.'" I swallow hard. "You're saying that these families here all carry a set of stones with them?" I point at the folders my grandpa had put together.

"No. If the Moray clan had possession of all seven sets of stones they wouldn't need to increase their numbers by using unborn children. They would've been so powerful that they could take whatever they wanted."

"Then why these people? And why me?"

"I'm not sure about that. The only conclusion I can come up with is Bridget Bishop and Elizabeth Proctor were their first victims. Each of them would have been given a set of stones to keep the curse alive, passing them down from one generation to the next. The reason you have both sets is you're a descendent of both Bridget and Elizabeth."

"I just remember Blake telling me I have the bloodline of two." This is inconceivable, yet so is everything that has gone on. "That makes all this impossible now, doesn't it?"

"Why?"

"If the curse has been going on for hundreds of years, and you don't necessarily need the stones in your family to be one of the cursed, then there must be thousands of them out there."

His expression cements my fears.

"Yeah, I kinda got that impression, too," he says, "but there's a brighter side to all this."

"What could that possibly be?"

"The way I figure it, your feelings can control the stones because they contain both good and evil. So, as long as you're in control of your feelings and stay positive, you can fight this. And also . . ." He pulls a paper from Grandpa's folder. "Read this." He hands me the page.

"'The only one that can break the curse is the one that can carry the stones.'"

"Remember when I held the stones and they burnt my hand?"

"Yeah . . ." I pause and then think about Grandma, she too could hold the stones. "Oh, no—it can't be."

"It makes sense and you do have the right ancestors."

The donuts now feel like bricks in my stomach. I bound from my seat. "Okay, let's just say all this is true, can you tell me how I would go about stopping this? Look at all this stuff Grandpa put together, but obviously he didn't stop it, 'cause here I am, battling the same shit as everyone else in my family."

"Brie, if there's anyone who stands a chance, it's you." He reaches out to me. "You have to do this. I won't lose you now."

His words speak to my heart. It's hard to keep the donuts down as I fight to hold back the tears. I turn away. He comes up behind me and wraps his arms around my waist.

"We're halfway to figuring this out. Don't give up on me now." He turns me to face him. "You can do this." His lips touch mine.

Without warning an immoral feeling stirs inside of me. My extremities shake. Abruptly, I pull away.

"I can't," I gasp. "I have to be in control at all times."

"We're together now. I won't let anything hurt you."

"It's not me I'm worried about."

Josh's admission beckons to the darkness inside of me once again. He reaches out to me.

I hold my hand up. "Stop! You don't know what you

are doing. Think about it, Josh, this is about control and you're making me lose it. I know you're stronger than me, but you're no match for what's inside of me."

I glance at the scratches on his neck. "Whatever this thing is, it's incredibly strong. So let's not do that again, okay?"

He nods and makes his way back to the table.

I run my hands through the tangles in my hair then glance down at my body. My clothes are dirty and ripped from the struggle with Blake. I'm irritated and feel disgusting. "I need a shower." I sigh.

"There's a motel not far from here. We can hold up there while we figure this out."

"You think it's safe?"

"If Blake hasn't come after you by now, he probably thinks he's already won. According to all this, he won't be back until—well—you know," he mumbles.

"Unfortunately, I do." I keep a safe distance between us as we gather up our belongings and head for the car. "So, you really believe I can do this?" I ask.

"Yes, I do."

I'm comforted by his faith in me. "You said you went to Appleton. Did you ever find the old woman?"

"No, just charred remains of the building. I asked a few people. They say she moved away, but they didn't know where."

"She survived the fire, that's good."

He barks out a laugh, "Of course she survived, she's already dead."

"She is not. But remember the first time we went to her and how weirded out you were?"

"Yeah, well, that hasn't changed. I still think she's creepy," he admits.

The sound of his voice quiets my restlessness. "Keep talking to me, it's a great distraction."

"Eric and Jill are going to Mexico for spring break?"

"Her mom's letting her go?"

He shrugs. "Guess so."

He rambles on my behalf.

I finally get up the nerve to touch his hand. "I want to beat this."

"You will. There's no doubt in my mind." He squeezes my hand.

TWENTY-SEVEN

Hiding Out

———————————

The motel is far enough off the main road that it can't be seen from the highway. Josh parks in back and makes me wait inside the car while he gets us a room. I dig a few papers out of my bag to scan them again while I wait.

A sudden tap on my window makes me jump. "Holy crap, you scared me."

"Sorry." Josh snickers. "We have that room right there." He points to the door closest to our car. "I thought it would be good for the car to be close, just in case."

"Good thinking."

We waste no time getting into the room. With back-pack in hand, I head straight for the bathroom to take a much-needed shower. Removing my clothes, I'm shocked to see the bruises and cuts that cover my skin. I don't even want to think about what I've done to cause them. Suddenly, the stones' leaving my possession scares me. I grab for my jeans and dig out the pouch, putting it on the edge of the sink, so I'll be able to reach it in a split-second and I keep the necklace on.

It takes a little bit to ease my sore body into the flow of

the water, and I let out a sigh as the water stings my skin. Complementary shampoo and soap is a welcoming sight.

After an extended time, Josh knocks on the door. "You doing okay?"

"I'm fine."

"Just checking."

Finally feeling refreshed, I step out of the tub, wrap my hair up in a towel, then rummage through my bag for the extra clothes Grandma had packed.

Just being clean and warm sheds a little light onto the hopeless situation. The pouch with the stones gets shoved into my front pocket.

"Feeling better?" Josh asks, as I make my way over to him.

I nod. Sitting next to him and staring at the floor, I sigh. "Are you sure you want to be here?"

"There's no other place I would rather be." He wraps his arms around me and pulls me into him. A surge of excitement tingles throughout my body.

"Josh, you need to be careful."

"I know. It's just hard to stay away from you."

I want to be with him, but, under the circumstances, it can't happen.

He smiles. "I need to get out of here, don't I?"

"Yeah, you do."

He kisses my forehead. "I'm going to walk to the restaurant across the street. Do you want something?"

"No. I'm fine. I'm going to start looking over the papers again. We have to be missing something important."

"I'll be right back, you sure you don't want something?"

"Not right now."

.   .   .

THE HORROR we're up against dominates my thoughts. I stand in front of the mirror to brush through my hair when a formless cloud of gray rises up behind me. Unable to turn away from the mirror, I watch it expand and contract in unison with my breath. When I move, it moves. I redirect my thoughts to happier times, and with that the cloud starts to dissolve. My mind flips between good and evil. The cloud responds by fading with good thoughts and materializing with bad, proving to me once and for all that the evil is truly part of me.

I drop my eyes away from the mirror, throw my hair up in a ponytail and then grab the box from the nightstand and sit on the bed to go over all the information again.

So, if Grandpa, Grandma, and Mom were part of this thing, and none of *them* turned evil, there has to be something that I'm missing.

The newspaper clipping about the fire that destroyed the Bishop Farm gets laid to one side. On a separate piece of paper, I write down the dates of their eighteenth birthdays, then the events that followed. I scan through the rest of the family trees, trying to find someone else that has been circled but seemed to have a normal life. As for "normal," I look for a death certificate on them.

It's eerie to see that almost everyone in red has no record of ever dying. The few that do get their name written next to Grandma and Grandpa's, and then any information about their lives also gets written down, until all the names that Grandpa had records on have been accounted for.

It makes no sense. Leaning back against the headboard while trying to put it all together, I twist my mom's ring around my finger. Now I'm imagining how awful she must have felt, waking in the hospital, thinking that my biological dad had left her.

Grandpa and the hideous scars that he carried with him from saving Grandma from the fire come to mind. The love they'd had for each other must've been strong to survive that.

Then my thoughts turn to my dad, the one who raised me and never let me down. It finally dawns on me. Everyone who has beaten this had some kind of accident shortly after their eighteenth birthday. I look at the names listed then search through the box for any documents telling of the severity of the accidents. The people who I find information on had all been in critical condition. Some had even been pronounced dead before miraculously awakening. I remember Grandma telling me that Grandpa had to perform CPR on Mom. After looking more closely at the information, it becomes clear that all of them must have been brought back from the dead.

Could that really be the answer? I have to die?

Josh comes through the door. "Hey, I bought you a . . ." He stops when his eyes meet mine. "What is it?"

"I've figured it out."

"That's great— Isn't it?"

I quietly confess, "I have to die."

"What!" he blurts out, hurrying to set down the drinks, he comes over to sit next to me on the bed.

"It's true, it's all here."

"Slow down. Let me see what you've found."

I show him the paper I've been working on. "Look, everyone who beat this thing died. I mean, they didn't die permanently, but they all had something happen to them where they stopped breathing for a short period of time. My mom and the car accident, my grandparents with the fire, they were all in critical condition, and weren't expected to live. That can also explain why they weren't killed by the clan, if they had stopped the curse inside themselves there would be no reason to bother with them."

He takes the paper from me. "That can't be the answer." He frantically skims over the page.

"It is. Look here." I point to a name. "Here's someone who beat this thing. But, again, some awful tragedy happened to her right after her eighteenth birthday." I hand him the newspaper clipping related to her.

"Let's just say this is true—then you should be fine. Didn't you almost die at the lake?"

"I hadn't thought of that." My mind shifts to that night I almost drowned; it was Grandpa that coursed me into the lake. He wasn't trying to kill me; he was trying to save me. "Then why does Blake still want me?"

"I don't know," Josh places his hand on my shoulder. "But this is a start."

"A start to what? The end?" I drop my head into my hands. "All this is meaningless."

"Sometimes it takes a little longer to figure things out, but we'll get there."

"A little longer," I whisper.

"What?"

"That's it. Maybe I wasn't actually dead, or maybe I didn't stop breathing long enough."

Jumping up, I pace the floor while that night plays over in my head once again. Josh turns away and begins rifling through the papers, then the folders.

"I didn't die." Without any other explanation, I sigh, "You never had to perform CPR on me, did you?"

He shakes his head, confirming my fears.

"My only problem is that they only killed the curse in *them*. I mean, it still *lives.*"

Josh is quick to respond, "So, technically, that's not the answer we're looking for."

"It might have to be the solution for now."

"Then if what you say is true, Alex will have to face the same thing when she turns eighteen, right?" His comment sends a chill to quiver through me. "Look, Brie, we still have a few days to research other options, so let's just focus on that." He reaches over and picks up the drinks he had set down. "Here, I bought you a malt, it's strawberry. I know it's your favorite."

"Thanks."

We spend the next few hours searching through the information, putting the events into the order in which they had taken place. When we are done, the evidence undeniable—the evil inside of me won't rest until my very existence is lost and I've destroyed all those around me.

"I know now why Grandma was adamant that I know about Sean."

Josh whispers. "He never had a chance, did he?"

"No. That's why she wanted to make sure I knew what I was up against." My pain reflects in his eyes. "No matter how much I love you or my family, if this thing wins . . . I will kill everyone around me."

"I'm not going to lose you. Now, let's concentrate."

TWENTY-EIGHT

Finding Direction

I look through the book 'Boundless' once more. Chapter ten, titled 'Completion of the Curse,' catches my eye. I'm stuck on paragraph three, and read it several times not wanting to accept what's written. Finally, I get the courage to say it out loud. "Josh." I sigh.

"Yeah."

"I know who the others are. And why Blake needs me."

He gives me his full attention.

"The others are the ones that won't stand a chance without my help. My mom must have known this. That's why she was so sad when she thought she wasn't strong enough."

"Slow down," he says. "Start from the beginning."

"It states here that it takes three centuries for any spell cast for pure evil to reach ultimate power. Any time after that, if the originator of curse were to become one with a direct descendant of one of their first victims, their power would become godlike, never to be defeated." I grab his hand. "Think about it—I have the bloodlines of the original two. I can hold both sets of stones. That's why Blake wanted my mom. When he couldn't have her, he waited for me. If I fail, he'll go after Alex."

I bound from the bed and begin pacing once again. "With knowledge comes responsibility, remember? That's what the old women said."

"Brie, if it comes down to it, we know how to stop the curse in you."

I shake my head. "That's not good enough now. I know too much. They're not going to let me live. Blake will stop at nothing to make sure Alex becomes his. The first chance he gets he'll take her somewhere where she'll never be found. I'll give myself to him before I let her go through that."

"Wait a minute, let's calm down." Josh sighs. "We're looking at the people. Maybe we need to look at the stones. I mean, that's what gave the Moray clan their advantage. They obviously are part of this."

He pulls me back down next to him then plucks a book out of the pile and holds it up, 'Myths and Legends of the Underworld.' "I'll look at this one. You keep searching through that one."

"You would think there would be tons of books on these stones if they were believed to hold such power," I say.

"Yeah, you would think so."

"Hey listen to this." I read, "'The best way to evoke a demonic spirit is through water or flames.' – It makes sense now why Grandpa lured me into the water."

"It would've been nice to know that then," Josh says.

"Yeah." The last page lists the author and two other books he has written: 'Mystical Stones' and 'The Power Within.' "We need to find these books . . . and fast." I scramble to put everything back into the box, grab my pack, and start for the door. Josh follows with the box in hand.

As soon as I touch the doorknob, a sudden feeling of unease shoots through me. I stop.

Josh bumps into me. "What's wrong?"

"Something's not right." I press my hand against the door. "I don't think we're alone."

He argues, "Yes we are."

"No—I'm pretty sure I have been watched this whole time. We need to find another way out."

"Brie, come on, Blake wouldn't have been left you alone this long if he thought you were in control."

"They would have if they believed I was coming after you. The one thing I learned from Blake is that the longer you prolong the agony of someone's death, the more pleasure you get from it. I mean, Dad's dead. Grandma's probably dead, too. Who else do I have feelings for other than Alex?" My voice cracks. "You."

Josh moves in front of me and looks through the peephole. "I don't see anyone."

"I'm telling you, we're not alone."

"I'll just take a small peek." He cracks the door just a smidge, then abruptly shuts it. "We need to find another way out."

"Is it Blake?"

"No, but there are two people just standing out there."

"There's a window in the bathroom."

We bolt for it. Once inside, he stands on the toilet and pushes the oblong window open and peers out. "I don't see anyone."

"There's got to be, they wouldn't be that stupid."

He sets the box down. "Here's the plan, I'll make some kind of commotion out front, hopefully drawing all of them out. I'll honk the car horn if I think it's safe."

"I don't like that plan," I argue. "What else you got."

He shrugs, "That's it." He grabs onto me and holds me tight. "You get to the street on the next block."

"What about you? I can't lose you."

"They let me leave once to go to the restaurant. I'll just make it sound like you've asked me to go get something and I'll meet you. If they don't see you come out, I'm sure they'll figure that I'm coming back."

"What if it doesn't work?"

He kisses my forehead, "It will. Stay positive." An unconvincing smile crosses his face, "I got this." He disappears through the door.

Within minutes a loud noise coupled by shouting can be heard. I'm just about to scrap the plan when a car horn sounds. Without delay, I heave the box and backpack out the window before squeezing through. I land feet first. Snatching the bag and the box, I run.

A deep ravine in back of the motel slows my pace. The ground is mushy. At the bottom of the ravine, my feet sink clear up to my ankles in the mud. It sloshes onto my legs as I trudge on. Making it to the other side, I don't take the time to wipe the buildup of muck from my shoes. I just run.

Desperation settles in on me when I think about being alone. I mumble, "Josh is going to be there. But what if he's not there? Then what will I do? Stop it, Brie, think about Alex."

The road finally within my sights gives me renewed energy to sprint towards it. I'm relieved when my feet touch the pavement, but with Josh nowhere in sight, panic hits hard once again. "Oh, God, where are you?" I tremble.

His car rounds the bend at the end of the road. Within seconds I'm safely inside. "What took you so long?"

"Just before leaving the parking lot, I saw their truck." His brow rise. "Plumbers."

"What?"

"I hurried to tell you, but you had already left."

I breathe a sigh of relief, "At least that makes me feel a little better."

He grins. "Aren't you glad you took a shower?" He eyes my mud-splattered legs.

"It could've been worse." I sigh.

Turning around, he drives back to the highway.

"Where're we going?"

"The library. Even if we can't find the books listed, maybe we can find something else on the stones." He glances down at his phone. "It's not even noon yet, so we'll have plenty of time."

Needing reassurance, I ask, "We're going to be fine, right?"

"Of course," he says way too fast.

I rest my head against the seat. The constant struggle to keep focused makes it almost impossible to keep my eyes open. "I'm going to close my eyes, just 'til we get there."

"No problem." Josh turns on the radio. "Brie?"

"Yes?"

"It's nice having you back."

"Nice being back . . . I think."

"HEY, BRIE." I'm gently nudged awake. "We're here."

We're parked in front of the Library. I stretch. "That was quick, what'd you do, speed?"

"No, but you were sure out."

"Was I snoring?"

"No, but you were talking in your sleep—and the

253

things I found out were . . ." The lines in his forehead tighten. "Well . . . Wow."

"I did not."

"Come on, we have a lot of work ahead of us," he snickers. "But admit it—that was pretty funny."

"Ha—yeah—whatever."

Once inside the library, he heads to the section on Greek Mythology while I make my way to the Geology section.

I search through countless books on rocks and gems, but nothing is written about the Aluben stones. Discouraged, I pile the books back onto the shelf. Josh is sitting comfortably on the floor with several books open in front of him. As I approach, he asks without looking up, "Have you found anything?"

"Absolutely nothing." I drop to the floor next to him. "What about you?"

He keeps his face buried within a book. "Yeah, I found quite a bit."

"What are you reading?"

He points to the open books on the floor. "Start with those first. They're open to the pages you need to read."

One book titled 'Great Gifts of the Gods' told about seven sisters who received the Aluben stones, also known as the balance between heaven and hell, and how the strength in the stones is determined by the wearer. One sister, who was cast out of heaven, used the stones for revenge, upsetting the balance in them to evil. Then she scattered them among the earth.

"We already know this," I say.

He never looks up. "Read the next one that's opened."

The next one tells how inanimate objects can be used to accelerate the evil inside the wearer's soul. My attention goes to the necklace fastened around my neck.

"Josh?"

"Yeah?" he whispers.

"I remember Blake saying it will take longer without the stones. Do you think I should take them off?"

He shakes his head. "No, definitely not."

"I'll just put this book aside for now."

While reaching for another book, Josh points to the bottom paragraph. "Read that."

"Oh, this is good; 'The only way to wash away the finder's hold on the stones is to take them back to where it all started.' I'd say we're screwed."

"Not necessarily."

"How do you figure? This thing started in 1692 at the witch trials. Do you have a time machine that I'm not aware of?"

"Technically . . ." He looks up at me. "The curse started in hell."

"Oh, you're right. That does make it all better, 'cause hell is *so* much easier to get to."

"Actually, it is." He holds up the book he's reading. "It says the time between good and evil is one minute. That's when the unsettled spirit can walk between heaven and hell."

"An unsettled spirit?"

"It's a person who's dying, but not dead yet."

"You're not making any sense."

"It didn't make sense to me until I read the part that explained why good always prevails. It's because in the mortal world, evil dies in four minutes and good dies in five." He places his hand on mine. "You were right. Everyone that beat this thing must have died long enough to destroy the evil in them."

I gasp. "That's why the lake incident didn't change anything in me. I didn't stop breathing long enough."

Josh nods. "That's the way I figure it, too."

"But, Josh, I want to stop it permanently."

"You can." His brows draw together.

A thousand thoughts fly through my head as I scrutinize over our findings. The unsettled spirit that can walk between heaven and hell. The stones that need to be taken back to source of the evil in order to break the curse. The union between the creator of the curse—Blake and the one who can carry both sets of stones, me. And the fact that if Blake is to prevail, he will become indestructible.

Then it hits me. "Oh, my God—are you saying what I think you're saying?" I'm in complete and utter dismay.

A heartfelt anguish burns in Josh's eyes. He confirms my fear with a slow, steady nod. He touches my face, making the tears fall freely down my cheeks.

TWENTY-NINE

The Journey

We searched for the truth and found it. Now it's up to Josh to stay strong and complete what needs to be done. I remove the pendant from around my neck, then take the pouch with the other stones out of my pocket and let them fall to the ground.

"I'm so scared." I admit.

Josh gazes into my eyes. "Focus on me." He taps his fingers against my cheek. For a brief moment the paralyzing anxiety eases, giving me back the ability to move forward.

"You know what has to be done, right, Josh?"

"Yes." He places his hands on each side of my face and draws me to him. "Come back to me," he whispers against my lips.

"I will, just don't stop once you start." A lump sticks in my throat. With the stones out of my possession, the evil inside of me will be temporarily distracted, trying to obscure my reality.

"You're going to win."

"We won't have much time. I can feel the darkness already."

"If . . ." he starts to say.

Gently touching his lips, I sigh, "I love you—I always have." The icy water rolls over my feet and up my legs as I advance further into the water. Josh stays close behind me. "You need to hurry."

"I'm not sure I can do this." He hesitates.

"You can. You *must.*"

We have come out to our favorite spot, the pool of water that is fed by a natural spring. This is where the memories of my life are etched the most clearly in my mind. I came out here the night my mom died, to let the water wash over me as I cried. This spot is also where I first realized that I am hopelessly and forever in love with Josh.

Although ice crystals have begun to form along the bank, it hasn't been cold enough to freeze the water solid. My breath is taken away momentarily as I kneel. Josh's trembling hands grasp onto my arms as he waits for the exact moment that he will take my life.

"Don't stop until you're sure I'm not breathing." There's no stopping the tears now.

"But what if we're wrong?"

"Just remember, four and a half minutes, that's what I need in order to live."

"Four and half minutes," he repeats. Taking the stopwatch out of his shirt pocket, he tosses it over to where the stones lay on the ground.

Little black specks obscure my vision, making me shiver. "It's time."

Josh only has seconds to take control. If he doesn't hurry, his life will be in danger. "I love you." He says as the water rushes over my face.

The moment of truth has come. I gasp to rush the end along, but panic arises as the gush of wetness enters my lungs. My instincts for survival take over, fighting to free me from his grasp while screaming inside my head, *What if this is wrong? What if I die and evil lives on?*

He maintains his hold. A calming sensation washes over me, halting my struggles. I'm silent, watching my last breath bubble its way to the surface. A warm rush of energy explodes around me, freeing me from my earthly body and elevating me into the air.

Now several feet above the ground, I look down to see Josh still holding my lifeless body under the water. With no more fight, the waters are quiet.

It's surreal to watch my body being lifted from the water and laid onto the shore. His panic is undeniable as he pushes his fingers against the side of my neck, and then fumbles for the stopwatch. Staring wide-eyed at the watch, tears stream down his face.

At that moment, a brilliant glow appears before me. Mom emerges from the brightness, holding out her hand. Immediately I'm encompassed in the smell of her sweet perfume—Jasmine, as she wraps me in her arms. Swaying back and forth to the sound of her voice, I'm home. The feeling of eternity is powerful and exhilarating. Even the false sense of ecstasy that evil had forced upon me isn't any match for what this feels like.

She takes my hand, leading me further into the light until the darkness of earth is just a distant memory. The heavens open, revealing a place with such intensity that every part of me feels alive for the very first time. Irides- cent blue skies, along with the plush green landscape, glisten with vivid colors, as though millions of diamonds have been scattered throughout.

Pastel blossoms hug tree branches, and clusters of

vibrantly fragrant flowers dot the land. Variegated bands of birds paint the firmament, gliding harmoniously far and wide. And hovering just above the florets are hundreds of glittery kaleidoscopic butterflies. The soft scent of honeysuckle, lavender, and magnolia fills the air. My mind swims with wonderment.

Just standing in the midst of such grandeur, I'm in complete awe.

Soft melody of perfect harmony is all around me. My soul rejoices with exuberant perfection—perfection that is in us all. Mom stands there and watches me as I stretch my arms out to absorb as much of this place as possible. The significance of our existence is finally understood. Everything we fight for and everything we have to endure is to get us here, to this place. This is where we belong.

With Mom next to me, we walk side by side without speaking. She has a glow of content and is truly happy.

She turns to me and rests her delicate, warm hands against my face. "You have felt the splendor of heaven, now you must feel the horror of hell."

"*What?* I don't understand! I *don't* want to leave."

"Many will never feel what you have just experienced if you can't stop it."

"I'm not strong enough." Torrent panic shoots through me.

She holds me at arm's length. "I love you."

"Don't let go of me . . . *Please* . . . I want to stay."

She brings me to her and kisses my forehead like she had done so many times before. "I will always be with you."

With that, I'm catapulted into the murkiness of the underworld. Standing in the midst of a swamp, all the beautiful color that had surrounded me is replaced by a depressing sea of gray. Through the stifling humidity, the smell of decay makes me gag.

Leafless vines hang from twisted and gnarled branches of massive trees. Fingers of low-lying mist creep over the land as cries of the dead echo throughout. Translucent silhouettes appear from the blackness, reaching out for me. I try to back away from the horror, but my feet stay stuck firmly in the marsh. I search the distance for a way out, but a black void fills the outlying areas. I'm trapped.

Lost souls gather around me, the sorrow entrenched on their faces is heartbreaking. It's disturbing that this place holds so many. There's no escape from the never-ending torment that they'll forever have to endure. The hollow eyes of the lost make me cry.

A rush of urgency explodes inside me. With newfound strength, I yank my feet out of the muck and push my way through the ghostly figures. Clearing the trees, the dark haze lifts just enough for me to see my home in the foggy distance. Running toward it, I'm confused yet relieved that I've somehow made my way back home.

All too soon, it becomes apparent to me that this is wrong. The house is not how I remember it. Sheets of peeling paint entangle with contorted vines that hang from the structure. The once vast, solid porch is nothing more than rubble. Every window is shattered, leaving sharp pieces of broken glass protruding from the panes. Tattered and stained curtains hang outside the openings.

It takes all my strength to climb the rubble to get inside, opening the front door to come face to face with an even more depressing scene. Broken furniture and debris is scattered about. The walls are cracked and scorched. With every step, the floor snaps and pops beneath my feet. I look down. The floor is alive with thousands of roaches piled on top of one another, all fighting for space. Standing still, my shoes quickly disappear beneath the hordes of insects. I sprint for the kitchen as I strike at the bugs that cling to my clothes.

Upon entering the kitchen, I'm overpowered by a disgusting stench. The kitchen is in shambles. Most of the cupboards are smashed. Rotted food is scattered about, giving homes to the multitude of flies, maggots, and small rodents that found their way in.

Unable to look at the disarray any longer, I turn toward the living room to search the upstairs, when Josh's voice comes to me. "Brie."

Swiftly redirecting my attention to the sound, I bolt through the back door and out to the barn. "Josh, I'm coming!"

But it isn't Josh—it's Blake.

He lifts his hand to me. "I knew you would come." His eyes are ablaze. "Stand by me. We can stay among the living forever."

After seeing this place, his offer is tempting. Then I think of Mom, bringing to mind the forever *she* has. "Your forever can never compare to what I've seen."

"But, Brie, you can't stop evil, no matter how hard you try. You will have to face the fact that this . . ." His arms stretch open, "*is* your reality."

"No, it's not." I think about the stones. With that thought, a cold sensation burns in the palm of my hand, giving me the strength and power. I need to end this. "There are a few things you don't know about me." I raise my clenched fist, "I'm not some weak soul that you can control."

"Oh, you are so wrong." He laughs.

Opening my fist, I reveal both sets of stones, "I brought these back to where they belong."

His eyes narrow with contempt. "What's that prove?"

"The curse might have started with my ancestors, but it stops here. I'm taking my life back."

"That means nothing!" his voice booms.

"Oh, Blake, you're so wrong." The stones fall from my hand.

"You don't know what you've just done!" his thunderous voice echoes.

The stones come to rest in the dirt as he lunges for me, but then, without warning, I'm pulled backward by some unknown force. It takes me back to the path that brought me here. Through the house, out the front door, and into the swamp, to the exact place I'd entered the underworld.

My head spins as my body is brought to an abrupt stop. Everything around me is silent. A preconceived notion of what's about to happen heightens my anxiety.

Through the limbs of the tangled trees, a soft glow begins to grow. It strengthens until nothing around me is visible through the sea of white.

Please get me out of here. The area clears and I'm now standing in the middle of a field. On one side of me is the light of heaven and on the other is the darkness of hell. There's no doubt in my mind where I'm going, moving toward the light when Josh's pleas resonate from behind. I keep moving toward the light. Then he says the one word that makes me stop: "Alex."

My promise—that I would never leave—rings loud and clear in my head. The instant I turn toward the sound of his voice, I'm whisked away. I reach out for the light that is fading fast, but nothing can stop the momentum that is taking me back, back to a place that has left me with more questions than answers—a place that holds both good and evil—a place that challenges me mentally and physically, and yet, it's the place I need to be.

THIRTY

Moment of Truth

Warm lips meet mine. Then a breath of air fills my lungs, causing me to cough.

"Open your eyes, Brie."

Through a watery haze, Josh slowly comes into view.

"Just breathe," he says.

An onset of rapid, deep coughs immobilizes me. My head spins.

"Hang on, babe, you'll be okay." He rolls me over to my side. Within seconds, the water is painfully released, causing tremors throughout my body. When the last of the water finally leaves, I inhale my first real breath of air.

"Are you with me?" Warm hands rub against my arm. "Brie, talk to me." He wipes my face with the sleeve of his shirt. "Will you talk to me?"

"I'm here," I murmur.

"I almost couldn't bring you back. Don't ever ask me to do that again."

"How long was I . . ." My words come out in a painful rasp.

"*Dead!* You were gone for almost eight minutes."

"That can't be right."

"Well, it is." His voice cracks. "You might think you know everything, but you don't. I know a few things, too. Like you can bring someone back after several minutes if they died from the cold. Also, I started CPR on you at exactly four and a half minutes after you stopped breathing."

The possibility that it didn't work hits me hard. Closing my eyes to relive the last moments, Josh grabs onto me.

"Don't do that—open your eyes."

Tears roll out of the corners of my eyes as a cold shiver runs down my spine.

"What's wrong?" He hovers over me. "Are you okay? Maybe we should go to the hospital."

I shake my head. "No, just help me up."

He holds onto my arm and slowly pulls me to my feet. "Just take your time."

The world spins, my legs buckle. Josh scoops me up into his arms and carries me over to the fire that we had started earlier in the night. The raw night air stings my skin.

"We need to get you warm."

My lips quiver. "What about you?"

Without saying a word, he lifts my wet shirt over my head and quickly replaces it with a heavy sweatshirt. He then helps me out of my wet jeans and into dry ones. A pair of wool socks, winter boots, a coat, pair of gloves, and a hat completes my ensemble, but none of it stops the chills.

Josh changes into dry clothes then sits next to me. Pulling me onto his lap, he wraps a wool blanket around the both of us. His strong arms hold me tight. "Is this better?"

I nod. My stomach flutters with nervous tension while I

think about heaven and hell and what Josh had said about the cold. "Do you think it worked? What if I needed longer to make sure this thing is dead?" My teeth chatter.

"Brie, it was long enough."

"But what if—"

"Stop it. Just stop talking about it. It's over."

While waiting for the chills to diminish, my mind fills with all that I've been shown. Although very little time has passed, some of my memories of heaven are already fading away, like a curtain being closed across the window to the other world.

Disrupting my thoughts, Josh asks, "Do you feel any different?"

I shake my head. "That's what scares me."

"What was it like when you were gone?"

"There are no words that can describe it."

"Do you remember all of it?"

"The feeling is still there, but some of the images have already vanished."

"Tell me what you remember."

"Heaven is absolutely stunning . . ." For the next hour, he listens to me tell about my mom and what she had shown me. And also about the horrors that await those who lose their way.

"So there really is a heaven...and a hell?"

"Yes—and in some weird way, it comforts me to know that earth is just a temporary stop." It's overwhelming for me and I witnessed it, so I can only imagine what must be going through Josh's mind. "I don't blame you if all this makes you want to get as far away from here as possible. But this has changed something inside of me."

"It's changed me, too." He turns me around to face him. "No matter what, I'm not leaving you. I'm staying with you forever."

"I like the sound of that . . . *forever.*"

"I love you. You do know that, right?"

"I love you, too." I snuggle back down into his arms.

A light dusting of snow leaves the area with a fresh blanket of white.

"So, how long do we have to stay here?" he questions.

"I just wish I knew for sure it worked."

"Wait, I think there is a way to tell." He flips the blanket off his shoulders and jumps to his feet. "They've got to be here." He says, scanning the area where he pulled me out of the water.

"What are you looking for?"

He picks something up and hurries back to me. "Look." In his hand are four colorless stones.

"Are those my stones?" They're clear. "Where's the necklace and the bag the stones were in?"

"They're gone."

The emblem of the Moray Clan had vanished.

"You think it worked?"

"What else could it mean?" He drops the stones one by one into my hand. "Think about it—you've been without the stones for a while now, and you're still here."

I grab onto him with renewed excitement. "I can't believe it's over."

"It is." His lips meet mine. "Let's go home."

"What should I do with these?" I hold the stones out to him.

"I'd get rid of them, fast." He motions to the fire. "Throw them in there."

Suddenly, a light shatters the dark, and standing before us is my grandfather. A look of admiration flashes in his eyes as he points to my hand. I look down to see that the stones have come to life with swirling movements of light.

The air warms as he moves closer to me, his words

sound clearly in my head. *Always stay true to yourself. Accept the moments you can't change. Most importantly, never ever give up.*

He leans in and softly brushes his hand against my cheek. He whispers, "Your journey has just begun. Keep the stones safe—they will show you the way."

The light gradually diminishes. *"Grandpa, wait!"* My plea doesn't stop his radiance from fading away. Looking down, I see that the stones are once again clear as glass. It scares me to keep them, but it also scares me to think of them falling into the wrong hands.

Josh and I exchange a frightening glance, "You did see that, right?" I question.

"Ah . . . yeah!"

"Good, wanted to make sure I wasn't going crazy."

"I thought the creepiness was over."

"I think it is." Against my better judgement, I shove the stones into my pocket.

Josh kicks snow and dirt on top of the fire. "Let's get out of here."

For now, it gives me great pleasure to know that Blake and his clan have been defeated.

THIRTY-ONE

New Beginning
_____

The days pass quickly as the dead of winter gives way to the rebirth of spring. A lot has changed in my life and some things have stayed the same.

Josh and his family ended up staying in Kiel, and although they had already sold their home, they decided to rent until they could find a new place to buy.

I had pretty much destroyed my friendship with everyone those weeks I was . . . well . . . not myself. But the funny thing is, my true friends were quick to welcome me back into their lives.

I'm at the kitchen sink filling a five-gallon water jug, and a truck backfires, making me jump. Looking out the window to see Josh getting out of the 'purple beast.' (That's what he calls his truck.) It's still the ugliest thing I've seen on the road. He walks over to where construction on a new barn had begun a few days earlier.

Water spills out of the jug and over the side of the sink, soaking my shirt. "Crap."

Jill comes through the screen door. "Need some help?" she asks.

"Uh, maybe just a little."

She helps me carry the jug outside and lift it onto the tailgate of one of the pickups parked next to the barn.

Josh walks over to us. His eyes spark when he looks at me.

"Still going to the movies with Eric and me tonight?" Jill asks.

"Whatever Brie wants to do is fine with me," he says, grabbing onto me.

"Yeah, we're still in." I say.

"I think I'll go help your Grandma." Jill turns to leave.

"Hey, Josh, what do you think?" Dad asks, "Look any different than yesterday?"

"I can't believe how quick the barn is going up."

"It doesn't take long when you've got so many people helping." Dad smiles. "Only hope I can repay them one day."

"I brought the water out."

"Thanks, Brie." Dad pats my shoulder as he walks away.

I'd wondered why, on the night my dad was supposed to have died, the elevated feeling of euphoria didn't totally consume me. After the curse was broke, it was revealed to me that Josh had gotten to the barn in time to save my dad. All that smoke had been the perfect cover for them. The scars on Dad's arm from that night is a constant reminder how fast your life can change.

Some might think it was inconceivable to keep such a secret, but under the circumstances they had no choice. Even though, none of us knew what we were dealing with, it was clear that Alex would be next if I failed. Dad would have been her best chance of survival.

He stopped drinking after that night, telling Alex and me that we were more important to him than any drink.

Even though Dad still has a look of longing in his eyes when he speaks of Mom, it's made him feel better to know that she is happy and that we will all see her again one day.

Mom is always in my thoughts, but now I'm comforted by the things I've been shown. And late at night when I'm feeling alone, I know she's with me.

"I guess I better help," Josh says. "Maybe later we can sneak away."

I smile. "I'd like that."

Josh goes over to help Eric carry boards to the barn, while I head back to the house. Jill comes out of the backdoor, balancing two trays in her hands. "Your Grandma's enjoying this way too much." Jill says, "She even has pies in the oven."

I laugh, taking a tray from her. Three picnic tables are set on the porch and filled with a wide variety of food from neighbors and friends. It's been this way most of the week, and I'm sure will continue until the barn is complete.

Alex grabs onto me as I walk through the door. "Can you take me for ice cream?" she begs.

Grandma is fast to answer, "I don't think so, there's work to be done."

Alex huffs. "Oh, Grandma, it's so boring around here."

"I suggest you help get the food on the table." She hands her a few bags of chips. "Take these out there."

"I'll take you later, Bug."

She pushes through the screen door and trots out onto the porch.

Grandma turns to me. "I have something for you."

My chest tightens as she reaches under the cabinet, pulling out a bag of wildflower seeds. "I think you should spread them this year."

Although the secret we are hiding is wrong, I can't bear the thought of exposing the truth. At least, not right now.

"Yeah, I would."

She hands me the bag then touches the side of my face. "I love you Brie."

"I love you too, Grandma."

The front door is my best chance of getting away undetected. With everyone preoccupied, it makes it easy to slip away into the woods.

The soil around the oak tree is already filled with tiny sprouts of new growth from the flowers that had gone to seed in the previous year. Opening the bag of seeds, I scoop one handful out at a time and scatter them in all directions.

It's sad to think that there might be someone out there still holding onto the belief that Sean's still alive. One day soon, it will be up to me to find them and give them the closure they need and deserve.

With the last of the seeds leaving my hand, I sigh. "I'll never forget you." I pray that the decision to keep silent is right.

Walking back to the farm that has come to life with excitement again, I know for now . . . it is right.

About the Author

Cynthia Cain lives in the Midwest where – when she's not chasing after her dogs or hanging out with her children, grandchildren, family and friends – She stays busy working, writing and contemplating every paragraph she drafts. She loves to travel and is inspired by the places she visits and people she meets. She is a member of the Midwest Writers' Center and continues to advance her craft through conferences and online courses. A perfect evening to her includes a thunderstorm, a cup of tea and a spine-tingling book.